The Stellaster Archive

VOLUME TWO

Seeding the Wind

Frances Edington

Talking Stick

Whoever holds the talking stick has within their hands the sacred power of words – only the one who holds the stick may speak

but must speak the truth about personal understanding and experience

First published in 2018 in the United Kingdom by
Talkingstick an imprint of
Archive Publishing
Shaftesbury, Dorset, England

Designed at Archive Publishing by Ian Thorp

© 2018 Archive Publishing
Text © Frances Edington, 2018

Frances Edington asserts the moral right to be
identified as the author of this work

A CIP Record for this book is available from
The British Cataloguing in Publication data office

ISBN 978-1-906289-44-7 (Paperback)
ISBN 978-1-906289-46-1 (Trilogy Presentation Set)

All rights reserved. No part of this publication may be reproduced, stored in a retrieval system, or transmitted at any time or by any means digital, electronic, mechanical,
photocopying, recording or otherwise, without the prior permission of the publisher

Cover design created by Ian Thorp

www.archivepublishing.co.uk

Printed and bound in Cornwall by TJInternational

ACKNOWLEDGEMENTS

Seeding the Wind would never have been published without the encouragement and support of my good friend, Hazel Marshall. As editor of four published books, she was the ideal person to suggest improvements, so if the book reads well, it is in no small part due to her wise guidance but I take full responsibility for any defects in style or content.

Many mentors and teachers have ignited my interest in matters philosophical and chief among them must be the gurus of the Siddha tradition whose wisdom has brought light into the lives of many, many people — including the writer.

My only concern is that I may have misinterpreted their teachings in this work of fiction. That aside, I owe my existence to their benevolent grace.

My thanks also go to Ian Thorp of Archive Publishing for his help and guidance in bringing this book to publication.

CONTENTS

Acknowledgements v
Introduction vii
Prologue xi

Chapter

1. HARBINGERS OF DAWN 1
2. TWIN-TALK 12
3. TRACKING A TRAITOR 32
4. MAKING PLANS 40
5. VERSILLA 63
6. SRIANDRA 79
7. JUBILEE PRIZES 88
8. DECEPTION 104
9. DISAPPOINTING NEWS 110
10. BIOSPHERES 123
11. BANDERENE 136
12. FIRESTONE 147
13. DEVASTATION 163
14. RETRIBUTION 175
15. PLANNING THE END GAME 189
16. PREPARING TO LEAVE 204
17. THE THIRD EXHIBITION 218
18. A TWIST IN THE TALE 230
19. A NEW EMPEROR 244
20. ARMAGEDDON 259

INTRODUCTION

Stories of one sort or another have always delighted human beings; favourites are retold from generation to generation to become just as crucial a part of a tribe or nation's cultural identity as its gene-pool, geography or history. So far as we know, story-telling is a uniquely human activity; no other species displays this behaviour.

Stories are a product of the creative imagination — that undervalued capacity of mind that provides so much of the richness of our daily experience. Scientists may scoff at Imagination as a purely subjective function, preferring to nail their colours to the objectivity of facts gleaned though careful observation. But it is an inescapable fact that scientific *theories* and *hypotheses* are what have rendered those observations *meaningful* and given Science its astonishing success in modern times.

And theories and hypotheses are, after all, only another mode of story-telling.

It is not only Science that resorts to story-telling: philosophers, theologians, mystics and other thinkers have always told stories as a way of sharing their insights into the mysteries of life. There must be a myriad creation stories, religious parables, heroic epics and the like most of which attempt to answer the Great Questions that have exercised the human mind for millennia.

Why should this be so? Because most people love listening to (or reading) stories but not everyone likes listening to a sermon or lecture or reading a scholarly dissertation. It was for this reason I chose to use the medium of story-telling when investigating a question that has exercised my mind for many years, as it has the minds of many before me.

The three books that constitute *The Stellaster Archive* are my attempt to answer the question: *What is it that differentiates human beings from all other species?*

Some writers have suggested that humans did not originate on Earth but came as aliens from another planet. It's an interesting idea but there is very strong evidence against, as anyone who has studied embryology will attest. Human beings clearly evolved on Earth from other terrestrial species — or at any rate our *bodies* did.

But it is our *mental* powers and capacities that distinguish Mankind from the other animals, not our physical qualities. It is our use of language (not merely the *capacity to communicate*, which appears to be universal) plus the emergence of what is generally referred to as *civilisation*, a few millennia ago. Civilisation was a sudden development in the ponderous context of Evolution — even of *humanoid* evolution — which suggests the intervention of some sort of external agent or influence.

The possibility occurred to me that, though our physical bodies are fashioned from Earth materials — materials that remain on Earth when we die — *our minds are formed of a different, more subtle substance, one that might well have had a non-terrestrial origin*. If so, what was that origin?

There is nothing to suggest that the mind remains with the physical corpse after death — indeed there are plenty of studies that suggest the exact opposite — which tells us that mind and body are different entities that have become *associated* during the period of our lives on Earth but part again at death.

If mind and body have different origins, is it possible that the human mind did not evolve on Earth but, like those earlier suggestions, came here from another world and was transplanted, by some means unknown, into the body of an Earth creature? Surely it is not such an outlandish proposition.

What if the mind of a person *could* be transplanted into someone else's body? The yogis of India know a thing or two about the quite extraordinary qualities and capacities of mind. During my studies in India, I came across hints that such mind transplantation is a possibility. Those hints gave birth to a story that has assumed epic proportions over the years as I worked through the implications of my *tongue-in-cheek* hypothesis.

The Stellaster Archive is that story and recounts the final years of Stellaster, the fifth of Sol's rocky planets. An ancient prophecy has foretold the coming of a meteor that will totally destroy this world, home to angels, elves and dwarves. What can be done in the short time available to save a few remnants of the unique civilisation that angels have developed on this world over the millennia?

The Wrath of Time — Book One of a trilogy — introduces the angels charged with planning for the coming catastrophe; in particular, we follow the fortunes of Calthea-Tai, a crystallographer who has been charged with recording the remarkable achievements of civilisation for posterity. But it will require a great deal more than an extensive knowledge of crystals for Calthea to address her mission; first she must understand the nature of mind and how one mind communicates with other minds.

Book Two — *Seeding the Wind* — takes the story forward; three spaceships are dispatched to other worlds carrying carefully selected refugees; they will have to establish a new civilisation on a world lacking a biosphere; can they survive for more than a generation or two? Back on Stellaster, arrangements must also be made to support those who cannot escape the coming annihilation.

The final book of the trilogy — *Echoes in the Mists of Time* —

brings the story up to the present. Four angels have escaped the devastation in the inner Solar System by taking their tiny space-shuttle on a loop into interstellar space, surviving their long excursion in a state of deep hypothermia. In Part One of *Echoes — Homeward Bound —* we accompany these angels as they re-enter the Solar System and begin searching for other survivors from the destruction of Stellaster.

In Part Two — *Guardians of the Ruby Globe* — we meet Bartholomew Thornhill, a student of London University. One day Bart is given a mysterious ruby globe in mysterious circumstances; who sent it and what is it for? He discovers the answer to the first question but not to the second.

Part Three — *Of Men and Angels* — describes the encounter between the four angels of the space-shuttle with Bart and his companions. Each side has questions it wants the other to answer but things are not that simple. What does emerge is the fact that human beings are *hybrids*, part mammal and part angel.

Human bodies are made from the substance of Earth; they have evolved in exactly the same way as the other species of this planet. But human minds have a totally different origin; they are our inheritance from the angels of Stellaster. It is for this reason that Bart and his fellow humans can communicate with the angels from a vanished world, which had a different system of Evolution.

So that is the thesis underlying this work of the creative imagination. It is up to the reader to decide whether it illuminates their understanding of what it means to be human.

Frances Edington,
Littlehampton,
13th August, 2018

PROLOGUE

London, Late July, 2003:

Leaping down the stairs, four steps at a time, Bart was as graceful and sure-footed as a mountain goat. Out in the Islington street that was his current home, he broke into a steady jog, heading for the underground station at the Angel.

My, but it was hot!

A sudden blast of wind sent empty coke tins tumbling in the gutter and crisp packets spiralling up into the air and suddenly all light drained out of the day. Bart glanced behind him to see a purple cloud advancing at pace from the west. That same moment a flash of lightning split the cloud and a simultaneous clap of thunder announced the imminent arrival of rain. Lightly clad as he was, Bart realised he was in for a soaking.

He happened to be passing a deeply recessed shop doorway so lost no time in seeking shelter. Facing him was a glass door bearing the legend:

The Bric-a-Brac Shop, Est. 1868, Prop. Josiah Soames.

He must have passed the shop a hundred times on his way to the Angel yet had never noticed it before. He pushed his way in to find a veritable Aladdin's Cave. At the tinkling of the door bell, an old man entered from a back room.

'Good morning, sir! Can I interest you in anything in particular?'

'Actually, I came in to shelter from the rain. May I browse?'

An elephant's foot sported an odd assortment of umbrellas, walking sticks and an old cricket bat. Bart was mad about cricket so, slinging his sports bag on the glass counter, he drew the bat out to examine it more closely.

'Will you forgive me for a moment, sir? I have something for you.'

The shopkeeper retreated to the back room, returning in a couple of minutes bearing a heavy parcel wrapped in brown paper and tied with string.

'This is for you sir. It was brought in some time ago. I've been waiting for you to claim it.'

Bart stared at the old man in disbelief.

'But you don't even know who I am!' he exclaimed. 'This is the first time I've ever set foot in your shop and I'm certain we've never met before.'

'That's as may be, Mr Thornhill, but this box was left for you and we've kept it safe for when you should call in to collect it.'

'But how do you know my name? Are you a magician of some sort?'

He examined the innocent-looking mind-reader standing before him and his amazement grew by the minute.

'Never mind that sir. I'm no magician; I'm just the keeper of your parcel. Don't you want it after all the care we've taken of it?'

'But what is it?'

'I have no idea! We were asked to keep it safe and out of the damp, so my father put it in the storeroom where it's warm in winter and cool in summer.... Don't you want to open it?'

Josiah Soames placed the parcel on the glass counter. The dusty brown paper was tied with jute string, now yellowed with age; over the central knot was a large blob of red sealing wax with a faint insignia in its centre. Bart cut the string on either side of the seal, carefully peeling away the fragile paper to reveal a wooden block about nine inches square. Carrying it over to the window where the light was a little better, he noticed that five sides of the box were etched with strange patterns but the sixth was smooth.

Closer examination revealed a fine line running round four sides. It was obviously a box with a lid. Bart prised off this lid then brought the two sections back to the counter. Fitting into the baize-lined wooden case was a further cube of polished black stone; this slid out easily. Bart placed it on the counter beside the wooden box.

'I wonder if it's like a Babushka doll; you know, those Russian dolls that fit one inside the other? Let's see if there's another box inside this black one.'

Again Bart found and prised off the lid but this time, instead of another cube, he found a globe packed tightly with crushed silk. It was dark and shiny, possibly made of the same substance as the box and measuring about five inches in diameter. Bart held the globe up to the light but it was totally opaque. He could learn very little about his mysterious acquisition.

'What is it, Mr Soames; an obsidian crystal ball? If so, I'm surprised it was left for me; I'm an astronomer not an astrologer; it must belong to a fortune-teller. Have you ever seen anything like it before?'

'Can't say I have, sir.'

'How did you get it? You said it was left some years ago? How long ago?'

Bart's questions could barely keep pace with the thoughts flooding his mind. It was a mystery and no mistake. The old man scratched his head.

'Well now, when did that man come in? I was still a school-boy so it must have been around the last year of the war — yes, it was 1945. A man came in with that parcel. He said he'd lost a leg in India and been shipped home to get an artificial leg. As he was leaving Bombay, some chap he'd never met before asked him to bring the parcel to my Dad in London. He gave him instructions to help him find us.'

'He told us: *you're to keep it for a young gentleman named Bartholomew Thornhill who'll come in to collect it; it may be some little while. Be sure you don't give it to anyone but Bartholomew Thornhill. It's important so please don't let us down.*'

'But Mr Soames, in 1945 I wasn't even born! My parents didn't meet till 1980 and I wasn't born till 1982. How can this be left for a person who won't be born for almost forty years? I can't think the parcel is meant for me. It must be for some other Bartholomew Thornhill who never showed up to collect it.'

'That's as may be but I don't believe it for a moment. The man said it might be some time. Anyway, *Bartholomew Thornhill* isn't a common name. Had it been *John Smith*, there might be something in what you say. No sir, it was meant for you all right. Now are you going to take the box so I can rest happy I've carried out our side of the bargain?'

'But how do you *know* I'm Bartholomew Thornhill? It's all pretty mysterious! You took one look at me and went off to fetch this parcel. I'm amazed I can tell you. That's almost as spooky as getting the box itself.'

'There's no mystery to that, sir. You put your bag on the counter when you took up the cricket bat. It's got your name on the label: *Bartholomew Thornhill, Imperial College, London*. When I saw that, I knew our task was over at long last. At least, I *hope* it's over. I don't want to have to keep that parcel for another sixty years.'

'Well you may have solved one mystery Mr Soames, but it certainly doesn't solve the main one: why the box was left for me in the first place? What am I meant to do with it? He said it was *very important*, you say? But what's it for?'

'You'll have to find that out for yourself, sir. We was only asked to keep the parcel till you came in to collect it.'

* * * * *

How Bart discovers the origin and purpose of his mysterious globe will be told in Volume Three of *The Stellaster Archive*, entitled *Echoes in the Mists of Time*. The actual story of how, when, where and why this and four other globes were made began in Volume One, *The Wrath of Time* and concludes in this volume, *Seeding the Wind*.

The Wrath of Time, follows the story of Calthea-Tai, a crystallographer who has been charged with recording the unique culture of the angels of Stellaster for posterity. This has become necessary because the complete destruction of her home, the planet Stellaster, has been prophesied by an unimpeachable source — Oracle.

Calthea must find a way of fashioning information storage devices that will keep her recordings uncorrupted for centuries, possibly for millennia. Her extensive knowledge of crystals will be insufficient to address the subtler the aspects of her assignment so she is sent to be trained by one of the foremost thinkers of the day, Professor Gylan-Bahle.

Volume One concludes with Calthea completing this part of her training with the Seraphim, a sect of angels who devote their lives to spiritual pursuits and the healing arts. The story of her assignment and the mission of which it forms a part is told in the present volume, *Seeding the Wind*.

VOLUME TWO

SEEDING THE WIND

Chapter 1

THE HARBINGERS OF DAWN

Through the emptiness of space, Stellaster journeyed along her destined path around Sol, revolving on her axis as she had done since Time Immemorial; that turning brought the city of Cander Imperia into night. Profound stillness engulfed the entire valley; citizens slept beneath the star-strewn sky; nothing stirred; even the guards stood motionless at their posts.

* * * * *

In all that stillness, one soul had been abandoned by sleep. Lord Versain paced the roof of his Ducal Palace, halting now and then to gaze out over the valley. For many nights sleep had refused to grant solace to his troubled mind; the darkness of the valley was indistinguishable from the darkness pervading his soul. Never had he felt so overwhelmed by darkness; it was an alien state he could neither account for nor shake off and that darkness was threatening to paralyse his entire being.

What had caused it? At first no insight came but then an answer began to take shape in his mind.

Since his early schooldays, Girilayne-Bahle had been a constant factor in his life, shaping his character and his mind. She'd continued as his guide and mentor as they worked together to set up the community. It had been a joint endeavour and now she was gone. He reminded himself that he was bound to feel some emptiness of soul at the loss of such a dear and close companion. Everyone had to face the loss of loved ones sooner or later; death wasn't a rare or unexpected phenomenon; people had been dying ever since angels first appeared in the world.

So why had Girilayne's departure left him feeling so utterly bereft?

Then insight came: the community had been a secret project, kept well hidden from the outer world. Always before, he'd relished the challenge of setting up this clandestine and highly illegal project whilst at the same time carrying out his official duties. He had thoroughly enjoyed living his double life, juggling two incompatible roles; he'd given the community the time and attention it needed whilst keeping that aspect of his life scrupulously hidden as he strutted about at Court playing his role as Royal Duke and Commander-in-Chief of the Imperial Forces.

He'd been well aware of the risks they'd taken — they'd broken several rigidly enforced laws — yet that had never stopped him from doing what was necessary, no matter how illegal. Now it was beginning to dawn on him that he'd only been able to take such a light-hearted stance because Girilayne had shouldered the responsibility; he'd merely been a figurehead.

But Girilayne had gone and he must accept responsibility for the community and its work. Why should that have made such a difference?

In the past he'd felt like a soldier carrying out the orders of his superior officer so had been spared personal accountability. Why couldn't he go on like that? Yet he knew he couldn't because he'd begun to see things in a new light. Unconsciously, his inner *conviction* had begun to waver; he'd begun to question the prophecy and that was like a canker gnawing away at his soul.

Girilayne had been absolutely sure they'd been sent to carry out this rescue mission. She'd been convinced that a meteor would strike Stellaster and that her life's work — and his — was to prepare the world for that disaster. Always before, he'd been content to ride on the back of her conviction.

Since her departure — not consciously, but in the depths of his soul — he'd begun to doubt the truth of the prophecy and therefore their justification for all the things they'd done. Always before he'd been sure that what they were doing was in the Empire's best interests so their actions were morally justified even if they were technically illegal.

But that position only held good if the prophecy was true.

He'd relied on Girilayne's faith in the prophecy because that faith was based on many interviews with Oracle. The day after her *Farewell* he'd escorted Calthea to Srivalian and had requested an audience with Oracle; he wanted her assurance that she'd support him in this work as she'd supported Girilayne. It had been a shock to have his request denied. He'd never been turned away before but then he'd never requested an audience before — Oracle had always summoned him — but why must she turn him away at the time of his greatest need?

Something else was nagging him too, something crucial to the safety of the community. He'd been about to mention this to Girilayne but she'd told him of her intention to enter the caves and the shock of that had put this other issue out of his mind. Then at her Farewell Ceremony, something had triggered his sense of danger but he couldn't remember what it was; all he knew was that the two incidents were related. Undoubtedly this other anxiety was a factor in his present depression.

As the Duke paced up and down, his thoughts gnawed at his confidence and his spirits spiralled ever deeper into a pit of despair. He urgently needed someone to help him climb out of that pit. Where could he find such a confidante? Calthea was definitely not the right person; anyway she was in retreat at Sriandra. Gylan-Bahle would only lecture him on the need to give grief time to run its natural course. Vyvyan-Varenne had been a close friend for a long time but their friendship was based on mutual respect; he dreaded Vyvyan seeing how helpless he'd become. It seemed there was no one he could turn to for the support and reassurance he needed so very badly.

At that moment, Versain noticed the first signs of dawn lightening the eastern sky. Perhaps he'd catch the *dawn miracle*.

As a young cherub, he'd rise early in hopes of catching the fleeting miracle that sometimes appeared at dawn. Often he'd be accompanied by his twin Versilla; she'd been every bit as enthralled by this strange phenomenon. They'd find themselves a vantage point and wait for the sky to pale, then they'd fix their eyes on the eastern horizon, each determined to be first to catch the magical line in the sky. They'd watch the delicate shimmering line rise in an arc spanning the sky in advance of the rising sun. Then they'd stay till daylight swamped the line, just as it swamped the myriad stars of the night sky.

If he caught the dawn miracle this morning, Versain would take it as an omen of hope, a sign that all would turn out well in the end.

* * * * *

High, high in the sky, the gossamer wings of the harbingers caught the rays of the rising sun. They were the only species known to inhabit such a rarefied habitat; they floated upon the upper surface of Stellaster's atmosphere at its boundary with the vacuum of space.

Their habitat was extraordinary in another way: the harbingers occupied a narrow strip of the sky thousands of miles long yet only fifty yards wide and spanning from pole to pole. This elongated strip bore no relation to the land below but kept a constant position in relation to the sun — the harbingers kept the sun ever rising over the eastern horizon and therein inhabited another boundary, the boundary dividing night from day.

Harbingers were very delicate beings three to five inches tall with a wing span much the same; those wings were gossamer fine and scattered the sun's rays into all the colours of the spectrum. Millions upon millions of these tiny creatures inhabited that narrow strip of the outer atmosphere. They spent their lives dancing in and out of the rising sun's rays, twisting and twirling in sheer delight, wings shimmering now red, now green, now blue, now golden.

They were a social species, extremely vocal, chattering away to each other in a constant sing-song that sounded like a flock of twittering birds. Harbingers enjoyed a well developed culture that expressed itself entirely through song and dance. The spectacular arc made by these creatures was visible from the ground for a few minutes in the paling skies of dawn.

No harbinger had ever been found on the ground; to drop even a few feet below the surface of the upper atmosphere was to court death since the tiniest increase in pressure would crush their delicate frames to dust. So not many angels knew of this species and were quite unaware of the true nature of the daily phenomenon that early risers named the dawn miracle.

* * * * *

With the eastern sky growing paler by the minute, Versain, eager to catch this dawn phenomenon, flew to the highest point of his palace roof. Within moments, he spotted the fine crescent shimmering just above the horizon and felt his spirits soar in joyful remembrance. On more than one occasion he'd flown with the harbingers.

The first time, he'd just graduated from the Academy; he'd been with a group of cadets making their first flight to Stellaster's moon, Verastra; the cadets were escorted to the moon, but were required to find their own way back to camp. He remembered how he'd planned his flight to re-enter Stellaster's atmosphere at the site of the rising sun; it would be an ideal opportunity to study the dawn miracle.

He only identified the harbingers when he was very close; their wings were scintillating in the rays of the rising sun, which from his vantage point, still lay below the horizon. Only when he was within a few yards of that shimmering line did he realise it was composed of living creatures. When he was sure they weren't afraid of him, he come closer and eventually joined their ranks. He spent an hour flying up and down the line in the midst of a cloud of fluttering, chattering creatures who were obviously just as curious about him as he was about them.

He'd been thrilled to be welcomed into their ranks in that way. Over the years, he'd even come to understand something of their language.

Now, seeing that sparkling line sweeping across the sky, Versain realised that this was another of Stellaster's treasures that would vanish for ever if and when their world was destroyed. He must think of some way of preserving them. Yet how could such incredibly delicate creatures be transported safely to another world? The Duke resolved to discover some means of saving at least a few of these exquisite, life-loving creatures; he'd raise the issue at the next meeting of the Paradisia Council.

Then Versain remembered that Versilla had loved the harbingers every bit as much as he did. Should she come to know of the fate in store for them, she'd want him to do everything in his power to save some of them. Then inspiration struck: he'd been trying to think of someone to help him overcome his demons yet hadn't thought of the most obvious person; his twin had a heart as big as the universe; who better to drag him out of this black pit of despair?

In the past, he and Girilayne had taken the greatest care to keep the existence of the community secret from the outside world and from the Emperor and Empress in particular. They'd felt it would place too great a burden on the shoulders of the new Monarchs as they tackled the daunting task of reviving a people brought to its knees by the tyrant's cruelty. It would only have added to Versilla's burden had she known of her twin's illegal activities.

In addition, Emperor Wellbeloved was not a person to be trusted with such a vital secret. He was an open-hearted, gentle soul but quite capable of blurting out confidential matters to the wrong people at the wrong time. Empress Serenity was an entirely different matter; his twin was the epitome of discretion; with her, a secret remained a secret unless there was good reason why it should not. Perhaps it was time he told Versilla what he'd been up to these past few years; he was sure she'd appreciate and respect the need for absolute secrecy. She was also in a position to protect him should things threaten to unravel.

The Duke returned to his apartments in a far happier state of mind. Daylight had erased the beautiful dawn-bow but seeing it had left him with a great deal of the harbingers' cheerful optimism. Perhaps this black depression might at last begin to loosen its grip.

Later that morning, he flew to the Imperial Palace. As he approached the compound, he saw several groups of angelas and cherubs all heading in the same direction and recalled that Empress Serenity held open court from ten in the morning till three in the afternoon. It was clearly not a good time for a confidential talk but he could at least arrange a time for a private meeting later in the day.

The Empress was about to take her place on the dais as the Duke entered. She greeted her brother in surprise.

'My Lord Versain! We seldom see you this early; indeed we seldom see you here at all these days. Where have you been hiding yourself?'

She held out her hand and he carried it to his lips as required by etiquette, making a formal bow and murmuring:

'Imperial Majesty.'

She looked up, smiling with pleasure but then exclaimed:

'Versain, whatever's the matter? You look dreadful! Your aura's lost its glow and where's the famous banter? *Imperial Majesty* indeed! You need a rest my dear brother; you've clearly been overworking. I shall arrange with Wellbeloved for you to take a good long holiday from your obviously onerous duties.'

'It's not a holiday I need, but a talk with *you*,' he said quietly, trying to avoid being overheard by her attendants. 'I need your wisdom Versilla, but this isn't the time or place. Can you spare me a couple of hours later? I'm afraid we'll need at least that amount of time; there's a great I need to discuss with you.'

'How intriguing! I've some appointments this afternoon but I can safely leave them to Vinchetta — you remember Vincheta? She's Wellbeloved's cherub — or rather she was a cherub a long time ago; she's now my chief attendant.'

'I remember her in her teens; I haven't talked to her since. Wasn't she keen on Geology? I seem to remember being dragged out on some expedition with a bunch of tweens to study the rocks of Cander Heights and being quizzed by Vinchetta; she wanted to know the name of every rock.'

'That would be Vinchetta! She's highly intelligent, you know. I'm grooming her to be the next Empress.'

'It's not up to you to select the next Empress, it's up to the Council — as and when the time comes — which it won't for many years. Anyway, why choose one of Wellbelloved's offspring rather than one of your own; they'll be the right age, by the time….' He paused.

'You mean *by the time we're due to enter the Caves* so why not say so?'

'I have no problem with that; I didn't know whether you had.'

'Look Versain, we can't talk now. Stay and watch if you like, but I shan't have time to talk till the audience is over. There are always more people wanting to see me than I can deal with. Come back at three and I'll give you all the time you need. I'm curious to know what's brought you here at this particular time when you've been clearly avoiding me for goodness knows how long. I only see you at Court functions and even then you invariably arrive late.'

Versain retreated to the back of the hall; he wanted to observe how his twin handled her official duties. At Court receptions he'd often watched as she carried out her social obligations and been pleased by her grace and dignity. How did she carry out her work as Monarch of the Angelas?

When the Empress saw that the Duke had decided to stay, she sent Vinchetta to explain proceedings to him.

'Your Royal Highness, you see the three lines?' Vinchetta whispered in his ear. 'Outside, the attendants sort arrivals into those with official business — they come up in the right-hand lane; those who've come to pay their respects to Her Majesty are directed to the centre line and we reserve the left lane for nine-year-old cherubs who come during their final year in First School. They visit the Empress as the grand finale of a week-long visit to the Capital.'

'Why no tweens?'

'Her Majesty goes on tour to the provinces three times a year and visits the Mother Houses and schools then; she doesn't want tweens and students coming here when they should be studying. Anyway, by visiting the settlements Her Majesty can assess for herself how well the schools and Mother Houses are being run.'

'Isn't that the job of the Schools Inspectorate and the Motherhood Supremo?'

'It is, but by visiting in person she can see whether the inspectors are doing a good job. I can tell you my Lord, it's a very foolish person who is taken in by Her Majesty's serene presence; she may live up to her Imperial name in public but woe betide the Mother who falls short in the care of her charges or the teacher who fails to inspire her students to achieve their best. Her Majesty is very tough if she notices carelessness or indifference; a teacher or Mother could well find herself re-training for a far less interesting career.'

'She's a hard task-master — mistress — then?'

'Oh no, my Lord! Not if you mean she's *unfair*. If the Empress sees excellent practice, she's the first to praise that person and rewards them far more generously than anyone could expect. Her Majesty is much loved and admired, not least because of the high standards she demands. She inspires us to strive for levels of excellence we never knew we were capable of.'

At this moment there was a buzz of excited chatter and about twenty cherubs in the charge of three teachers were ushered into the hall; they advanced up the left hand lane towards the Imperial throne in a barely controlled stampede. The Empress was talking to a group in the right line and Versain noticed with approval that she was not in the least distracted by the boisterous surge of the cherubs.

She completed her conversation with the angelas who bowed and left. Only then did she turn to greet the excited newcomers. She addressed each cherub as she was introduced and gave her a small gift from the table at her side. She then spent a few minutes talking to the teachers before signalling her attendants to escort the cherubs to the side of the dais.

'They're being invited to stay and watch,' Vinchetta explained. 'After a few minutes they'll be escorted to the Royal Mother House. That's the highlight of their holiday; it's a good way of getting them out of the hall without feeling sad at leaving the Empress. We expect three First School visits today; sometimes there are more.'

After a while Lord Versain thanked Vinchetta for her commentary then, impressed by what he'd seen, left in search of his *aide-de-camp*. He needed to brief Devallian who would have to cover for him during his meeting with the Empress later in the afternoon.

Chapter 2

Twin-Talk

Shortly before three, the Duke returned to the Empress's Palace. In an archway leading to her Court, a dwarf was lurking in the shadows, obviously waiting for him. It was very unusual for a dwarf to speak to a member of the Royal Family unless he had been summoned so the Duke was on his guard.

The fellow bowed respectfully enough and waited until given leave to speak. When he did, he turned the Duke's world upside down.

'Great Lord, I am Sujinka. There is something I have to report. This morning I went to see Dorka at the university; I knew he would give me good advice as he is known to you. Dorka said I must see you myself, Great Lord; he said I must report to you what I have heard as soon as I could find you alone; he said I must choose a place where no one would overhear our talk.'

'This sounds serious, Sujinka. Dorka was right to send you to me. Please tell me what it is that is troubling you.'

'Great Lord, I work at the Palace barracks in the place they call *the Mess*. Three evenings ago, I heard some officers discussing something. They seemed very excited. I was working close by so could not help hearing what they said. They didn't seem to notice I was there.'

'*I'm sure they didn't!*' the Duke thought ruefully; dwarves were seen by most soldiers as little more than furniture, not as intelligent beings with ears and brains.

'Did you overhear the subject of their conversation?' The Duke asked.

'I did, Lord. One of the officers had just returned from the moon and boasted that something secret was going on there the others wouldn't know about. He said he'd heard this from a person who worked at the secret place; he said not even the Council or the Emperor knew anything about it. He said this secret place was being run by an illegal group headed by a person at Court.'

'Did the officer name the person at Court?'

'No Lord, he didn't. I don't think he knew who it was himself. I thought he was just bragging. Then the next evening I heard the same officer telling the same story to different officers; this time I thought it was more than just boasting. It seemed to me he was trying to get these other officers to join him in some sort of action. I don't know what, because they left the Mess.

'Then again last night, this officer was telling his story to a third group; I felt I should say something because this lot seemed keen on making trouble. If they'd been going to report to their senior officer, I'd have said nothing, but it sounded like they wanted to get something for themselves. If there's treason involved, why didn't they say they'd report it to their superior officer, or even directly to you, Lord?'

'Sujinka, you've done right in coming to me. If there's anything going on that shouldn't be, the sooner I find out the better. Do you know the name of this officer?'

'He's a captain in the Surveillance Corps Lord, but I don't know his name. I think it should be easy to find him because of his plumage; he has grey wings with rusty red tips and his body plumage is rusty red all over.'

'Thank you for coming to me Sujinka, and for being so discreet in dealing with this. I would like you to keep the matter to yourself until I discover what it's about. Will you promise not to tell anyone else? It was fine for you to speak to Dorka, he is trustworthy, but I wouldn't like anyone else to know until I've investigated.'

'Great Lord, I give my word. If I should hear anything more, should I come and tell you?'

'Yes do. But please don't go out of your way to try and overhear conversations; you could put yourself in danger. I must thank you again for coming to me; it needed some courage I believe.'

The Duke was well aware how deeply respectful of authority all dwarves were so he was impressed that Sujinka had felt brave enough to report his suspicions to the Comander-in-Chief in person. The dwarf bowed deeply and took his leave in one direction; a badly shaken Versain continued on his way in the other.

As the Duke was entering the Audience Chamber, he met the Emperor also on his way to see the Empress. Wellbeloved greeted Versain with his usual *bonhomie*. Since the Emperor was incapable of hiding his feelings, the Duke was reassured that he at least had not yet heard of any illegal organisation operating on Verastra.

What should he do now? He must certainly confide in his sister this very day, trusting she'd understand their reasons for setting up the community in secret and in breach of so many laws. He had to wait on tenterhooks whilst the Emperor conferred with his consort, hoping she wouldn't make any compromising remarks about her brother's sudden and urgent request for a private interview.

To the Duke's relief, the Emperor left after a brief word. Versilla could now devote the remainder of the afternoon to her long-estranged brother.

'What's this about, Versain?' she demanded as soon as they were alone. 'Shall we talk here, or would you prefer to walk in the gardens?'

'Oh, let's walk outside, somewhere where we can talk in complete privacy.'

'Good gracious! You *are* sounding mysterious, my dear Versain. Let's go to the Crystal Grove; no one will be there at this time of day.'

Every dawn, the Empress led the dawn *Obeisance* in this grove but now it was empty and bathed in afternoon sunshine. They walked for a time in silence; she was giving him plenty of time to tell his tale. When he began, it was in a tentative tone that contrasted strangely with his usual air of self-confidence.

'I spent a sleepless night fraught with worry and didn't know who I could to turn to for comfort and relief. Then I watched the dawn miracle and that reminded me there's only one person in this world who knows me to my core, only one person I can turn to with complete confidence and trust.

'We've not seen very much of each other these past few years Silla, and I admit that was deliberate on my part.' The Empress was delighted that her brother had used the diminutive of her name; it told her he wanted to renew their old intimacy. 'I kept away,' the Duke continued, 'because I know only too well your ability to see things people wish to hide and I have very definitely had something to hide.'

'Good gracious, Versain! Now you're beginning to worry me. Have you been leading a double life?'

'That's just what I mean! You have this uncanny ability to put your finger right on the spot. Yes, I've been leading a double life — and taking great care you wouldn't get to know about it.'

'But now you're telling me yourself, so something must

have changed.'

'Yes, something's changed and I can't keep you in the dark any longer; in fact, it's now essential that you *should* know.'

'Well I'm glad to hear it. Have you had an unhappy love affair? Has someone close to you died recently?'

'The latter. What's changed is that Girilayne-Bahle went into the Caves just a few days ago leaving me utterly devastated and feeling totally abandoned.'

'Now you're talking nonsense, Versain! Girilayne was killed in an accident at least ten years ago. You can't still be mourning her; I know you were close but it really isn't healthy to be mourning her after all this time.'

'But there you're wrong, my dear Silla. Girilayne *wasn't* killed in that accident. In fact, the accident was carefully staged so that we could get on with our work — our secret work. But a week ago she finally entered the Caves and ... '

'I don't understand what you're saying, Versain.'

'I knew this was going to be difficult.'

'Well, you must do your best. I'll listen, but you'll have to help me understand. You've obviously been carrying a heavy burden; I want to share that burden if I can. I know you wouldn't do anything wrong or illegal, or stand by if someone else did, so Girilayne must have had good reason for staging a fake death.'

'She did. Look Silla, I'd better start this story at the beginning; it all starts with Girilayne anyway. Do you remember how she was appointed as my tutor when she was still very young and totally unqualified for such an appointment?'

'I recall there was a great brouhaha at the time; but we were only ten, weren't we? So we wouldn't have taken much notice of Palace gossip.'

'It seems that Empress Wonderful was told by Oracle to give her the post.'

'*Oracle*? Why would Oracle have anything to do with Palace appointments?'

'She had everything to do with this appointment. Empress Wonderful wasn't like the old tyrant: she had the greatest trust in and respect for Oracle. So when she was told that Oracle wanted her to appoint an unqualified commoner as tutor to a Prince of the Alphaline, she didn't ask questions; she just did as she was told.'

'Yes, but *why* did Oracle want Girilayne appointed as your tutor?'

'That's the crux of the matter. Girilayne had been having strange dreams. She consulted a seraph, who took her to see the Chief Seraph, who arranged an audience with Oracle. The outcome of *that* was Oracle's insistence she be appointed my tutor.'

'It all sounds extraordinarily complicated, Versain. But what did the old tyrant say? Surely it was *his* responsibility to arrange for the education of you princes once you reached ten.'

'I think he was only too happy to see one of his potential rivals given a tutor who would pose no threat to his authority. Remember how paranoid he was about possible contenders to the throne? — he must have rubbed his hands in glee that this prince at least was in the hands of an angela and not some scheming, power-hungry tutor who'd connive to get his protégé into the seat of absolute power.'

Versilla laughed at her brother's accurate description of the deposed despot.

'So Girilayne became your tutor. What happened then?'

'Her appointment was hugely significant in the long run. As you know, the tyrant was mistaken in believing I posed no threat to his throne because it was I who led the insurrection that toppled him. You may be surprised to learn that it was

Girilayne, under orders from Oracle, who masterminded that crazy adventure.'

'You're not serious? How come? Surely Girilayne was no longer your tutor by then — you were at the Academy and she'd gone somewhere else.'

'She'd gone to Bilwinia to be Calthea's tutor.'

'So she had! I'd forgotten she was poor dear Calthea's tutor.'

'It was Girilayne who sent Calthea's first crystal recorder to you at Court and it was Girilayne who brought Calthea to you to receive the Imperial Prize.'

'I'd never made that connection till now. But it was *you* who asked me to persuade Calthea to become a Royal Mother, though I don't think you let on to her that you were the one who chose her and not I.'

'In fact, I didn't: *Girilayne* told me to get you to approach Calthea.'

'Goodness, Versain! What a tangled web and it's all tangled around Girilayne. Please go on with your story. I'm intrigued to know why Girilayne's accident was staged. I do recall at the time thinking you weren't as devastated as I'd expected. But I was seeing you less at that time; I was still getting to grips with my Imperial duties.'

'That was the beginning of my double life,' said the Duke. 'By the way, I know you were unhappy that I wasn't chosen as Emperor, having led the Galliards in our bid to free the world from that monster.'

'Indeed I was! It was unforgivable to pass you over — you, the people's hero. It seemed extraordinary to me that they should choose sweet, gentle Servenken to be Emperor not you but then he invited me to be his Empress and I saw that as a sort of recognition of your role in the revolution. You didn't seem in the least upset at being passed over so I accepted the honour on your behalf, as it were. I still believe you'd have made a wonderful Emperor.'

'I'd have made a *terrible* Emperor; it would have driven me mad! I'd never have been out of the public eye and that would never have suited our mission.'

'What mission? Oh, you must be referring to your *double life*.'

'I am. To backtrack a little: what Oracle told Girilayne was that she'd been sent specially to… '

'Sent? Sent by whom; sent from where?'

'Yes, well, that's all part of this tangled web. Girilayne always said she'd been sent here by the Immortal Powers because of an imminent threat to the future of the world. She said her assignment was something she'd been born to undertake, though I now think that was probably put into her head by Oracle. Anyway, Girilayne was convinced that she and I and Phillestra were all sent to… '

'Versain, you're not making sense. *Phillestra*? Come on! This is fantasy, surely? Phillestra is not yet six years old; surely you can leave that small person out of this fantasy … '

'It's not fantasy whatever else it may be; it's an extremely serious situation. What Oracle told Girilayne was that at a point in the not-too-distant future, a meteor will strike Stellaster, a meteor massive enough to destroy the entire world.'

There was silence as the enormity of this statement sank home.

'Oracle maintains,' he continued gently, 'that the people I've named have been born at this time to rescue whatever can be rescued of our unique culture before our planet with its population of angels and others is smashed to smithereens.'

'You really believe this story, Versain? You really believe the world is about to vanish in a puff of dust?'

'Until a few days ago I hadn't the slightest doubt; I believed the prophecy to be true; after all, it was Oracle saying so; but since Girilayne's departure, something has changed and for the past week my mind's been racked by doubt. It's why I'm in this terrible state. The things we've done can only be justified if the prophecy is true. I'm being driven mad by the thought that we could have got it all wrong. If we have, a lot of brilliant people will have put their lives in jeopardy for nothing.'

'In jeopardy? How so?'

'Girilayne needed to disappear from society because we were ready to establish our community in ... '

'What community?'

'That's what I'm trying to tell you, Silla!' the Duke snapped in frustration. 'We've brought together the best minds we could recruit to work out a plan to save what can be saved of our culture for posterity.'

'But if the planet is destroyed, where will those people live?'

'That's one of the things we're working on; we've brought together a team of brilliant people — scientists, scholars, thinkers — many of them personally known to you and greatly admired by you. Sometimes, the only way to extract someone from society has been to stage an accident, as we did with Girilayne and with Calthea.'

'*Calthea* is with you?'

'Yes; her so-called accident was another dramatic divesion.'

'But her body was found by dwarves. They buried her in the local Caves.'

'The dwarves were acting on my orders. Actually, I kidnapped Calthea on her way to a meeting with the Senate. I have to tell you she was not entirely pleased — not until she found that Girilayne was behind the plan and was there to brief her and help her settle into her new home.'

'And where is this *new home*?'

'Our community is based in the Quartz Mountains.'

'The Quartz Mountains! And how many are there in this community of yours?'

'You sound exactly like Calthea, Silla! We have a hundred people based in the mountains and several more working on a construction site on Verastra.'

'What are they constructing?'

'Three huge spaceships. You ask where people will live if this world is totally destroyed; the answer is that we will have to establish communities on other worlds, communities that must include angelas and cherubs. Spaceships will be needed to carry them to their new homes since angelas and cherubs can't fly long distances.'

'And all this is being done in total secrecy, Versain? I've heard no rumours of any community which, given the scale you've mentioned, is quite an achievement. How have you managed to keep such a large and complex enterprise secret all these years? How have you kept it supplied?'

'I'd better confess: we've broken pretty well every law on the Statute Book. I've been able to draw on supplies and services in my position as Commander-in-Chief. We've also been able to recruit the very best people, specialists crucial to the success of our many endeavours. Girilayne was brilliant at persuading people to join us even when they realised there could be no return to their old lives. Our people are virtual prisoners in the mountains but they've willingly agreed to abide by our strict rules and are fully committed to the success of our mission.'

'And who precisely are these brilliant people you've enticed away? They can't be all that famous or we'd have noticed. All our luminaries couldn't suddenly fall victim to fatal accidents without somebody commenting on the fact.'

'Well, that's another law we've broken. Some recruits were due to go to their eternal rest but agreed to be *rescued* after their Farewell Ceremony to give us a few more years of their expertise and experience.'

'But surely it's impossible to *rescue* someone, as you delicately put it. The caves are very closely monitored; the system doesn't permit escapes.'

'The Caves are run by dwarves and dwarves owe me special allegiance. Before the Insurrection, dwarves suffered more than most at the hands of the tyrant. As I was leader of the Galliards who sent him packing, they now see me as their saviour. If I want anything done, I have only to ask a dwarf.'

'You mean there are *several* death-evaders in your community? Oh, Versain but that's so dangerous! You know what a horrible fate is in store if they're caught — and for anyone who has helped them. How could you take such enormous risks?'

'It's strange, isn't it; you didn't bat an eyelid when I confessed to purloining supplies, yet you tremble at the notion that someone might defer their right to eternal rest. Our elders have offered us their expertise to ensure a future for our species — there won't be a future for anyone or anything without their contribution. It's strange how deeply the Death Law has become imbedded in our psyche.'

'It's not strange at all. The law was introduced by Magister who knew that if he succeeded in getting angels to give up their constant warring — which he did — and if seraphs continued to hone their healing skills — which they have — the population would begin to increase and that increase would accelerate rapidly until the planet became seriously overpopulated.

'Nothing has changed to make that insight any less valid. The Motherhood Programme controls births and the Death Law ensures that births and deaths remain in balance. There are no exceptions: not even an Emperor or an Empress can extend their stay in this world by so much as a day once their

Due Departure Date has arrived. You know this as well as I do.'

'But something *has* changed, Versilla — the threat to the survival of our planet. Surely the prophecy justifies *any* action that will ensure — or seek to ensure — the survival of our species.'

'But that's the whole point, Versain! *Is* this prophecy a reality, or a figment of Girilayne's imagination? After all, there've been many prophecies of doom before and without exception they've all turned out to be hoaxes.'

'It isn't Girilayne's prophecy; it's Oracle's; that's what makes it so difficult to doubt. But the possibility that it might not be true is driving me crazy. Until Girilayne left I hadn't a vestige of a doubt that it was true; I had a strong intuition that she was right — that I had been sent to lead a team charged with saving our culture from the coming devastation. But now I'm torn by doubt.'

'Then why not request an audience with Oracle? Surely she's the key. Wouldn't it be better to share your concerns with her? I have no idea whether your tale makes sense or not. Anyway, don't you have someone on your team who can prove this meteor is on its way, who can verify the prophecy by direct observation? Don't you have astronomers you can call on?'

'Yes, we have Professor Kritten, but … '

'*Kinver-Kritten* is with you?'

'Yes, we recruited him a couple of years ago.'

'Oh Versain! You really do have famous people working for you.'

'But even the best astronomers with the very finest telescopes, can't confirm the prophecy and they can't prove that the meteor's *not* there either. We're left with a big dilemma: do we shrug our shoulders and say, *this so-called prophecy is just moonshine*! or do we turn our minds to what can be done, in case it turns out to be true?'

'So what solutions have you come up with? Is setting up communities on other worlds your sole strategy? What if those communities don't succeed, what if the new worlds prove unsuitable habitats in the long run?'

'The settlements are only one of a number of avenues we're exploring. Many of us believe it's the only practical answer because we'd be preserving our species as well as our culture. But as you say...'

'But if *angels* don't survive, who else could benefit from our culture?'

'Well, we're planning to make permanent records of the best of our civilisation in the hope that those recordings will fall into the hands of intelligent beings on some other world and that they might benefit from them.'

'That's utter nonsense! Name one species in either of the other biospheres that could benefit from our notion of a civilised life. You can't! Not even dwarves or elves have the intellectual capacity to adopt all aspects of our way of life yet they evolved from the same ancient ancestors as we did.'

'It's possible that an intelligent species might visit the Solar System from outer Space; they'd come across our recordings and so be able to introduce features of our civilisation into their own.'

'That's pure poppycock and you know it, Versain. What evidence is there that *any* alien species has visited the Solar System in the past four billion years? None!'

'You can't say that, Silla. We've no direct evidence that the creatures presently living in the three biospheres originated on these planets. Life could well have been seeded from some other world and evolved on the planets those seeds happened to land on in different ways. I do agree however, that there's pretty little chance of non-angels adopting our way of life.'

'I'm glad to hear you say so. I always thought you had

more common sense than most.'

'Thank you for the compliment; but we shouldn't dismiss either possibility out of hand. There's another reason for making recordings of our culture. Let's suppose we succeeded in establishing settlements on other worlds, for several generations the survivors would have to deal with the enormous challenges of daily life in an alien environment; they'd soon forget the finer aspects of our culture.

'But once they'd established a firm footing and the future was assured, they'd have more time for art, music and drama; that's when these recordings would come in to kick-start a new era of civilised living; they'd be able to replicate a little of what we've achieved on Stellaster in the course of our history. All would not be lost.'

'That makes more sense. But it does depend upon the survival of these new settlements. Which worlds do you have in mind to colonise?'

'We believe the only practical possibilities are the moons of Earth and Mars and possibly one or two of the Jovian moons; the planets themselves present serious problems. The most promising world is Luna; it's a lot smaller than Stellaster but its surface is not so very different from our own; the main problem is the intensity of the sunlight. Phobos is a possibility but it's very small; Deimos is just an ugly rock.'

'We already have bases on Luna and Phobos,' The Empress responded. 'that should make it easier to set up settlements. Angelas and cherubs could be brought in to join the angelis already based there. You've been to those worlds yourself, Versain; do you think they could replace Stellaster in the long run?'

'No other world could possibly *replace* Stellaster; we'll just have to make the best of what's available. But I do believe a community could be established on Luna, given luck and a successful voyage. I'd be hesitant to put my hopes on Phobos; it's too small to provide a permanent home for a reasonably-sized population.'

'Can you wait before launching these spaceships of yours? I mean, can you wait for clear evidence that this meteor really is on track for a direct collision?'

'We simply don't know; it's one of our chief concerns. We have no actual date for the collision — except that Oracle says it could be in about ten years' time, when there's some sort of special astronomical conjunction. We'd all like an early sighting of this meteor as that would give us plenty of time to carry out our plans but comets in the Solar System often appear with little warning. Do you remember the comet five years ago — the one they called *Stinger*? That was first observed as it was passing Jupiter's orbit; we'd have had barely a month's warning if it had been on a direct collision course with Stellaster.'

'So what's your plan? Will you send these expeditions off even before you know for sure that the prophecy is talking about a real threat?'

'What would *you* do, Versilla? If you were told by Oracle that a meteor was on its way to destroy our world, would you really wait for visual confirmation, even if it meant there'd be no time to take effective action? Would you really just wait and see? Wouldn't you put your full trust in that extraordinary being and make every possible effort to get at least one spaceship away before disaster struck?'

'Oh Versain, I really don't know. But I *would* want a personal assurance from Oracle that this isn't just a challenge she's set to test your character or something.'

'Well, I *did* ask for an audience as soon as these doubts emerged. The fact is, she refused! I've never heard of Oracle refusing a request before; but I'm no expert in such matters.

It's mostly been Girilayne who had audiences, not me; it was Girilayne who was told what our future course of action must be. I've been summoned on occasion but it's been to brief me on some specific aspect of the mission.

'I simply cannot understand why Oracle should refuse my request. I feel very vulnerable because of that refusal so I had to come and talk to you. But there's also something else.'

'What else?'

Versain stopped and his companion stopped too; he turned to her and she was relieved to see how much brighter his face looked: *he's almost back to his old self*.

'This morning I watched the dawn miracle,' Versain said, 'and I remembered how we used to get up before the dawn and compete to see who'd catch first sight of the harbingers. It reminded me how close we'd been, how in tune with each other's thoughts and feelings. I realised how very much I'd missed that. Then, something happened on my way to see you just now, something deeply troubling.' To Versilla's dismay, the cloud once more darkened her brother's brow.

'What! This afternoon?'

'Yes; just before I met you I was waylaid by a dwarf who works at the barracks; he'd overheard some gossip in the Officers' Mess and felt compelled to report it to me. Someone's been talking out of turn about our work. One of our own people must have let the cat out of the bag and put our entire operation at risk. If this rumour should take hold, things could turn nasty very rapidly.

'Luckily, I can rely on the dwarf's discretion; but I need time to track down the culprit. I've had a niggling worry that there might be a weak link in the chain and this report confirms what I'd only vaguely suspected before.'

'What's the risk you face at this moment, Versain? I suppose I'm asking: *is there any way to neutralise this rumour before it can cause trouble?'*

'What's being said is that there's a construction site on Verastra belonging to a secret organisation that's run by a member of the Court — luckily the rumour doesn't name me — and that neither the Emperor nor the State Council knows about it. I must stress Silla, that Wellbeloved must remain ignorant of my work till we're ready to tell him and the public about the prophecy.'

'Why? Wellbeloved isn't likely to panic when he hears you're running a secret organisation, Versain. He's fully aware that you should be Emperor. He turns a blind eye to your many absences from Court, even when you've promised to be present.'

'I know that, but he *is* likely to blurt out something inadvertently, maybe in front people who'd be only too delighted to cause trouble. He could say something that would create widespread panic. You know very well that it's hard for our much-beloved Wellbeloved to keep a secret — he's kindness itself but he's not discreet.'

'I take your point.'

For a time they walked in silence, the Empress deep in thought. She stopped in her tracks:

'Versain! I think I have the answer. In three years' time it will be our Jubilee, the twentieth anniversary of our coronation. Why don't you present your spaceship project as your secret contribution to the festivities? Now that you've told me about it I can easily say I've known about it all along but have been under oath of secrecy so that you could present the spaceships to Wellbeloved as a special surprise.

'You could arrange for the first launch to take place during the celebrations, couldn't you? That could work very well as a cover story, don't you think? Anyway, it would get you off the hook if this rumour spreads.'

'My first impression is that it could work.' The Duke walked in silence for a while, also deep in thought. 'But it would serve no useful purpose if you were to be accused of participating in our illegal activities. Let's think about your idea, shall we? But thank you Silla, your suggestion takes a load off my mind; it gives us a way out if this rumour threatens to blow up in our faces.'

'I don't suppose you'd let me visit your community, would you Versain? I'd love to see what you've been up to all these years. In a month's time I will be taking a three-week retreat at Sriandra; I could make an excuse to break it for a couple of days and visit your community. What do you think?'

At this moment the ruby pendant hanging around the Royal Duke's neck began to vibrate signalling an urgent message.

'Versilla, will you forgive me if I take this message? It could be urgent.'

'What message? If you've been carrying a recorder around all this time, it can't be *that* urgent.'

'Of course!' the Duke laughed 'you don't know of Calthea's latest invention. See this?' he drew the ruby pendant from behind his royal sash.

'You've seen this before but weren't told of its unique uses. It's one of a set made by Calthea, they're tuned to the same frequency. If a wearer of one ruby wants to contact either of the other two, he or she sends a signal on their own ruby and that causes the other two to vibrate.'

'Do you need to listen to your message in private? Shall I leave you?'

'No need. They're like quartz recorders — mind-to-mind transmission. Let me see what it's about and then we can continue our talk.'

For a few moments, the Duke held the pendant against his

forehead, listening intently; when he carried it to his throat, the Empress knew he was sending a reply. Once more he listened then replaced the pendant behind his sash.

'Well Versilla, that was Gylan-Bahle. He... '

'Professor Bahle! — the Imperial Prize Laureate? I thought he'd long since left for... Oh, I see, he's another of your famous elders. I'm sorry; you were going to tell me about your message.'

'Gylan isn't an elder; he was one we had to 'kill off' to capture for our mission. He's just confirmed the identity of our gossiping culprit. The moment he mentioned the name I knew that this was the fellow who was responsible for the rumour. For the past week I've been racking my brains to remember an incident that happened at Girilayne's Farewell. I couldn't recall it. Now I remember that this engineer, who was working on the spaceship programme, tried to speak to me at the moment I was saying my last *goodbyes* to Girilayne.

'I probably snapped at him — told him to get lost or something. What I'd seen but couldn't recall was the look of hatred in his eyes. I knew that look meant trouble. It seems this fellow was sent to Verastra by his chief with a message for the spaceship crew and hasn't been seen since. Gylan fears he may have fallen into the hands of the authorities; I believe he's in hiding having started these malicious rumours.'

'You believe this engineer might cause trouble?'

'I believe that's his intention. I've had my doubts about him for some time now, though I never suspected he'd turn traitor. I still have a great deal I want to tell you, Silla but I must track down the gossiping officer in the barracks and initiate a search for our rogue engineer. Will you forgive me for having disrupted your afternoon?'

'Don't give it a second thought, my dear Versain.'

'In spite of this terrible news, I feel a great deal better for having talked to you.'

'I'm glad of that; it's been far too long since we opened our hearts to each other. Come back as soon as you can to complete your story. Now, you must act as fast as possible to stop this rumour gaining hold. Will you tell me if there's anything I can do to help? And please, send me a message if there's the least sign of imminent danger? Will you promise?'

'I promise. And thank you again from the bottom of my heart. I knew I could rely on you to listen and not fly off the handle at the dreadful things I've done.'

'You've told me *why* you did those things, which makes all the difference. You asked me what I'd have done in your place, and I realise I'd have done exactly what you did — I'd have done anything, legal or illegal, for the slightest chance of saving some of our people — even if those actions put my life or my reputation on the line. Now for goodness sake go and deal with this problem.'

Chapter 3

TRACKING A TRAITOR

Leaving the Empress, the Duke flew to a safe-house on the outskirts of the city; he'd frequently met Girilayne here as they could be assured of privacy; they'd mull over plans for recruiting community members or discuss future strategy. Having the house available had saved many a night-flight to the mountains. He'd arranged to meet Devallian here to discuss Gylan-Bahle's message.

That message had confirmed the Duke's suspicion that the missing engineer, Davrinka-Danyetta, was the origin of the rumour reported by Sujinka. Ever since the fellow had posed his question about the prisoners on Deimos, the Duke had thought him a misfit: the fellow lacked compassion. Versain preferred the company of open-minded people like Girilayne and Gylan; the Danyettas of the world were frequently at the root of the problems besetting society in his view.

He remembered how Danyetta had tried to collar him at Girilayne's Farewell with some request or other. He'd brushed him aside, irritated at the fellow's total lack of empathy; he'd had no thought to the consequences; what a mistake that was proving to have been.

Danyetta is the sort to take offence at the least rebuff, he mused. *A put-down in public would be unbearable to a person of his ilk and that always spells trouble. Now I shall have to suffer the consequences of a moment's inattention; I can only hope his spite won't be directed at others in the community. The fellow is dangerous; he must be found and silenced; he seems to have persuaded this officer in the Surveillance Corps to become his ally. He must be found and silenced too.*

He had to tread carefully: he might wield immense power but he couldn't go bursting into the Officers' Mess to confront the trouble-maker. A visit in person by the Commander-in-Chief would set tongues wagging even more vigorously. Devallian must investigate and must do so with discretion; it would be a good test of his ADC's diplomatic and problem-solving skills.

When Devallian arrived, they got straight down to business.

'You heard Gylan's message, Captain?' The Duke enquired abruptly.

'Yes, my Lord. Do you think Danyetta might have fallen into the hands of the Verastra authorities? It's almost a week since he vanished, a long time without news. Could he have been arrested, put under pressure and started spilling the beans?'

'I don't think it needed pressure for him to *spill the beans*; he's obviously been doing that of his own accord — and not to the authorities either.'

The Duke repeated Sujinka's account then told him about the incident at Girilayne's Farewell.

'He probably left for Verastra directly after the Ceremony, still smarting at his public humiliation. I believe he's a traitor to our cause and could well be hiding out somewhere in hopes that this fellow he's been bragging to will get other officers to take action. I dare say he plans to lead a band of trouble-makers to Paradisia; I dare say he hopes to be proclaimed a national hero.'

'I'm not surprised, my Lord. I didn't like Danyetta. It's a dangerous situation, isn't it? He knows about the spaceships and the community, and that many of the people there are.... '

'Quite so! Many of our *elders* are indeed in the gravest danger as a result of his spiteful talk — as is the entire enterprise. I'm giving you responsibility for finding this braggart at the barracks. Deal with him as you think fit but be careful not to create more problems in doing so. I'll go to Verastra. The Master may have more information than he passed on to Gylan. Keep me posted Captain, but I don't need to know the details of what you're up to. Just deal with this fellow; if you need advice, of course you can contact me.'

Devallian was both surprised and delighted at being given this assignment and at the way he was being addressed — as a competent officer and no longer a trainee. It was the first time he'd been given such an important assignment without the Duke spelling out how it was to be done. He was being put on the line and was thrilled; at last he was being given a chance to prove himself; yet he was well aware he mustn't underestimate either the difficulty or the importance of his task — at any rate, he'd give the assignment his best shot.

'Should I join you on Verastra when I've dealt with the situation here?'

The Duke paused before replying.

'No; on reflection, I'll leave Verastra to you too, Captain. I'll go to Paradisia. They'll be concerned about what has happened to Danyetta. I'd like to consult our people there; someone may know where he is. When you get to Verastra, find out everything you can from Master Tang and follow up any leads. We must get to Danyetta before he causes any more trouble.'

'You seem convinced he's in hiding, not the victim of an accident or in custody, my Lord.'

'My intuition tells me so. I don't trust this fellow and that's unusual; generally, I trust our chosen people implicitly. His disappearance, coinciding with this rumour of a secret construction site on Verastra, smacks of cheap revenge. We must act on the assumption that Danyetta is responsible unless and until we discover otherwise.

'By the way,' the Duke continued, 'when you meet Master Tang, please enquire whether it will be possible to launch the first spaceship in *three* years' time, not five. Ask him if it is possible to complete construction of at least one ship that early.'

'Has the meteor been sighted then, my Lord? Is that why you want to bring the launch date forward by two years?'

'My reasons for seeking the Master's advice are my business, Captain. You have your orders and I'd be grateful if you'd apply your mind to them and refrain from engaging in speculation.'

The Duke's sudden return to his usual abrupt manner didn't upset his young *aide* in the least; in fact Devallian was considerably relieved. He'd been worried sick by the Duke's deepening depression; he'd feared his health might be breaking down. His chief had been juggling two totally incompatible roles for far too long; each made heavy demands on his time and energy. Now that Girilayne was no longer there to deal with day-to-day affairs, the strain on the Duke had been only too visible.

Devallian would not easily forgive her for deserting the Duke at such a crucial time, putting her desire for peace and rest above her duty to support him. These cogitations were interrupted by the Duke.

'Have you completed your rapid-flying course, Captain?'

'The training my Lord, but not my final assessment.'

'Well, a trip to Verastra will give you a chance to practice. Are you confident enough to use rapid-flying for your flight?'

'I could, my Lord, but I'm barred by my oath.'

'I'm sure the Chief Seraph will forgive you this once; you'll save many hours.'

'But I gave my oath on *The Words of Magister*, my Lord; that bars me from using the technique unless I'm with my supervisor.'

Devallian was unhappy. He was taken aback by the pressure being put on him — unfairly in his opinion — to break an oath sworn to his seraph supervisor. But the Duke couldn't resist the temptation to increase the pressure; it amused him to put the young captain in a moral dilemma.

His *aide* possessed a strange mixture of qualities; one moment he could be the consummate athlete showing astonishing creativity and courage; he was also highly intelligent — he'd passed out of the Academy at an early age and with flying colours. On the other hand he was often over-obsessive about rules and regulations.

Devallian had the makings of a great leader but, in the Duke's opinion, that would only happen if he learnt to use discretion; he needed to learn when he was justified in breaking the rules and when he wasn't. Sometimes he'd launch into a hare-brained scheme without thinking through the consequences for himself and others. Such lapses might be excused in a youth of sixteen but no longer.

In the present crisis Devallian would need to show far better judgement than he'd done in the past or Versain would not be able to appoint him as Commander of the Luna Expedition. How the commander of that expedition behaved would set the tone for an entirely new era; his values would become the values of the community, his actions a model for how that community conducted itself.

Responsibility for ensuring Devallian's fitness for such a responsible role rested fairly and squarely with the Duke and was weighing heavily on his mind. Both the tasks he'd assigned the young captain required discretion; he would need to think things through carefully and then accept responsibility for his actions. As a mere aide he'd been shielded by the Duke but now he was being treated as an officer, required to make his own decisions and to live with the consequences.

To turn the screw a little more tightly the Duke added casually:

'It's up to you to decide, Devallian. You know how important it is to nip this rumour in the bud. Time is of the essence. But I won't over-ride your conscience. Just deal with things to the best of your ability and report back. Before I leave, let me ask you what you understand to be the essence of rapid-flying?'

'The *essence*, my Lord? ... '

'How does rapid-flying work? How is it possible to travel such long distances so easily and so rapidly using rapid-flying rather than conventional flying?'

'We weren't taught that on the course.'

'I'm not asking what you were *taught* but what you *understand*. Why does rapid-flying give you such an advantage? Think it through; I'm sure your oath bars you from using the technique for personal gain, such as competing in a race.'

'Yes it does, I swore to that as part of my oath.'

'Well, you must have come up with some explanation for these restrictions.'

'At first I thought it was part of the Wizardry you were teaching me but my supervisor never uses the word *Wizardry* or even *magic* so I put that idea aside.'

'Oh, Devallian!' the Duke burst out in exasperation, 'Haven't you guessed yet that all this nonsense about *Wizardry* is just a game I've been playing?'

The captain's face was a picture of astonishment. He could not visualise his august commander indulging in anything as frivolous as a *game*!

'I told you that the things I've been teaching you were Wizardry because that allowed me teach you techniques that demand more maturity of mind than you possess at present. We cannot wait for you to achieve that maturity so I've had to resort to trickery to help you perfect these skills in time for your assignment. Let me ask you this: have you never heard athletes talk of finding themselves in *soul-mode*?'

'Yes, of course; we all strive to find ourselves in soul-mode during a race. It's the most amazing sense of freedom and empowerment. It feels as if some other being has taken over your body and is operating it with an amazing degree of efficiency. It's impossible *not* to win if you find yourself in soul-mode.'

'Doesn't that suggest an answer to my question about rapid-flying?'

'Oh!' Once more, Devallian's face registered astonishment. 'It never occurred to me to link them. But yes, I suppose my training could have been about how to get into soul-mode deliberately. Generally, an athlete has no control over that state; it's a gift from the gods and you feel incredibly grateful to receive it — especially when you win. But you can't summon it at will.'

'So you've experienced soul-mode when sand-surfing?'

'Yes, occasionally; and when I did, I always won. Also once when I was flying, the time I took part — unofficially, as you will recall — in the Champions Race. I found myself in this amazing space. It didn't seem I was flying at all — I was being carried. It lasted only a few hours but I'll never forget the sensation.'

'And isn't it like that when you are rapid-flying?'

'I've never thought of it like that. I've been too focused on my instructions. But it's true; I do lose all sense of being *me*... but not quite like in soul-mode. Perhaps that's because I'm not on my own but always with my instructor.'

'Think about it. You're being trained in rapid-flying for a reason. Ask yourself why the state you experienced is called *soul-mode*. Also, Captain, I want you to be far more aware of what you're doing, why you're doing it and the consequences of doing it. Now, I must be off. There are things I must do before heading for Paradisia. Meet me at my palace at sunset; I may have further instructions.'

Without a backward glance the Duke left.

Chapter 4

Making Plans

Cander Valley was bathed in the rich glow of sunset as Lord Versain prepared to head for the Great Mountain Range; he gave his final instructions to Devallian then leapt from the roof of his palace high into the air. As the Duke made a wide circuit over the valley, the last rays of the setting sun caught his magnificent golden wings so that they appeared to catch fire. It was a sight Devallian had witnessed many times but had never ceased to marvel at. The captain was in awe of his chief, and in particular, in awe of his flying skills. The Duke was a champion flyer who could out-race all but the swiftest professional athletes — not that the Duke competed in races these days; he had little time to spare for recreational sports.

For his part, Versain never ceased to marvel at the sight of Cander city lit by the amber hues of sunset, its many spires and domes flashing gold against the purple shadows that were rapidly flooding the city's narrow streets. With powerful sweeps of his wings, the Duke gained height then swung eastwards towards the badlands.

Flying provided the ideal opportunity to review the events of the past twenty four hours. In that time everything had changed, but most significantly, his state of mind had changed. One might think that Sujinka's news would only have deepened his depression but it had had the opposite effect: he felt as if a great weight had been lifted from his shoulders.

Versain had always been at his best when engaged in action or planning future action; it was *uncertainty* that had brought him to the brink of madness; he'd been powerless because he didn't know what action would be safe to take and what might only make matters worse. Now that he knew the nature of the danger he faced, he could make appropriate plans and take the necessary action.

There'd also been his meeting with Versilla. He'd always known that he relied a great deal on Girilayne's guidance but he hadn't realised how much he'd relied on her emotional support as he charged about the world like some knight errant. The sudden withdrawal of that support had left him in a vacuum that had paralysed him, body, mind and spirit. Now that he'd resumed intercourse with his twin, all his old self-confidence had returned; instead of paralysis, he felt empowered by enthusiasm. With Versilla's help, he knew he could tackle the work he'd been born to undertake.

A third factor had contributed to his present state of euphoria: there'd been signs of a new maturity in his aide; he suspected that Devallian had at last outgrown his post as *aide de camp* and was now ready to assume greater responsibility. The two tasks he'd been assigned would be a good test of that; if he handled them well, the Duke would be able to assign him other tasks that would lighten his own load. He knew he was a tough task-master but that was intentional. Master Tang was fond of saying that metal was made strong through much hammering, only then could it be fashioned into reliable swords — and spaceships.

Yes, all that had happened in the past twenty four hours had effectively driven away his depression leaving him happy and surprisingly content. The Duke now turned his attention to his journey. It needed a special kind of focus to enter soul-mode; he'd been taught that — just as Devallian was being taught the technique now — but what the young captain didn't realise was that soul-mode was only the prelude to something a great deal more mysterious.

Soul-mode could reduce the time taken for a journey but only by ten or fifteen percent; it would have been impossible for the Duke to maintain his complicated life if he'd had to spend umpteen hours flying between Cander, Paradisia and Verastra. A few seraphs were Masters of the Mind; they knew how to do things most people never even suspected were possible. These secrets were jealously guarded and only ever revealed to angels at the express order of Oracle; she had given such an order to enable the Royal Duke carry out his mission.

Soul-mode acted as a gateway to a mystery the Duke still did not understand; by focusing his mind in a certain way he would enter a state very like meditation and that put him into soul-mode; then, by following a few further prescribed steps in the prescribed manner, he'd be at his destination in an instant. It was something he still found hard to accept yet on many occasions he'd benefited from this miracle.

He'd had to disguise this miraculous ability to avoid idle speculation; but that had been made easy by reason of his unconventional and secretive mode of life; the Duke was widely regarded as a law unto himself and any comment on his comings and goings was treated as mere gossip.

Having arrived in Paradisia within an hour of setting out, Versain was able to retire to the cliff-side cave previously occupied by Calthea during her training; the cave was now his base in the mountains; here he had enjoyed many a good night's sleep before he had to launch into a full day's work.

Waking soon after dawn, the Duke went in search of Vyvyan-Varenne. Before she'd vanished from Court two years before, Marima Varenne — then Motherhood Supremo — had been second only to the Empress in the realm of angelas. In those days she and Lord Versain had been close friends and regarded as the ideal couple, each a perfect complement for the other, each blest with impressive physical stature, each wielding enormous power in their respective spheres of influence.

Even before joining the Paradisia community, Vyvyan had been a supporter of the Duke's mission — and not merely a passive supporter. For ten years she'd helped to further his work in many vital, though always clandestine ways. It was she who'd master-minded the abduction of a Royal Mother and half a dozen proto-cherubs from the Palace Mother House on the morning after Phillestra's arrival there.

This heinous crime had been perpetrated at the Duke's request. He had his reasons; he wished to limit the number of cherubs being brought into the world at a time when few were likely to reach adulthood because, unless they were selected for one of the expeditions, they faced inevitable death in the coming disaster. Girilayne had recruited the Royal Mother to join the community and her apparent abduction was Vyvyan's way of bringing her to Paradisia.

Then rumours began circulating that Vyvyan was secretly involved in an illegal enterprise and Girilayne and Versain had had to engineer another of their *tragic death scenarios*. It was announced that Marima Varenne had contracted a serious infection whilst inspecting a hospital for cherubs run by the Seraphim — who were party to the plan from the outset. The infection was highly contagious so visiting was banned; that meant that her apparent death was witnessed only by her seraphina attendants.

Vyvyan's Memorial Ceremony had been the highlight of the social calendar that year, with a distraught Empress proclaiming the Eulogy for her departed friend. Since joining the community, Vyvyan had been made responsible for the selection of personnel for the expeditions; she was also special adviser to the Hybrid Project. She had never felt happier or more fulfilled; not for a moment did she miss her life at Court; her one sorrow — and it was a significant one — was the loss of her friendship with the Empress; they had been bosom pals since their school days.

From the moment she appeared in her amphora, Vyvyan had been unique; no one could remember ever having seen a spirit-light blaze with such brilliance, nor in such a glorious shade of emerald. That spirit-light had never faded. As a cherub, Vyvyan had been highly intelligent but also very difficult to control. She wanted to go where she wasn't meant to go; she demanded to take part in games that were too advanced for her; she pushed boundaries because those boundaries were clearly only there to frustrate her insatiable desire for new experience.

When she was ten and due to start Second School, Vyvyan had flatly refused to join the class of tweenlas, as custom demanded; she insisted that she be allowed to join the class of tweenlies because their curriculum was a great deal more interesting. Recognising that there was little chance of peace unless a solution could be found, Empress Wonderful came up with a plan: Versilla would attend the same class as her twin Versain, and Vyvyan would attend as Versilla's companion. This compromise gave Vyvyan what she wanted without the Empress seeming to have given way to her demands.

In the years following, Vyvyan had become a close friend of the future Empress and through her, of her brother. In fact, she became like a third twin; they were often referred to as *the three V's* or more often as *the terrible V's*. They'd remained friends ever since. When Versain asked Vyvyan to join the community, she'd been thrilled but felt that being asked to keep her work secret from Versilla was a betrayal of trust.

The Duke however was intransigent; his sister must *not* learn of this aspect of his life because it would put her in a dangerous position should it become known that he was involved in an illegal enterprise. Vyvyan accepted this explanation and kept her promise. It had been especially hard for her to withdraw from the world without saying goodbye to her lifelong friend, but that had been a necessary sacrifice if she was to play her part in the Duke's extraordinary enterprise.

Vyvyan had been unaware of Girilayne's true role in the community, which was precisely as Girilayne wanted it, so when she suddenly announced her intention of entering the Caves, Vyvyan hadn't realised how deeply his old tutor's departure would affect Versain; for her, the Duke was merely losing his deputy in Paradisia.

Now, she was delighted to see his familiar form striding across the courtyard towards her office and rushed out to meet him.

'Versain! How lovely — we weren't expecting you.'

'You're looking well, Vyvyan. I've come to deal with this wretched Danyetta business. Is there any news of him?' The Duke's tone revealed his anxiety.

'The engineer missing from Verastra?' she responded casually, 'No, I don't think so. You'd better ask Gylan, he's been dealing with the matter. Why? Is there a problem?' Puzzled at his concern, she added, 'Do you think it means trouble?'

'Hasn't Council met to discuss his disappearance?'

'Gylan was waiting for you to come. Anyway, without Girilayne, we're not sure who's authorised to convene Council, not that that matters since we'd certainly have met if anyone had thought this matter urgent. Why are you so worried?'

'I don't trust the fellow. It's just my intuition but I don't feel I can trust him.' He told Vyvyan of the rumour circulating in the Officers' Mess and of his own encounter with Danyetta at Girilayne's Farewell, then added, 'There'd be dire consequences, should the community or the construction site on Verastra be discovered by the State authorities.

'I've always before been in a position to divert attention from our work. But if I'm the one suspected, I'll be powerless to protect the people we've brought here — many quite illegally.'

'Look Versain, we all know the risks we're taking; we were all happy to accept your invitation to play our part. We believe in our work — believe in it *passionately*. If that means we're at risk, so be it; we'll face any consequences that may arise. In any case, we've a good defence if we tell the Emperor and the State Council what our work is for. I don't believe there's a soul here who feels in the least *guilty* for what they're doing; I don't believe any court would think it wrong either, especially when they hear that not one of us stands to benefit from our endeavours, though hundreds of our fellow angels very definitely will.'

'That's a comforting view, Vyvyan; but it doesn't allow for the less attractive side of our nature. I have many enemies, as anyone would in my position, and some who'd be only too glad to see me brought down a peg or two — and it won't be just a peg or two if I'm found guilty of treason.'

'And you really believe this fellow would shop us out of spite at being snubbed in public? That would be petty-minded; he must know what's at stake for us as well as for the future of our race. Surely you don't suspect him of deliberate betrayal?'

'Till he's found and questioned we have to suspect the worst. I'd like to discuss this with Council members today. Are they all here?'

'You're in luck; the Master flew in yesterday but Malgan is on a visit to Luna and Calthea is still in Sriandra.'

'That's fine; Calthea hasn't joined Council yet and Malgan isn't crucial to the discussion I'd like to have. Can you contact the others; we can meet in my cave at midday but I'd like a word with Gylan first. Could you ask him to join me if he's free?'

Soon after reaching his cave the Duke was joined by the professor. The terrace was bathed in morning sunlight so they were able to bask as they talked.

'Whatever is wrong, Versain? Vyvyan sounded very cagey when she asked me to meet you here. What's worrying you?'

'It's this wretched business of Danyetta. What's been done to trace him, Gylan? It's vital we find out why he's vanished. I want to know what he thinks he's up to.'

Again he described the palace rumour and the incident at Girilayne's Farewell.

'I see,' Gylan replied thoughtfully. 'Danyetta is probably the sort who harbours a grudge, which prompts him to act out of spite. But would he really want to destroy work he's been part of? Surely he must know the consequences of bragging like that? Surely he can't hate you so much that he'd do such an evil thing?'

'Devallian believes he has a rigid mind and a rigid way of categorising people; I tend to agree. I gather he didn't cover himself in glory when he appeared before Council. If he's taken a dislike to me, then I dare say he won't be overly concerned at any collateral damage he inflicts just so long as he gets his own back at me.'

'I do hope you are wrong, Versain. It was clearly an error of judgement to bring in someone with such a deep flaw in his personality. I must accept my share of the blame; Girilayne consulted me on his selection. But, you know, we've had only good reports from Master Tang on his work with the spaceship programme; apparently he's made many useful contributions.

Oh, I do so hope you are wrong.'

'So do I! But if the fellow has mischief in mind, the sooner we find him the better and we must correct any damage he's done already. Devallian is dealing with the officer at the barracks; then he'll fly to Verastra to consult Chorton — though I gather the Master is here, so he'll miss him.

'If Danyetta *does* create trouble,' the Duke continued, 'my chief concern is for our time-expired elders. I simply cannot risk their being humiliated, arrested and tried. I propose that, at the first hint of trouble, every elder immediately enters a Cave of Eternal Rest; at least they'll be safe from arrest, even if we do have to lose their services. How does that proposal strike you?'

'I understand your concern, Versain. Being arrested and tried for death-evasion is not an experience anyone would savour; but it doesn't outweigh the privilege of being part of this venture. It's true that if there are no death-evaders here when the authorities come looking, there'll be less risk to the rest of us, and though it would be a pity for our elders to be forced to leave before their work is brought to a successful conclusion, I'm sure they'll be ready to make that sacrifice and remove themselves from the scene to guarantee the safety of the project.'

'Yes. But Gylan, how can our work possibly succeed without our experienced and respected elders?... Anyway, that's the plan I shall propose.'

They fell silent as they contemplated this plan. A couple of hours later, their colleagues arrived. The terrace was just wide enough to accommodate the five of them; Versain and Gylan commandeered the terrace pillars leaving Vyvyan, Master Tang and Maestro Arbrecht-Betaline to take their places against the cave wall on either side of the cave entrance.

'I've asked you here because we need to discuss a number

of matters that have come up since Girilayne's departure.' The Duke began. 'The most urgent of which concerns the disappearance of Engineer Davrinka-Danyetta.' the Duke gave a brief account of Sujinka's report and his own views on Danyetta's disappearance.

'We need to discuss the probable consequences of Danyetta's possible breach of trust. I would like you to consider a plan that would remove any risk to our highly valued elders should our activities become known to the authorities. I also wish to discuss an aspect of our future work that I'd hoped Girilayne would have taken on — the final stage of our mission. I have a suggestion relating to that. Are there any other matters we ought to address as we are together?'

'Versain, who should deputise for you when you're not with us?' the Maestro asked, 'We need to know who can call a meeting of Council and who should act as your deputy in Paradisia.'

'I believe the best person would be Gylan; he's familiar with all aspects of our work and can consult me at any time. Are you happy with that?'

Everyone agreed, so the Duke continued.

'Chorton, what can you tell us about the disappearance of Danyetta?'

'Davrinka accompanied me to the Farewell Ceremony, as you know. I had to stay on here so I sent him back with instructions for the crew on Verastra. I returned a couple of days later and was surprised to hear that my instructions had never been delivered. Davrinka had always proved reliable before so my first thoughts were for his safety.

'I made discreet enquiries at the Embassy on Verastra and was told he'd been seen chatting with officers of the local garrison; it didn't seem he was under arrest or in any kind of trouble. After that he seems to have vanished. Of course, he had no right to be at the Imperial base as it's off limits for community personnel.

'I sent a message to Gylan to let him know the situation and asked if Danyetta had returned to Paradisia. I thought he might have fallen sick — it never occurred to me he might be up to no good; I'd no idea he felt alienated. He's a hard worker and a good designer. I'd always found him fully committed to his work; it never occurred to me that he might do anything to put that work at risk.'

'Thank you, Chorton. Has anyone anything to add?'

Gylan responded.

'When I received Chorton's report, I made enquiries but no one at Paradisia had seen him since Giri's Farewell Ceremony. I asked our dwarves to let me know the moment he was found here or anywhere else. We all know about the dwarves' remarkable communications network — goodness knows how it works but it's highly efficient — so far they've had neither sight nor sound of him. That's all I can tell you.'

'Fine, so Danyetta is missing and we have no idea where he went after he left Verastra. Can we assume he *has* left?'

'Oh, I'm sure we can,' the Master replied. 'There are very few hiding places on the moon and our dwarves would certainly have found him if he was still there.'

'Does anyone have any idea where he might have gone; has he any friends he might have turned to for help?'

'He worked on Phobos for some years.' The Master said, 'He was engaged in designing armaments for the forces; that work has proved invaluable to us in the spaceship project… '

'If he's flown there,' the Duke interrupted, 'he'll find his old friends have all departed. There's only a tiny garrison on Phobos now and all have been posted there within the last two years. If he's hoping to find old mates he'll be disappointed. But we should certainly make enquiries there.

'So, we have a missing colleague and reason to believe he may be a traitor to our cause, which brings me to my idea for protecting our elders.' Versain outlined his plan that anyone beyond their DDD should avoid arrest by immediately entering a Cave of Eternal Rest.

'My Lord, you are suggesting that our elders will have to depart permanently,' the Master spoke again, 'but this may not be necessary. Recently Chunka took me to a cave system near here to look at a particular gemstone we need for the spaceship motors. This system has several openings into the valley, one not far from here. We hadn't known about this cave system before because we'd never asked for this type of gemstone.

'Apparently these caves are used by the dwarves for ceremonial gatherings and are not usually shown to angels. The system is an extensive labyrinth of tunnels with a large central chamber formed of pure crystal that's bathed in sunlight for most of the day — only those familiar with the cave system would ever find their way into that chamber. We could adopt your plan my Lord — assuming we get the consent of the dwarves — but the elders need only *take shelter* in this crystal chamber; if it is a false alarm, they can be restored to us as hale and healthy as when they went in.'

'That's a marvellous idea, Master!' The Duke's smile spoke his relief. 'I'll speak to Chunka; the dwarves are our good friends and I'm confident they'll agree. Let's proceed along those lines, shall we? Good!

'Now let's turn to the challenge that will soon be upon us — the time when we must inform the State Council about what we've been up to and why. I'd thought we might have at least five years before reaching that stage but there may be a reason to advance that by a couple of years.

'I was talking to my sister yesterday,' the Duke continued, 'and she reminded me that it will be the twentieth anniversary of the Coronation in three years' time. Might we not invite the Emperor and Empress to launch our first spaceship as part of the Jubilee celebrations? It would be the perfect cover story if our work is discovered.

'We could say we've kept the spaceships secret because the launch is intended as a surprise. What do you think? Could we get one of the spaceships ready by the time of the Jubilee?'

'Speaking for the expeditions,' Vyvyan said, 'we might be able to assemble a ship's complement by then but I very much doubt whether Calthea's recorders could be ready in time for the Jubilee. How critical is it that each expedition carries one of her recorders?'

'I wouldn't think the recorders are critical;' the Duke responded, 'we could always send them on at a later date. What do you think, Maestro?'

'Calthea is still in Sriandra so hasn't even started the project;' Arbrecht replied, 'Vyvyan is right, I can't see how the recorders can be ready in three years. But surely the point is whether Chorton can get one of the spaceships completed in time.'

For some time the Master remained deep in thought.

'So far, we've been working on all three spacecraft in parallel.' he said after this long pause. 'If we focused all our efforts on one ship, we *might* be able to complete it in three years but it would....'

'I'm sorry, Master, but I must push you even harder,' the Duke interrupted. 'We'll need at least six months to test, commission, staff and load the speceship. It won't have the same significance if we simply invite the Monarchs to inaugurate a test flight; we need to be talking of an actual launch, to be sending an expedition off to a new world.'

'Hm, you're pushing me there, my Lord,' Chorton replied, tapping his slide-rule on the flat of his hand. 'I'd hate to make a promise I can't keep; two and a half years is a tight deadline. I don't say it's impossible because I don't like to be negative; I can see that your plan has considerable merits; it would certainly solve a number of problems.'

'Just give the matter some thought, Master. We are talking about the possibility of a launch during the Jubilee; no one will be held to account if difficulties crop up that make that impossible. There's another point we must consider.' The Duke turned to Professor Kritten, 'Which of the chosen satellites will be in a favourable position at the Jubilee, Kinver? That will decide the spaceship's destination.'

'I'll need the exact date before I can do my calculations, Versain.'

'The Coronation was held at the three-quarter-year festival seventeen years ago so our proposed launch date is that same festival in three years' time. When might you have an answer?'

'Oh, I think four days should be sufficient.'

'Good. Then let's meet again in a week. Please keep this proposal confidential for the present. We need to consider all practicalities before we throw the idea open to wider discussion. I'd also like us to keep the situation regarding Danyetta under wraps till we find out what he's been up to. In the meantime, I will consult Chunka about possible access to this crystal cave as a retreat for our elders.'

* * * * *

Vyvyan and Gylan stayed behind after the Master and the Maestro had left. Versain wanted to tell them more about his meeting with the Empress.

'Vyvyan, I told Versilla about several of our people but I didn't mention you. Having pressured you into keeping your work secret from your dearest friend, I couldn't then reveal your involvement without your consent. What I suggest is that I invite Versilla to pay us a visit in secret and that you organise her schedule and escort her around Paradisia. What do you think of that plan?'

'Nothing would give me greater pleasure. But why the sudden change of mind, Versain? You said Versilla must be kept in ignorance for her own safety as much as for ours. What's changed?'

'A lot has. When I joined Girilayne twenty years ago, the world was in turmoil after years under the tyrant. Versilla and Servenken were newly crowned and faced enormous challenges in rebuilding the confidence and trust of the people. It was not the time to tell them of Oracle's prophecy or of our efforts to prepare for the disaster.

'When you joined us some years later — you'd just been appointed Motherhood Supremo if I recall — there were still pockets of dissidents troubling the Monarchs; if it had became known that the Empress knew of our illegal community it would have placed her in a very dangerous position.

'What's changed is that the world has changed: I watched Versilla performing her official duties and saw how much she's achieved within her own domain. She's universally loved and admired so in a far stronger position to take knowledge of our work on board. She wants to be involved now that I've told her about that work.

'As I'm sure you both know, I'd always assumed Girilayne would be around to tell the world about the prophecy; my mentor was immensely wise and skilful; she'd have been the ideal person to handle that stage of our mission; she'd have ensured there was no panic or alarm. I'm sure you agree, Gylan.'

'I certainly do. Giri would have been the ideal person.'

'I'm aware that I'm *not* competent to handle that stage of

our work but as I was talking to Versilla, I realised she was the perfect person to mastermind that final phase. As Empress, she's uniquely placed to organise preparations for the final days, but inviting her to join the community could have unforeseen consequences, so I'd like us to discuss this idea before I approach her.'

The professor had been nodding his head in agreement during this speech.

'This is an inspired notion, Versain. I don't know the Empress personally but I do know her reputation among my female students and colleagues; they invariably speak of her in glowing terms. Yes, you have my whole-hearted support.'

'What about you Vyvyan, would you welcome your friend as a secret member of our team?'

'How could you think I wouldn't, Versain? The ending of our friendship has been my one and only regret since coming here. If Versilla wants to see what you've achieved, I'd love to be the one to show her. But how can that be organised without putting her reputation at risk?'

'She's due to go on retreat to Sriandra very soon and can easily slip away to visit us during that time; only the Seraphim will know and they're part of the team already. For her protection, we should make sure she doesn't meet any of our time-expired elders; it would place her in a dangerous position should it become known that she'd been consorting with people that the State, in its ignorance, regards as criminals. She knows there are elders here but she's the model of discretion and will certainly not do or say anything that might harm us.'

'In that case, how could we possibly object, Versain?' Vyvyan teased.

'Good. So I have your approval. I'll discuss this with Versilla as soon as I get back; I'll ask her to bring forward her visit to Sriandra so she can visit us very soon — the sooner the better, as far as I'm concerned.'

'There's something else we need to discuss.' Vyvyan added, 'As you know it's my responsibility to select the people who will make up the three expeditions; I've come to realise that there are some very difficult problems involved.'

'What difficult problems?'

'Firstly, we need to be highly selective in choosing those who will found the new civilisations. We will need to choose a well-balanced mix of genes to give future generations the best chance of long-term survival; that means we need to select people with robust bodies and resilient, versatile minds. We must select only the best characteristics of our race and avoid including people known to have genes carrying any risk of disease or disability. That is obvious I think.'

'It is; I don't see where the problem lies.'

'The problem lies in the selection process itself. I'm stuck here so can't visit the outer world to supervise the selection process. I had no chance to ask Girilayne what plans she had for dealing with this problem. The plain fact is that I don't have access to the people I need to assess. The same applies to the Hybrid Project; the selection process for that poses even greater problems; we'll be looking for different qualities in any case.'

'Different how?'

'For the Hybrid Project, the physical characteristics of potential subjects will be of little concern because they'll be shedding their bodies anyway.'

'I don't understand. Are you saying that the subjects you choose will die in the process of becoming hybrids?'

'Their bodies will die. The challenge is to keep their mind from slipping away as we attempt to transfer it into the hominid's body; that is the essence of the project. Not only do we face the problem of selecting suitable subjects without being able to interview those subjects for ourselves; we cannot even tell potential recruits what project we are recruiting them for or why.

'You must realise Versain, mind-transfer is a very delicate process that requires the services of a highly skilled mind-surgeon and a proficient psychotherapist. The mind-surgeons and psychotherapists are in Sriandra so their selection and training is not the issue. It's the choice of candidates for the settlements and the choice of subjects for the Hybrid Project that is exercising my mind at the moment.

'In fact, I've come to the conclusion that the very secrecy of our mission is placing impossible constraints on my ability to carry out this assignment. I'm not sure we can achieve anything today, but I felt you should be aware of the situation.'

'Have you any thoughts on the matter, Gylan?'

'Vyvyan and I have discussed this at length; it is indeed a perplexing problem. We have come here to the mountains to plan, organise and initiate various projects in secrecy; we have also vowed never to visit the outside world or to let anyone in the outside world know of our existence. But as Vyvyan has said, once we come to the matter of choosing members of the public for our various projects, our hands are tied. We have prayed for inspiration to show us a way out of the dilemma but so far no solution has been revealed.'

'Perhaps this is something I could discuss with Versilla.'

'That would be a great idea,' Vyvyan agreed. 'She might think of a solution. Now I'd better leave, Versain; I'm due to meet members of the Hybrid Project. Please let me know when Versilla plans to visit — you must know how much I'm looking forward to seeing her again.'

As soon as Vyvyan had left, the Duke took out his ruby pendant.

'I must contact Devallian, Gylan; why not listen in then I won't need to brief you about what he's been up to.'

Devallian answered the Duke's call within seconds.

'I've been to the construction site but Master Tang isn't there, my Lord. I dare say you've already met him in Paradisia. I'm in Verton Colonia at present. I flew to Verastra straight after sorting out the business at the Mess. You could say I've dealt with *the mess at the Mess*.'

Devallian's attempt at humour was accurately transmitted by the responder but was met by a reprimanded from his chief who wished to point out that flippancy was out of place in this crisis; he should make his report in a more professional manner.

'Sorry, sir!' Devallian quipped in a cheery tone that totally negated his apology but continued in official mode. 'I believe I've silenced the fellow Danyetta was trying to recruit to his cause. His name is Turven Chixon; he's a captain in the Surveillance Corps just as Sujinka reported. I told this Chixon bloke that you'd hand-picked him to lead a platoon to root out a gang of terrorists who've been causing trouble for a long time.

'I told him we'd had the best sighting in a very long time, showing they were operating out of the northern badlands; I said our latest reports pinpointed a location in the Rottenhill area, which, as you know my Lord, is riddled with caves and criss-crossed by deep chasms.

'The stupid fellow was extremely gratified to be chosen and is determined to be the one who finally nails these terrorists. I said there might be a promotion if he found either the miscreants or their operating base. I believe we can rule him out as a possible focus for trouble for the next five weeks at the very least.'

'Why that specific period, Captain?'

'I told him he shouldn't feel rushed in his assignment as we know only too well how difficult the terrain is in that area. I said he shouldn't feel he had to give up and return to the barracks in anything less than five weeks. He took that as a sign that we were giving him plenty of time to prove himself competent in a difficult operation.'

'That sounds a good solution to the problem, Captain. Now, what about the other officers he's been bragging to?'

'Oh, it seems Chixon is regarded as something of a bar-acrobat.'

'A *what*?' The Duke was mystified.

'He spins tales in the bar to make out he's more important than he is. People think he was just showing off, trying to make out that his posting to Verastra had been a lot more exciting than it was. I believe, without him there, the tale will fizzle out — it already has, in effect.'

'How did you get to Verastra?'

'I used the rapid-flying technique, my Lord. I remembered what you'd said about soul-mode and since I already know what that's like, I used the technique to get into soul-mode. It felt just like when I'm sand-sailing, not at all like when I'm with my supervisor.'

'And how much time did you save?'

'It was astonishing. I made the flight in six hours less than usual. Normal flying would have taken sixty hours at the very least, possibly a great deal longer.'

'And now what?'

'I couldn't locate Master Tang, so I couldn't put your question to him so I…'

'Forget about that;' the Duke responded sharply, 'I've seen the Master and am dealing with that matter myself. What about Danyetta? Have you contacted our *eyes and ears* in Verton Colonia yet?'

'I have, my Lord. It seems Danyetta asked one of them if there was a group leaving for Phobos in the next few days as he had to make an official visit there and preferred to fly in convoy. It seems there was a platoon of soldiers leaving next day. I assume he joined them because no one here has seen him since. Should I contact our *eyes and ears* on Phobos to track him down?'

'Yes, do that but you needn't go yourself; send one of our agents. Tell them to keep Danyetta under surveillance and to be sure to stop him from leaving — get him arrested as a suspected outlaw if necessary. But please make it clear he's not to be interrogated by anyone but you or me. I don't want the fellow spinning his tales in the bars of Phobos. When you've dealt with that, return to Cander. I'll be back by tomorrow morning; we can review any damage done when you arrive. I believe we may have successfully snuffed out the conflagration, at least for the time being.'

The Duke tucked his pendant away.

'What was all that about terrorists, Versain? Are they a problem?' Gylan asked.

'Those outlaws have come in handy more than once;' the Duke chuckled, 'they provide me with an excuse to escape Court functions so I can visit Paradisia or deal with community business in the city.'

'Do they exist?'

'They used to, many years ago. After the fall of the despot, his close henchmen and several members of the Palace Guard fled to the northern badlands in a bid to escape justice. We were hunting them down for a long time, but it's at least five years since we heard of any outlaws operating in that region. Nevertheless, a few baddies might still be lurking there and I make good use of that remote possibility. Devallian has shown commendable imagination in getting this troublesome officer out of the way without stirring up his revolutionary zeal in the process.'

'I agree. Then he mentioned *soul-mode*; what was that all about?'

'Aren't you familiar with the term, Professor?'

'I've heard athletes speak of being *in soul-mode* but I can't say I know exactly what they're talking about.'

'Very occasionally, a sportsman will experience a state of extraordinary focus; it seems as if an outside force has taken control of your body and is operating it with consummate skill; it may happen when you are under intense pressure, perhaps competing for a prestigious trophy. It's as if your actions have been taken over by a power immeasurably more skilled at your sport than you've ever been.

'It's a truly exhilarating feeling, hard to put into words but the most exciting thing a sportsman can experience.'

'Then you've experienced *soul mode* for yourself, Versain?'

'Indeed I have.'

'It occurs to me that this *soul-mode* of yours has similarities to the state we call *inspiration* or *intuition*. In a state of *inspiration*, Intellect comes under direct control by the soul. It sounds as if, in the state you call *soul-mode*, the body comes under similar control; the difference being that in *inspiration* it is the mind that is controlled by the higher power whilst in your *soul-mode* it is the body. Do you follow this?'

'It's a fascinating notion, Gylan. The state of *soul-mode* is something any athlete would give his wing feathers to be able to summon at will. It seems that Devallian has finally made the connection between *soul-mode* and the technique of *rapid-flying* he's being taught by the Seraphim. Is there a technique you can use to gain access to this state of *inspiration*?'

'There is. At Persinnia we teach a technique with this very aim in mind; indeed I've been teaching that technique to

Calthea. During *contemplation*, the mind learns how to open itself to the deeper wisdom of the Heart.'

'Why did you teach Calthea this technique? Is it relevant to her assignment?'

'I believe it will prove crucial. Only when Calthea finds out how to access the wisdom of her Heart will she find ways to record our culture for posterity. It is no small challenge to capture the diversity and richness of our civilisation in some form of permanent record.'

Chapter 5

VERSILLA

Once back in the capital, Versain lost no time in paying the Empress a further visit; that afternoon, they walked again in the Crystal Grove.

'Delightful as it is to talk to you Versain,' she said apologetically, 'I'm afraid I can't stay long. There's a brilliant playwright in town and the premiere of his new play is being performed this evening. *Please* come. It's so long since you attended a cultural evening at Court and this play is said to be very amusing.

'The author is famous for his wit, scintillating dialogue and telling caricatures. I'm told the new play is a pastiche on Court life and parodies both the Emperor and me — all in good fun I'm assured. I'm sure you'll enjoy it. Who knows, he may even take a dig or two at the Royal Duke.'

'But Versilla, I'm far too busy to spend an entire evening at Court, even with my highly esteemed sister.'

'You told me your work was all about saving Stellaster's remarkable culture for posterity yet you show little interest in that culture. Anyway, you've obviously been working far too hard for far too long; an evening of amusement and relaxation will do as much to restore you as several days in retreat at Sriandra.'

'OK, I'll spend the evening with you but only if you promise you'll give me a couple of hours tomorrow. A great deal has happened that I'd like to tell you about.'

'Just tell me you're in no immediate danger and that the problem you went to sort out has been sorted out.'

The Duke gave both assurances and promised to attend the performance. In fact, he enjoyed the evening far more than he'd expected; the play was just as clever and amusing as Versilla had predicted and elicited much laughter from the audience who appreciated the all-too-accurate portrayals of Court life. It was a long time since the Duke had laughed so spontaneously. As his twin prophesied, the evening drove away the last vestiges of his depression.

Next afternoon they walked again in a sun-drenched Crystal Grove.

'You told me you'd like to visit our community in the mountains, Silla; I was there two days ago talking to Professor Bahle and someone you know very well; both were enthusiastic at the prospect that you might visit them.'

'Who is this person I know *very well*? Another of your famous *death-evading elders*, I suppose?'

'No, this time it's another of my *dramatic death scenarios*. How would you like to meet your old friend Vyvyan-Varenne again?'

Versilla stopped dead in her tracks and stared in open-mouthed amazement at her brother.

'*Vyvyan*! Don't tell me you snatched Vyvyan from the jaws of death!'

'Vyvyan was never in the jaws of death. She was visiting a hospital run by the Seraphim and, since the Seraphim are our collaborators, they helped me spirit her away under the very noses of her Imperial friends. I confess she was very upset at being asked to leave without saying goodbye to you and even more upset when she realised she might never see you again.'

'Then why did she agree to go?'

'Vyvyan had been working for us ever since she was appointed Motherhood Supremo — in secret of course — but then there were rumours of her involvement with an illegal organisation so we asked her to join us in Paradisia full time and...'

'*Paradisia*?'

'It's what we call our base in the mountains. Anyway, Vyvyan is very eager to show you what we've been doing. How good are you at flying, Silla? Could you fly as far as Verastra? If you can, I'll show you the construction site and the spaceships. Master Chorton-Tang is in charge there; he's studying your suggestion that you and Wellbeloved might launch one of the spaceships at your Jubilee. Everyone is very enthusiastic about that idea.'

'Of course I'd like to see them; but flying to Verastra is beyond my powers. But Versain, surely the launch will have to be from the moon; how will you get everyone there? Most angelas can't fly that far and cherubs certainly can't.'

'Of course, how silly of me! We've built shuttles that ply between Paradisia and Verastra; anyone not able to fly there takes the shuttle; that includes dwarves and some angelis too because not everyone is a champion athlete. I'll take you there by shuttle or, if you prefer, Chorton can come to Paradisia and describe his spaceships.'

'I'd rather see them for myself.'

'Let me look into it. In the meantime there are a few things you could help us with Silla, things Girilayne would have handled had she been around. But it depends on whether you're prepared to join our mission, whether you feel it's safe for you to become a member of the team. I'm sure there'll be many risks if you do.'

'I've been thinking of little else since our first talk, my dear

Versain. *Of course* I want to be part of it; I'm upset that you've kept me out for so long — it looks as if you didn't trust me, just as you don't trust Servenken.'

'I have a very high regard for our beloved Emperor; as well you know; I just don't trust his discretion though I definitely trust *yours*, which is why I've told you about us. I didn't tell you before — indeed, took the greatest care to prevent you getting as much as a whiff of it — to protect you. You faced an uphill battle after the Insurrection and needed all your energy to heal our deeply traumatised people; your reputation also had to be shielded from your brother's highly illegal activities.'

'But, Versain, that aspect of my work was completed many years ago. Empress Wonderful took many risks to protect her Domain from the worst excesses of that dreadful tyrant, so my task was far lighter than Servenken's.'

'I'm glad you don't give the tyrant his title; I never do.'

'He didn't honour his position so why refer to him as if he had. Wonderful protected us young angelas, but what was happening to all you young angelis almost broke her heart — she told me so. She was devastated to see tweenlies she'd nurtured as cherubs being exposed to the truly sadistic whims of that madman.

'After our Coronation, Servenken faced a daunting task restoring trust within his realm. Since mine was in much better shape, I offered to take responsibility for his Second Schools and colleges; that allowed me to take care of all the young people just entering adult life; they're back in his domain now, still being well cared for.

'So for quite some time I've been looking for something to challenge me. I've had the Mother Houses rebuilt and I've been planning to up-grade our First Schools but if Stellaster is about to be blown to *kingdom come* that would be wasted effort.

I may as well offer my services for something that will be more useful in the long run.'

With this assurance, the Duke briefed her on his visit to Paradisia.

'I'll bring forward my retreat at Sriandra.' The Empress responded, 'Whilst I'm there, I shall request an audience with Oracle; she may be prepared to see me even if she won't see you. I'll ask her advice on how to prepare our people for the coming disaster. Can you arrange for me to visit Paradisia during my retreat? I'll also discuss with the Chief Seraph how we can solve this problem of selecting members for the expeditions and for this Hybrid Project of yours, though I must say, I have serious reservations about that strange scheme.'

'What reservations?'

'I question the morality of foisting an angel's mind onto an unsuspecting Earth creature. I'm even more concerned at imprisoning an angel's mind in a body that has evolved to live in a way we consider bestial and immoral.'

'You seem to know a lot about Earth's creatures.'

'Of course I do. Vyvyan and I shared your education remember; we weren't constrained to studying Court etiquette and the life-cycle of the cherub like other tweenlas; we studied Maths and Science, including the biology of Mars and Earth. Earth biology was my favourite subject.

'In fact, for many years I've ensured that tweenlas study a richer curriculum. It's why Calthea was able to graduate in a technical subject like crystallography; she wasn't limited to Motherhood or teaching or a career in the Arts. Funnily enough, it was far easier to introduce these changes in the turmoil following the Insurrection than in more stable times. It's strange how war and revolution bring major advances in science as well as developments in society in general…'

'We're shaken out of our complacency.' Versain responded;

he'd always loved these discussions with his twin. 'Disruption forces us to find new ways of surviving in a threatening environment. In times of peace, the world values its old traditions and considers change as a threat to the established order.

'For instance, with this meteor threatening total disaster, you'd be amazed at the spate of new ideas and brilliant inventions pouring out of the community every day. We've never had much of a metal industry, yet these days the mountains of Verastra are alive with dwarves mining ore, smelting it in the lava-flows of Mount Varenta, then working the metal into panels for our spacecraft to specifications that flow from the drawing boards of our designers at an amazing pace.

'We have workshops in elfin settlements producing some of the finest lenses ever fashioned for our new telescopes. Other workshops are making windows for the spacecraft to extremely advanced specifications.'

'Elfin settlements? How can you be using elves for work that isn't authorised by the State Council? I thought the settlements were closely supervised.'

'They are; but one of those supervisors was none other than Girilayne-Bahle. We have friends and helpers in some surprising places Silla. And now I hope we'll have a helper within the Palace itself.'

'Of course I'm going to help. By the way, I presume these *friends and helpers* are in society; you're not referring to people in the community?'

'Correct. People we approach are happy to offer their support, practically and morally but always in secret, because they still hold positions in the public domain.'

'Then I want to know who they are so that I can give them *my* support. I don't want to do anything that might embarrass or harm them. In fact, I may want them to help me with the assignments you've given me. In other words, I want to become a member of your Secret Service, Versain.'

'Then may I be the first to welcome you, Silla? I can give you the names of our volunteers and will let them know that you've now joined our merry band. May I tell them they can come to you if they need help?'

'Of course you can! Perhaps we should have a secret password for community business; then I'll make sure they can speak to me in private. Perhaps *Girilayne* could be our password; she seems to have been an important person in your mission.'

'She was; and for my self-confidence as well; that's why I miss her so much.'

'She was also crucial to your survival. Did you know?'

'How do you mean?'

'She saved you from execution. I didn't see much of you after the Insurrection so I couldn't tell you. When the Empress heard that you and your bunch of hotheads had been arrested for treason, she appointed me her Protector of the Imperial Jewels, which meant I had to be with her at all times. As your twin, I was in great danger from the tyrant; she didn't want the Palace Guard arresting me on some trumped up charge so she even made me sleep in her personal suite. She also sent for Girilayne, who was in Bilwinia at the time.'

'That must have been a few days after my arrest; I'd asked Arbrecht Betaline to persuade Girilayne to go into hiding.'

'I didn't know that. Anyway, the Empress sent out agents to find her, when they did, she sent Girilayne to Oracle to find out how to save the four of you.'

'But why ask Girilayne to find out?'

'Because Oracle had appointed her as your guardian.'

'She wasn't my guardian; she was my tutor.'

'That's not what Empress Wonderful told me; she said

Oracle had appointed Girilayne as your guardian because you were going to play a dangerous role in the future. So when you were in danger, it was Girilayne she sent for to protect you.'

'And what did Oracle say?'

'Something about getting you transferred from the Palace gaol to the city gaol.'

'Well, that clears up something. Girilayne told me very little of what happened at that time; in fact, I didn't even know she'd played a part in that strange business — except that she had advised us how to start the rebellion.'

'Please tell me, Versain! I was beside myself with terror. It seemed obvious you *had* been the instigator and so faced imprisonment and certain death.'

'We knew we were guilty as charged and that the tyrant wouldn't entertain a plea for mercy. In fact, we'd pretty well accepted our fate. Then late one evening I was secretly handed a note by a guard; it told me to demand a lawyer as was my right. The note even gave the name of the lawyer I was to ask for. I did that because the wording of the note suggested that it had come from Oracle.

'I was very surprised when my demand was granted; next day this lawyer came to see the four of us in prison. His name was Taitaillin, he was barely older than I and...'

'I know Taitaillin, Versain; he's a member of the State Council.'

'Of course he is. At that time, he was only recently out of Law School but he held a civil warrant for our arrest — for a breach of the peace. We didn't understand what was going on but he said this was our only chance of survival.'

'That's very strange, Versain. How could the City demand the arrest of people already in custody at the Palace?'

'Taitaillin quoted a statute that gave Civil Law precedence over Imperial Law. The tyrant was fuming because he'd wanted a swift public execution as a high-visibility reprisal for our audacity and as a warning to others. But there were no legal grounds on which to could refuse.

'Taitaillin argued his case with the State Council and won the day. The four of us were taken then and there and locked up in the City Gaol; it wasn't much of an improvement on our previous accommodation but we weren't about to complain. Then Taitaillin told us he would be acting as our Defence Counsel and a famous and highly respected lawyer, Liberelli, would lead for the Prosecution. It transpired that Liberelli had been our lawyer's tutor and was widely acknowledged as the best legal brain in the land.

'Of course, our hearts sank. But Taitaillin reassured us that our trial would be a *cause celebre*. It seemed the whole thing was to be a carefully staged courtroom drama aimed at toppling the tyrant by public acclaim. We'd been arrested under the Civil Law because they'd found two citizens who'd been wounded during our attempt to overthrow the Palace Guard — not badly, but enough for their purpose.

'The charges were *Breach of the Peace and Malicious Wounding*. The Prosecutor was such a renowned lawyer that the tyrant hadn't bothered to have him replaced by one of his own cronies. He'd assumed the City's intention was to find us guilty then we would face the far more serious charge of Treason.

'I wish you'd been there, Silla. It was a courtroom drama all right, with a very cunningly written script. Liberelli, started the prosecution in bombastic style, waxing ferocious in his condemnation of these young hotheads who'd caused physical harm to bystanders by their irresponsible behaviour. He played the part marvellously.

'Then our young Counsel gets to his feet all hesitation and deference to his mentor; he was *abjectly* apologetic as he submitted with the utmost humility that maybe we'd been justified in taking the course of action we did because we were following the letter of the law. Very gradually, he led the court through a tangle of legal niceties that had my brain in a twirl and must have given the Judge and jury bad headaches.

'But it was all good, sound law. Liberelli and his young assistant — for that's what our Defence Counsel turned out to be — had constructed a clever legal dialogue that led the court point by point through the foundations of Civil Law, a legal system based, as you know, on the teachings of Magister. They argued the case so slowly and carefully that everyone present was able to follow their logic.

'Taitaillin closed his speech for the Defence by quoting a stanza from *The Words of Magister*. You'll be familiar with it: *Tyranny is the greatest crime a ruler can commit against his people; it is so great a crime as to justify any angel in taking action to remove that tyrant from power. Indeed, I would go further and say that it is no less than treason for an angel to put his own safety before his duty to end tyranny by the swiftest means available.*

'After that speech, the Judge called a recess. Generally, a recess lasts for at least an hour and everyone rushes out to bask in the sun. That day, not a soul moved from the courtroom — except for the newshounds, who could hardly wait for the Judge to leave the bench. Inside the court, the excited chattering rose to fever pitch; we knew those two lawyers had conjured up something truly remarkable.

'Outside, I was told, the newshounds were rushing about telling everyone to get to the courthouse before the recess ended. As you know, the courthouse faces Festival Park and I gather the entire park was filled to overflowing by the time the Judge came back into court; even the students from Imperial at Cander had deserted their lecture halls to be there. Everyone knew something historic was happening.'

'I do remember that terrible, marvellous day, Versain!

The Empress had sent a couple of observers to the court and they came rushing back with the news. She couldn't leave the Palace herself, by then it was too dangerous, but she sent me with an escort of trusted attendants and I was in Court in time to hear your acquittal.'

'Yes, I saw you were there and realised our relationship might now protect you rather than endanger you — as it had until then. You'll remember what mayhem it was when the jury announced its *not guilty* verdict. Then the Judge made his extra-ordinary speech about how we weren't hotheads but heroes who had set an example for each and every angel of the best standards of devotion to duty etc. etc.

'The next few months are something of a blur; so much was happening so fast. The only sad consequence was that we hardly saw each other in the aftermath; you were busy learning to be an Empress and I was helping Servenken to hunt down and capture all those who refused to accept that the world had changed and changed for the better, I trust.'

'It was a great time, but a terrible time too, Versain. The worst was the danger our beloved Empress was in. Now I was able to protect my protector. The mob was howling for her to be arrested and tried alongside that tyrant; it needed immediate action by all who loved her to keep her safe until things settled down.'

'What happened, Silla? I remember that for several days law and order in the city broke down completely.'

'A group of us escorted the Empress to Sriandra under cover of darkness. I've never been so terrified in all my life. I wasn't used to the dark at the best of times, but with hoards of outlaws trying to get out of the city and you lot hunting them down, we were in danger of being attacked or ambushed, especially when we stopped to rest. Actually, it was one of your Galliards who helped us to escape.'

'Who was that?'

'It was one of your fellow-revolutionaries, Prince Altrix.'

'Trixie? Yes, he was one of us. Later, Servenken posted him to the Embassy on Luna, I believe.'

'Well, the moment you were released, you asked Altrix to find me in the crowd and escort me back to the Palace. I told him it wasn't me that needed his protection but the Empress; it was his idea to take her to Sriandra. Without him to show us the way, I don't think we'd have made it. It took five long days to get our endangered Empress to the safety of the Seraphim and even then we couldn't relax till we knew she'd been accepted.'

'She asked for sanctuary?'

'Yes. The Seraphim knew she was no criminal but a caring and compassionate Monarch, so she was given sanctuary. We stayed with her for ten days; then the new State Council needed her advice on the best way forward. She stayed in the city only a few days then returned to Sriandra; she wanted to keep out of the way whilst the new State Council sorted out the mess. She returned to Sriandra alone; she insisted that my place was now with our people.'

'I wish I'd known her better, Silla; she sounds a wise and caring Monarch.'

'She was also very brave. Only those who were close to her know how much she did to protect the domain of angelas from the ravings of the tyrant. It was risky because that so-called *Mighty* had become more than a little mad towards the end — at least, that's the excuse she gave for his excesses.'

'I'm so glad she was given a proper Royal Farewell. From what you say, she deserved no less.'

'Were you there? I don't remember.... '

'No, I was on Phobos. When Servenken was chosen to become Emperor he asked me to visit the colonies to ensure there weren't any troubles brewing. He was afraid they might demand that I be made Emperor, or something of the sort. I was only too happy to oblige having no wish to mount the throne in his place. So, there was a good send-off for Empress Wonderful in the end?'

'It was a very moving ceremony. People began to realise just how *wonderful* an empress she'd been; she'd protected us during those terrible years. Everyone took her to their hearts and wanted to be there to say *Thank You*. If I earn even a modicum of the gratitude showered on Empress Wonderful, I'll have done extremely well.'

'From what I hear from various friends at Court and in Paradisia, you've nothing to worry about on that score, Silla.'

'Paradisia? Oh, your community. But how could they know? Surely they're out of touch with the world.'

'Not so; we try to keep them entertained with all the latest gossip; we aim to make life interesting and ensure they still feel connected to the outer world. After all, it's that world they're devoting their lives to saving. Girilayne was a great asset; she travelled here, there and everywhere.'

'How could she if she was officially dead?'

'She joked that she had the perfect cover: she was a supervisor of domestic servants and so treated as a non-person. She boasted that she could go anywhere and talk to anyone, even to people who'd known her quite well in the past, and she wouldn't be recognised because of the work she did. There was only one person she took the greatest care to avoid.'

'Who was that?'

'You!'

'Me? Why me?'

'Because, she said, you look people in the eye when you speak to them, no matter how humble; and very few people do that, especially when they're discussing the employment of elves and dwarves.'

'Isn't that an exaggeration? I'm sure most people look at the person they're talking to — how else can they establish a rapport?'

'I seldom look people in the eye,' Versain responded. 'It's how I keep a barrier between me and them. I'm not proud of that but I recognise the habit in myself. It's different when *you* speak to people; I watched you during your audience and you did just what Girilayne said: you *looked* at each person and they left feeling they'd been the only person you'd spoken to that day.'

'Well, I'm flattered you think it a virtue; it's quite unconscious — I didn't realise I was doing anything quite so intrusive.'

'Oh, for goodness sake, Silla! Don't start looking at the floor — or the ceiling. It's greatly to your credit that you want to relate to people; I just don't have that same desire. Girilayne told us a funny story about how you once almost caught her out. She'd been in one of the Mother Houses discussing some problem when you made an unexpected visit and there she was, trapped in a room with only one door, and you coming in at that door.'

'I didn't see her — I'd definitely remember if I had.'

'She said she did the only thing that came into her head; she dropped to the floor and began scrubbing, goodness knows what with.'

'You know, I believe I *do* recall the occasion, Versain. I was so upset that this poor angela should have come to such a sorry pass as to have to work as a domestic servant. I was about to speak to her, then thought she might feel embarrassed so I let it pass.'

'Girilayne knew perfectly well that, had you looked her in the eye, you would have known who she was. She said she could make sure other people *didn't* see her, but that trick would never work with you because you are always so aware, so *present*. She said you were one of the few people she knew who actually *lived* each moment of each day. That's quite a commendation.'

'I'm surprised she knew me well enough to be able to say any such thing.'

'Of course she knew you; she was close to us all in Second School; she may have been my tutor but she would have seen almost as much of you and Vyvyan since you attended my homework tutorials, remember?'

'So we did; it was so long ago. And now she's gone.'

'Yes, and now she's gone and I'm learning things about her I never knew when she was alive. But there's one good thing, Silla: we've resumed these discussions. I've missed them. I'm so glad you've agreed to join us. It will help fill the void Girilayne has left in my heart.'

'I'm glad too. I'm looking forward to contributing whatever I can; in particular I must think about how we're going to prepare people ahead of this disaster. I must consult some of these friends of yours who are already involved.'

'It would be a good starting point; many of them hold positions of influence.'

'Once the prophecy is made public there could so easily be widespread panic. In fact, ruthless people could even try to hijack your spacecraft to save their own lives; there could be something close to civil war if we don't take precautions.'

'That's why we kept the prophecy secret. One thing you should know, Silla: all of us who've joined the community — whether in the mountains or in the world — have vowed that we will not ourselves be chosen for any of the expeditions. We will work tirelessly for the preservation of what little can be saved, but that *little* will not include us.

'This doesn't apply to Devallian, by the way. He's never

joined the community though I employ him on community affairs. He's in training to take command of the third expedition. Everything he does for the community is in preparation for the heavy responsibilities he'll have to shoulder in the future.'

'But Versain, isn't Devallian a trifle young for such a responsible position?'

'I hope we'll have seven or eight years before the third expedition leaves; he'll mature a great deal in that time. In fact, his youth is an advantage as the journey to Luna will take some years; the spaceships travel quite slowly. He'll be a mature adult by the time he takes on the challenge of establishing a settlement on Luna. The plan is for him to train Phillestra, who will become Empress when she comes of age.'

'You mean to send Phillestra on the third expedition?'

'I do, she has always been destined for that; it's why she was born.'

'That's a bit mysterious, Versain… '

'When I asked you to arrange for Calthea to join me in bringing a royal cherub into the world, it was because that cherub was destined to play a part in this enterprise.'

'What you say baffles me, Versain, but I'm glad Phillestra will have a chance of a full life, so I'll accept your explanation. You know, I'm glad you're giving me these things to do; this terrible prophecy could so easily persuade one to give up. I really do need to ask Oracle for an audience; I need to assure myself that her prediction is true and not some test she's set you for the betterment of your soul.'

Chapter 6

Sriandra

Two weeks later, Empress Serenity visited Sriandra for her annual retreat. On this occasion, her attendants remained behind and only the Royal Duke accompanied her. The Palace was alive with gossip at the recent resumption of relations between the royal twins after many years of seeming estrangement; there'd been a number of suggestions for this sudden reconciliation but none came near the truth.

Soon after arriving, the Empress was informed she'd been granted an audience with Oracle. In preparation for this important event she went into silent retreat for three days. On the day of her audience, she flew to Srivalian alone; she was met by a seraphina who escorted her into the interior of the pyramid — just as all visitors were escorted — and placed at a pillar. The attendant left as soon as Oracle appeared.

Versilla had been in Oracle's presence more often than she cared to remember and each time the Great One appeared, she felt the same overwhelming reverence for this mysterious and powerful personage. She bowed till her head touched the surface of the pillar and remained thus till Oracle's extraordinary voice bid her rise.

'Empress, it is good to see you. Come, kiss my hand, we will talk for a while.'

The hand extended to the Empress was almost transparent;

the skin was fine and shone with the same diamond-like radiance that lit Oracle's face. Versilla barely touched the sacred hand before retreating to the safety of her pillar. She knew of old that the radiation zone around Oracle could drive all thought from her mind; she had come with a purpose and needed to remember that purpose.

'You wished to see me, my child?'

'Yes, Holy One. My brother, the Royal Duke has invited me to help him with the work of his secret community. I wish to know if this has your approval, and if so, to ask for your blessing and your guidance so that my efforts will advance and not hinder his important mission.'

'I am glad you have come, Empress. It is, as you say, an important mission and now that the Duke has lost his mentor, he is in great need of your support.'

Oracle paused and Versilla knew from past experience that Oracle was probing deep into her heart; this was the part of an audience she most dreaded — there was no place anyone could hide from that penetrating scrutiny. After a short period the soft resonant voice continued.

'Lord Versain has been assigned the hero's role in this drama. It is not generally realised that a hero requires levels of sustenance not provided by even the strongest sunlight; the role demands what only a devoted angela can provide.

'It was the responsibility of Girilayne-Bahle to provide that sustenance and she did so faithfully up to the time of her departure — a departure that I ordered. At that time, Lord Versain requested an audience, which I denied. He had recognised his urgent need for someone to take the place of his mentor and I wished to see to whom he would turn; he has turned to you Empress, and he could not have chosen better.

'More important than any specific task or responsibility you accept from your brother will be your role as his confidante and faithful supporter. A hero needs the unconditional love of an angela who cares passionately for his soul yet has no desire to steal his limelight. A hero depends upon the genuine admiration and trust of that supporter; you can fulfil that role to perfection Empress, if you choose to do so.

'You have earned your own limelight and so have no need to usurp the Duke's. You have fully justified my trust in recommending you to succeed the late Empress; you have sought neither recognition nor reward for your achievements. The Empire was on the point of collapse and is now healed and flourishing; that is due in no small part to your care and compassion.

'But let us return to your reason for coming to see me today. In what way may I help you to fulfil this new role?'

'Holy One, it may be a great indiscretion for me to ask and yet I must do so, both for my brother's peace of mind and for my own. This prediction you have made concerning Stellaster's destruction: is it a test of the Duke's character that he should accept the prophecy without question or does the prophecy tell of an event that will actually take place?'

Again there was a long pause; the Empress feared she might have overstepped the bounds of protocol by asking so direct a question. It was usual in an audience to *hint* rather than ask something straight out, as she had done. Yet she had to make her question clear, if only to rescue her brother from the distress of his recent doubts.

After a long silence Oracle sighed deeply.

'Ah! You wish me to give you assurances, dear Empress that the universe will not continue to move in accordance with its Destiny; you wish me to tell you that the Immortal Powers will intervene to rescue this one small world of the myriad worlds that crowd the heavens.'

Again Oracle paused.

'Prophecy is a strange gift my dear, and not always welcomed by those who might best benefit from it, especially when it speaks of things they would rather not hear. Let me say just this: we are not sent to this world to be safe nor to be in control of our lives nor to satisfy our myriad desires; we are sent here to fulfil the intentions of those who sent us.

'It sometimes happens that the Immortal Powers allow us the illusion of Free Will and we live for a time in the mistaken belief that the choices we make determine the course of our lives; then something happens that is so far beyond the scope of our powers to comprehend, control or even influence that we are forced to accept that we are but pawns in a complex game that we do not understand.

'That is all I am able to tell you, my child. Do what needs to be done and do it to the very best of your ability; that is all that can ever be asked of you. If you accept the challenges that are presented to you, you will have my support and my blessing — always. And now Empress, this audience is at an end.'

These words were the cue for Versilla to prostrate and leave; an attendant came to lead her out into the weak polar sunlight. She left immediately and spent the rest of the day basking alone in the slightly stronger sunlight of Sriandra. She had much to think about yet even after many hours of intense contemplation, she still could not decide whether Oracle had been *assuring* her that the predicted meteor was still on course or had been *reassuring* her that the Immortal Powers were bound to intervene to save their beloved world.

What had been made abundantly clear was that she had Oracle's blessing for joining her brother's mission. Perhaps that was all she could have expected. Oracle had never been famous for making things easier or clearer. At least on this occasion she had been given confirmation of her future duty.

* * * * *

The next evening, the Empress was chief guest at a ceremony presided over by Chief Seraph Godwinian. It was attended by the entire community of the Seraphim; Calthea was also there, so the Empress finally met her supposedly-dead protégé.

'Your Imperial Majesty,' Calthea murmured bowing low, 'it is a great pleasure to see you again. May I request an appointment to talk to you tomorrow?'

'Calthea dear child, how are you? I am very pleased to see you especially as tonight is the anniversary of your marriage on the sacred festival of Verastrom.'

'Yes Your Majesty; it is why I have been given permission to attend.'

'You have my blessings for this special celebration; I hope it brings back many happy memories — as it will for me. Meet me tomorrow morning after the *Obeisance*; we can have a long talk as we bask.'

'I'm very sad not to be spending this special evening with my cherub, Your Majesty, but the Royal Duke has other plans for my life and hers. I am resigned to the fact that I shall not see darling Phillestra again — or at any rate not for many years.'

'But why, Calthea? Surely Versain can find a way for you to meet Phillestra without risk to you or the community? When I get back, I'll ask him if a meeting can be arranged… Oh! I think we'd better take our places; the procession is approaching.'

The festival of Verastrom was celebrated at sunset and marked the rare event of Jupiter and Verastra rising side by side; this conjunction occurred once every five and a half years. In Cander Imperia, which lay directly to the south of Sriandra, most citizens would have spent the afternoon at fairs in the many amusement parks; in the evening there would be fireworks and dancing in Festival Park.

At the Palace, a special party was being held to mark the sacred anniversary of Phillestra's birth. Lord Versain had promised to make this a memorable event for the young cherub; he'd promised Versilla he would escort Phillestra himself during the celebration rather than delegating the task to Devallian, as was his wont. She would be allowed to stay up till well after sunset to watch the fireworks, which were bound to be an amazing spectacle.

Although the Empress was sad not to be at the Palace for an event so important to her adopted cherub, she was glad to be spending it with Calthea, for whom it was also an evening of great significance; it must be hard for her not to be spending this anniversary with the cherub she loved so much.

The Chief Seraph took his place at the northernmost pillar — the Great Pillar — of a ring of stone pillars in the centre of Sriandra's compound; other leaders took the remaining pillars with the rest of the community standing behind enclosing them in an outer ring. The Empress and other guests formed part of this ring.

A trumpet voluntary announced the opening of the proceedings; Chief Seraph Godwinian reminded the company of the great significance of this festival.

'At *Verastrom*, eighteen hundred and fifty four years ago, Coranda Magister first appeared in the city square of Sandolinia; it was the start of his short but world-changing ministry. Seraph was the first disciple to come to him; to Seraph we owe all knowledge of Magister's teachings, for he became scribe from that first day giving us both our own holy book, *The Secret Teachings of Coranda* and the holy book of the angels, *The Words of Magister*.

'To Seraph we also owe the name of our race, for over the years we Seraphim have become genetically separate from our angel ancestors. That day so long ago was significant in other ways: we count our years from the Year of Magister; we seek to lead our lives according to the precepts of Magister; our beliefs regarding death and what follows are illuminated by Magister's teachings. So at Verastrom, we Seraphim come together to re-dedicate our lives in service to Coranda Magister and to offer gratitude to our ancestor, Seraph.'

Godwinian paused for so long that the choir, thinking he had concluded his opening oration, took a collective breath in preparation for the first anthem. But he had merely paused for effect and continued in a quieter, more emotional tone.

'We know that this will be the penultimate celebration of Verastrom. Before another eleven years have passed, our beloved world will have ceased to exist. Only once more will we gather together to celebrate this great festival. So let us dedicate our prayers tonight to our beautiful, fated world and to our lovely, fated moon. Let us thank the Immortal Powers for the boon they have granted in sending us to be born in this world at the end of its immensely long existence.'

At last the choir was given its cue for the first anthem — a paean of praise to the Immortals for the precious gift of life. During the anthem, the Chief Seraph left the arena, to return a few moments later escorting the radiant figure of Oracle. There was a gasp of surprise; Oracle had never before been known to leave the Crystal Pyramid.

Godwinian led Oracle to the Great Pillar and took his place opposite. There was a long silence; then Oracle's voice rang out in her clear bell-like tones.

'Beloved Seraphim, it is long since I visited Sriandra. I come to bid you *Farewell*. I come to tell you that this is our final meeting. My work in this world is done and I am called to my eternal home, just as you will all be called sooner than you might have expected. I leave no successor; Oracle will reside no more upon Stellaster.

'You know the future that has been prophesied for this world, and the duty you owe to the peoples who share this world with you; I refer not only to the angel race from whom the Seraphim are descended but to the elves, the dwarves and the harbingers of the upper skies who also call Stellaster *home*.

'Many of you have been charged with helping to save the cream of Stellaster's treasures for posterity; it is the duty of the rest to assist them in any way you can. The treasure to be preserved is angel-culture, which is the gift of angel-mind. In the Seraphim angel-mind has evolved to even higher degrees of sophistication but let me remind you my children: our minds are but pale reflections of the Immortal Mind that created all worlds and all living beings.

'Fulfil your worldly duties to the best of your ability but let your chief concern be to arrive at the end of your life having attained what it was you came here to attain. Each of you knows what that is, for the goal for each is different. In the time remaining, each of you will be given assignments by your superiors; these tasks are designed to aid you on your journey to fulfilment.

'Give your entire commitment and your full enthusiasm to these assignments. Every effort made now will go far in securing your place in the next stage of your eternal journey. As the predicted disaster approaches, your greatest challenge will be to keep hope alive. This will be possible if you remember who you are and who you are not; that knowledge will serve as your map and compass in the difficult terrain you will soon be traversing.'

Oracle paused but not a soul stirred; after a while she continued.

'Tonight, we worship two heavenly bodies that will continue to shine long after Stellaster and Verastra have vanished from their ancient places. Magnificent Jupiter and

Life-giving Sol will continue to follow their destined paths in the firmament; they will continue to shine upon the remaining worlds of the Solar System.

'I leave you with my blessing and an invitation: when the final day draws near, I invite all seraphs and seraphinas to end their worldly lives in the Crystal Pyramid; it is the most sacred place in this world. I return there now and this body will never again leave its hallowed confines…. *Farewell*, my dear, dear children.'

Oracle left her pillar and made a slow circuit of the arena, touching each person in the centre of the forehead as she passed. She then turned away from the circle and walked, unaccompanied, away from the arena.

After a stunned silence, the Chief Seraph invited everyone to turn towards the sun, just setting in the south west. As soon as its rim touched the distant horizon he invited everyone to face south east, where the beautiful pink orb of Verastra and the great bronze orb of Jupiter were cresting the horizon side by side, apparently equal in size, and certainly equal in splendour — this was the moment of Verastrom.

The choir sang an anthem only ever performed during this rare event; Calthea recognised it at once — the hymn sung at the culmination of her Marriage Ceremony. That event lay in the past, yet it was as if she stood again on that distant plateau, about to join her consort in calling down a special cherub.

How odd! It was as if the flow of time had made a complete circuit so that the present merged into that earlier occasion and both were but part of all that had ever existed. Was she experiencing Eternity?

Chapter 7

The Jubilee Prizes

Time flows relentlessly into the future. Across the universe specks of stardust — some large, some small — follow their assigned paths, each sounding its own note in the symphony Time is orchestrating within the vast auditorium of Space. Two specks are of special interest: one, a planet with two moons, glides along its customary path around the star whose strong gravity holds it within a time-worn groove; the other, a chunk of dense matter, ejected during some ancient catastrophe, hurtles along the path of its own momentum. These two objects are destined to meet in a future cataclysm that is still some time and distance away.

Three times has Stellaster circled Sol since Oracle departed for another realm, and will circle seven times more before the score of Time's Great Symphony sets the cymbals clashing in a series of sharp discords that will shatter the measured harmony of the Solar System.

But for now, the planet pays loyal attendance on Sol and the meteor streaks through the dark emptiness of intergalactic space.

* * * * *

After joining the Duke's service, Versilla spent much of her time thinking about her assignments. She assumed they had several years before the public need be told of the fate in store for their world but there were less than six months before the first spaceship would be launched in the Grand Finale of the Royal Jubilee celebrations.

She'd racked her brains to come up with a practical way of selecting that ship's complement of passengers — the pioneers who would establish the first settlement. It was easy enough to decide the qualities needed; the challenge lay in selecting the individual passengers without revealing the reason for their selection.

They would have to resort to trickery on a grand scale but what form should that trickery take? Versilla wrestled with the problem without success until a flash of inspiration during a retreat at Sriandra revealed a way: they would hold a series of competitions as part of the Jubilee celebrations that would give every commoner a chance to win a place at the Grand Finale. The prize-winners would be taken to the moon, given a tour of Master Tang's great spaceship then set off on a short test flight, which would turn out to be not quite as short as they'd been led to expect.

A circuit around Verastra would become a trip to Phobos, and not just a trip but a one-way journey to a new life on an alien world. They would have to come up with an explanation as to why the spaceship failed to return to the launch site, but faking an accident would surely not be beyond the capacities of those who had designed and built the world's first spaceship.

Versilla discussed her idea with the Paradisia team who were enthusiastically in favour. Competitions were a way of identifying people of outstanding ability; the Paradisia team could ensure that the individual categories were designed to favour people with the qualities necessary for long-term survival in a hostile environment.

The State Council had already approved the Duke's proposal to hold the Finale of the Royal Jubilee on Verastra with the launching of the spaceship as a spectacular conclusion to month-long festivities. The royal twins explained to the State Council their idea of holding competitions that would give members of the public a chance to take part in the Finale. After all, it had been the public who'd actually deposed the tyrant thus paving the way for the coronation soon to be celebrated.

One advantage of the proposal — an advantage that was *not* revealed to the Council — was that, although the competitions would be public events, the reason for holding them could remain secret; they'd be designed in Paradisia, and many of the winners would be chosen by the Paradisia team, but the community's existence need not be revealed in the process. It was not yet time to inform the State Council and the public of the pending disaster.

The Duke hoped all three spaceships would have been dispatched before any announcement was made, thereby ensuring that the spaceship programme remained under Paradisia control. He recognised the risk of civil unrest — even civil war — once people realised that their lives would be forfeit when the meteor struck.

The competitions proved a great success; everyone wanted to take part because it would give them a chance to be at the Grand Finale of the Jubilee, which celebrated the overthrow of tyranny and the restoration of peace. They also wanted to see with their own eyes the metal monster that had been built in such secrecy on Verastra.

The month of festivities began with a great procession from the Royal Palace to Cander City. In a brilliantly staged durbar held outside the Courthouse, the heroes of the Insurrection — the Four Galliards and their lawyer, Taitaillin — were honoured by the Monarchs. The Emperor installed the five as Knights of the Grand Order of the Golden Wing; the Empress then presented each with a casket of fabulous gemstones from the Royal Treasury.

Finally, the city elders invested the Four Galliards with the Freedom of the City — Councillor Taitaillin was already a Freeman — after which the heroes were carried in triumph around Festival Park on the shoulders of cheering crowds.

In the following days, circuses visited most towns and settlements; plays were staged in town squares and dances in public parks whilst firework displays lit up the skies each evening, all of which proved extremely popular. The Monarchs were in constant demand to preside at these functions and the Galliards were pressed into attending several events each and every day.

Then there were the competitions: athletic games and tournaments in a variety of team and individual sports were held in every locality to decide those who would compete in the finals; these were held at the Jubilee Games in the third week of the festivities. A Jubilee Arts Festival held that same week displayed competition entries in various cultural categories including literature, art, science, and architecture. In the city, there were performances of plays, operas, ballets and concerts, all competing to win one of the greatly-desired Jubilee Prizes.

In fact, there was barely a day that did not see some sort of event being staged somewhere in the world and all were enthusiastically attended.

During this time, final preparations were in hand for the Finale of the Jubilee on Verastra and for the commissioning of the *New Enterprise*, the latter in the strictest secrecy. The Duke chose one of the Galliards, his close friend Altrix, as Commander of the first spaceship and the Empress appointed her chief attendant Vinchetta to be the expedition's Vice-Empress.

It only remained for the Paradisia supervising team to choose the names of those who would win a Jubilee prize. Often the winners were obvious — they'd won the final of their sport at the Jubilee Games — but many competitions involved submitting entries in advance; these were then judged in secret in Paradisia. After a check for any genetic problems in the Motherhood Archives, the final list of winners was compiled and presented to the State Council for public announcement.

* * * * *

Devallian leant against a dark rock on Meon, Stellaster's minor moon, basking in sunlight as he gazed up at Verastra floating above him. He'd been sent here to monitor the launching of the spaceship from Verastra's construction site, which was just emerging from the shadow of night. Stellaster herself lay below the horizon.

Two chains hung around the Devallian's neck: one bore his ruby responder; he would use it to keep in touch with Professor Bahle in Paradisia and with the Duke, who was at present escorting the royal contingent to Verastra for the Grand Finale. The second chain carried a small telescope through which he would observe the launch. During the past few years, the community's scientists had made remarkable advances in optics; his telescope might be small and light enough to carry around his neck but it was powerful enough to see distant objects and events in amazing detail.

Why the Duke had sent him to Meon to keep the launch site under surveillance he could only guess — and had done just that. The whereabouts of Danyetta, the missing engineer, remained a mystery; in the three years since his disappearance, not the slightest trace had been found of him despite thorough searches on every world within flying range. Danyetta had left Verastra with a platoon of soldiers and never been seen since.

Devallian didn't accept the popular view that the delinquent engineer had lost his way or over-taxed his strength during that flight, so he remained vigilant; he was convinced Danyetta was still alive and often quizzed the Duke for news of him. It was his opinion that his chief had sent him here because he feared Danyetta might attempt to disrupt the launching of the spaceship, thus causing the Duke no little embarrassment; it would be revenge for being snubbed in front of his colleagues.

It was barely dawn on the construction site, yet the area around the lone spaceship was already a hive of activity. The team's dwarves had spirited away the other two ships, but Devallian could not see where they'd hidden them; there was no sign of the dwarves either; this wasn't their day so they'd made themselves scarce.

A large grandstand stood alongside the spaceship. The invited guests, who had been brought to Verastra by shuttle during the night, were now taking their places in that grandstand; those shuttles had returned to Stellaster to bring the prize-winners. Another shuttle was bringing the royal party, including the Royal Duke; they would be last to arrive at Jubilee Park, the new name for the construction site.

* * * * *

Phillestra jumped to the ground; it was her first ever visit to the moon. The sun was well above the horizon but the globe of Stellaster was just vanishing below the opposite horizon. She was ecstatic to be accompanying the Monarchs to this historic event. Her friends at the palace were green with envy — why should she, a *half*-royal, have been chosen?

Countess Vinchetta had been chosen too, but as chief attendant to Empress Serenity no one questioned her selection, nor that of eighteen-year-old Sibylina Cyr; who had passed out top-of-class at Royal Second School; she had earned her place as much as any of the Jubilee Prize-winners.

The shuttle pad was at some distance from the grandstand so they had to fly; the guests and prize-winners were already in their places and eagerly awaiting the royal party. As the Monarchs approached the royal dais, a great fanfare of trumpets blared out in welcome; then the Imperial Orchestra broke into a Ceremonial March always played when welcoming the Imperial Majesties.

Phillestra was placed directly in front of Empress Serenity and so guaranteed a good view of the proceedings. First, there was a concert including a brilliant chorale written specially for the occasion. Then Lord Versain brought Master Chorton-Tang, the designer of the spaceship, to be presented to the Monarchs. Emperor Wellbeloved invested him with the *Imperial Prize for Technical Innovation*, and placed a fabulous ruby sash over his shoulder; he invited the Master to describe his masterpiece to the assembled company.

Phillestra was very impressed. Outside, the spaceship was a lattice of diamond-shaped panels that swept elegantly over its surface, reminding her of a snake in her favourite book, *The Amazing Diversity of Earth's Creatures*. Overall, it was shaped like a different Earth creature — the sea monster called a whale. But it was difficult to see how such a heavy object was going to fly, especially as it hadn't any legs or wings. How would it get itself off the ground? It would be a big embarrassment if it didn't!

Phillestra could imagine the faces of the organisers if, having brought all these people to the moon, the launch itself turned out to be a flop. She couldn't make up her mind whether she'd rather see the great monster leaping into the air or whether it might be more dramatic if it failed to make it off the ground at all.

Master Tang was explaining that the diamond-shaped panels were of three sorts; the translucent panels were windows that would allow the ship's occupants to look out and also to bask in sunlight; the dark panels were made of a special vitreous compound that was able to capture sunlight and produce a magical power he called *electricity*; the third sort of panels, the ones that gleamed like silver in the sunlight, were made of a light metal alloy specially designed to provide strength.

They were told the ship could carry over a hundred people in interplanetary flight but it was necessary to take off from the ground with fewer on board because of the strong pull of Gravity. The ship would take off today with only the royal party on board so everything should be fine. Anyway, they'd find out soon enough, Master Tang joked engagingly and everyone laughed with him, though a trifle nervously.

I wonder if the Emperor will demand that beautiful sash back if the monster fails to fly, Phillestra thought to herself. Master Tang now invited members of the royal party to accompany him to his wonder-machine for a closer inspection. They stood in a semi-circle beside the ship, which now towered over their heads. Only when you were this close did you fully appreciate its size.

The plan was for the ship to take off with only the crew and the royal party on board so that they would be its first passengers. The ship would make a short circuit around Jubilee Park a few hundred feet from the ground, it would then hover whilst those not going on the excursion disembarked; the Prize-winners would then fly up and board for a short trip around the moon.

Chief Seraph Godwinian stepped forward to address the assembly; he quoted a few verses from *The Words of Magister* as a form of blessing; his place was then taken by Emperor Wellbeloved who named the ship *The New Enterprise* and added a few words of his own in praise of this truly magnificent technical achievement.

Commander Altrix, whom Phillestra knew to be one of her royal father's close friends, invited the royal party to fly up to an opening in the ship's side where a metal panel had been moved to one side. To Phillestra's delight, as she entered the interior, Lord Versain pulled her to his side; clearly he wanted to show her over the ship that he himself had ordered to be built. Phillestra was ecstatic! She adored her royal father but saw far too little of him. She now understood why she'd been chosen for this great adventure. If the ship only existed because the Royal Duke had told Master Tang to build it, then it was his ship; so why shouldn't he invite his own cherub to its official launch?

The Duke, however, had a different reason for drawing his daughter from his sister's side. Versilla's chief attendant, Vinchetta would soon be leaving, never to return. The Empress was very fond of her protégé and though she herself had chosen her to lead the expedition's angela contingent, it was still going to be an emotional parting. She was grateful to Versain for ensuring she could give her full attention to Vinchetta during their last moments together.

Phillestra was both excited and nervous at what would happen as the monster leapt from the ground but it wasn't as horrendous as she'd feared. In fact, they rose very gently; she saw the ground slowly receding from her window. It was interesting to watch the grandstand becoming ever smaller as they rose higher and higher. It seemed that Master Tang could keep his fabulous sash after all. Nevertheless she was grateful for her father's hand resting lightly on her shoulder; it gave her confidence; but soon she didn't need that reassurance.

'Go and look out of the window on the other side,' the Duke gave her a gentle push and followed her across the interior. 'Tell me what you see.'

'That's Meon, isn't it? It's the dark moon floating in the sky.'

'It is — and a friend of yours is on that moon looking at us looking at him.'

'Who?'

'Can't you guess?'

'It's not Devallian, is it?' Phillestra jumped up and down in excitement.

The Duke held his ruby responder to his throat, as he often did, then placed it on her forehead. To her utter astonishment, she could hear the voice of her dearest, dearest friend as clearly as if Devallian had been standing beside her.

'Hello, Phil. Are you enjoying your flight in *The New Enterprise*? I can see you with my telescope but you won't be able to see me as I'm only a tiny black speck on this large black rock.'

'Royal Father,' Phillestra exclaimed in delight, 'I can hear Devallian's voice.'

'Hold the ruby to your throat and *think* something you'd like to say to him.'

It was a novel experience for the eight-year-old but she soon got the hang of it. She spent a few moments in silent conversation with her dear friend then reluctantly surrendered the pendant when her father held out his hand. The Duke spent a few moments in further conversation with his ADC, then stowed the device behind his royal sash.

'Do you remember your Mother, Phillestra? Do you remember Calthea-Tai?'

'Of course I do, I remember spending a night in her home but she disappeared the next day and Marima Serenity said I shouldn't think of her any more as it would only make me sad. Why do you ask?'

'Because this ruby responder was made by your Mother; it is one of her clever inventions. Did you know that crystal recorders were invented by your Mother and that they earned her the Imperial Prize for Technical Innovation.'

'What, like the one Emperor Wellbeloved has just given to

Master Tang?'

'Exactly like that.'

'And did she get a ruby sash too?'

'No. In those days, there wasn't this habit of presenting everyone with precious gems; the Master's sash was the Empress's idea; my sister seems keen to empty the Royal Treasury of all its best gems by dishing them out to anyone and everyone in sight.' The Duke chuckled at a private thought.

'I wish she'd give some to me!' Phillestra sighed wistfully, but was unheard.

The Duke was deep in thought. The casket of gems given him on the first day of the celebrations had astonished him at the time but he'd soon come to see how clever Versilla had been. By honouring the heroes of the Insurrection in this way, she'd been able to give him the very gems Calthea needed for her assignment.

Some day soon, the Duke thought, he would take Phillestra to meet her Mother again; their cherub was mature for her years and would soon be able to start training for the role she was destined to play later in life.

When the *New Enterprise* had completed her test circuit, the Emperor and most of the royal party left and flew down and took their seats in the grandstand. The royal twins did not leave, nor did Vinchetta, Sibyllina or Phillestra — the Duke had deliberately held his daughter back.

The Jubilee Prize-winners now flew up in batches and were welcomed aboard by Commander Altrix, the Empress and the Royal Duke. All were bright-eyed and bubbling with excitement as they stepped into the spacious interior of the ship. The youngest were eight-year-olds still at First School and the oldest no more than thirty five; the hundred had been carefully chosen to include a good mix of ages and sexes, temperaments and skills. These unsuspecting visitors would become the seed-corn of the future.

When all the prize winners had boarded, the Duke called Phillestra to his side; he spoke to her in his formal *Commander-in-Chief* voice.

'Phillestra, we are not here for our own enjoyment but to make the day special for the Jubilee Prize-winners. Do you see that group of cherubs over there? You've seen how the Empress goes about her work; show me what you've learnt from her. Go and talk to those cherubs.'

The Duke was impressed; this sheltered young aristocrat didn't shy away from her assignment; she wasn't used to meeting commoners yet responded immediately to her father's command, approaching the group with confidence. In fact, it was they who were suddenly shy and reserved; they hung back, dumbfounded that a member of the royal party should deliberately seek them out. Phillestra had her back to the Duke but he could see the anxious tension on the faces of the cherubs.

At first they stood back but Phillestra said something that encouraged them to approach her with eager enthusiasm; they replied to whatever it was she'd said and soon there was a huddle of laughing cherubs enjoying themselves to the full. The Duke, content to leave his daughter to her own devices, now turned his attention to the rest of the group. How were they reacting to this unique adventure?

This was his preferred stance — as watcher rather than participant — but he was seldom able to play the detached observer at Court; he'd be pestered by courtiers burdening him with their opinions, comments and complaints; they'd importune him for some favour or preferment, bending his ear on any and every topic.

Now he could stand back and savour the sweet taste of success. They'd done it! Master Tang had come up trumps with his fabulous spaceship. The passengers were expressing their delight at being part of this historic flight to Vinchetta and Sibylina; crew members were also busy putting the prize-winners at ease before they set off.

The Duke was reassured to see how well the new arrivals were getting on with those who would share the remainder of their lives. All was going well so he called Vinchetta over to accompany him to the ship's command centre; he found Altrix deep in conversation with the Empress. When he was free the Duke handed his friend one of two scrolls he'd been carrying; the other he gave to his twin.

'Trixie, these are your sealed orders. When you have left Verastra well behind, you are to read the contents to the assembled ship's company; break the seal in front of them so everyone can see you haven't seen the contents before you read the scroll to them. Nothing here will come as a surprise to you; it will certainly be a surprise to your passengers. I think you know that and are prepared for the shock that will undoubtedly be felt by these poor innocent victims — or lucky survivors; we have no way of telling which is likely to be the case in the long run.

'Each passenger will be given an edited version of your scroll; it makes clear that they are under military orders and must obey every instruction you give. It's up to you to soften that harsh message with kind words and the promise of a relaxed regime as long as everyone agrees to co-operate. I know you can do that.'

It was now the turn of the Empress to hand over her scroll.

'Dear Vinchetta,' she put an arm around her attendant's shoulder, 'this official citation appoints you my deputy on this expedition; it gives you full powers to act as *Monarch in absentia*. From this time, you are *Queen Vinchetta*; you will be addressed as *Your Majesty*. Sibylina will become a countess on attaining the age of twenty — two years to go but I'm sure they will pass before either of you has time to notice.

'We will receive regular reports of your progress — at least, we will for the next few years — but I think you already know that there is no prospect of us meeting again on this plane of existence. You have my blessings and my eternal gratitude for accepting this most challenging appointment. Be brave and give all the comfort and support in your power to those I am placing in your care.'

'Empress,' Vinchetta was fighting to control her emotions, 'may I ask where this title *Queen* comes from? It's not an angel title, I think.'

'It's from an ancient elfin tradition; the elfin people were ruled by queens in antiquity. I intend to revive the position of *Queen of the Elves* in the near future. We need to think of ways of enhancing the quality of life for all the people living on this poor doomed world; I believe this will bring joy to our small friends. I'm pleased you are bearing this so well; you could so easily be overwhelmed by the situation. Now let us embrace and part quickly.'

As the Empress made her way to the exit, the Royal Duke turned for a final word with his friend.

'It's not *goodbye* for us Trixie, I'll continue to visit Phobos from time to time. But you must make clear to the angelis strong enough to fly home that it is a matter of honour that they never attempt to do so. Point out that the angelas and cherubs in your community need to have complete confidence in their stronger members; they must know that they will not be disserted, not even when things get tough — as they are bound to do.'

'I'll certainly do that, Versain. I also give you my word that I shall never leave my charges till I leave them for my final rest. I'll do all in my power to keep our small community together and as happy as is in my power; we'll fight to survive through thick and thin — mostly *thin* I dare say though we shall do our best to remain cheerful.'

'I know you will, Trixie. It's why I chose you for this assignment; you have the reputation for running a happy ship.'

'May I ask a favour, Versain?'

'Of course — so long as it's not the cancellation of your posting,' the Duke laughed easily.

'When you send Balchin off with the second expedition to Jupiter, will you give him my blessings for a successful outcome? He faces a far greater challenge than I do. We already have a colony on Phobos; he'll be establishing a base on an unexplored world.'

'I promise I'll do that. But you know, we Galliards have forged a bond that transcends time and place; I'm sure Balchin will know he has your blessings even as you know you have his — and mine and Hugorin's.'

'Yes I do. These past few months have made that bond even deeper.' Then he added reluctantly, 'Versain, I believe it's time we set off. I look forward to meeting again in the not-too-distant future.'

The Duke tore Phillestra away from her group and they descended to take their places in the grandstand for the finale of the Finale — more anthems, more fanfares and more eulogies. At long last the programme came to an end and everyone could board their shuttles and return home.

It was the universal view that the Grand Finale had been a tremendous success; everyone was tired but thrilled. They'd seen the spaceship rise majestically into the skies of Verastra, justification enough for enduring the long journey to the moon and back. It had been a truly awesome happening, an emphatic demonstration of angel ingenuity and enterprise.

Exhausted after long months of eager anticipation as well as the excitement of the event itself, their only wish was for a good night's sleep. On the royal shuttle, Phillestra was already fast asleep held safe in her father's arms. In her very long life, this was a day she would never forget. The royal group travelled to the Palace, other shuttles took their passengers to various towns and settlements then returned to the moon, ostensibly to collect the prize-winners after their excursion around Verastra.

* * * * *

On distant Meon, Devallian watched as the *New Enterprise* left Jubilee Park on her long flight. There'd been no sign of trouble but his assignment wasn't over yet. He must now keep the spaceship in sight as it journeyed to Mars, keeping far enough behind not to be observed yet close enough to detect the first signs of trouble, should trouble arise.

Chapter 8

Deception

The day after the Finale, all the world was abuzz as the lucky guests who'd attended the Grand Finale described for their less fortunate friends the magnificent sight of the New Enterprise rising majestically into the sky above Jubilee Park. They couldn't praise the spacecraft enough or the organisation that had taken so many people to the moon and back without a single hitch.

But that widespread euphoria was not destined to last long.

On the second morning after her return, the Empress was enjoying a rare treat: a prolonged bask in noon-time sunshine; she was rebuilding her reserves after the gruelling schedule of the Jubilee celebrations. Versilla knew she'd have little time for relaxation once news of a missing spaceship reached the capital. Her peace was interrupted by the arrival of a flustered attendant who bowed and asked permission to speak.

'Whatever is the matter, Salcha?' the Empress admonished the young angela. 'Look at the state you're in! You must learn to comport yourself with calm dignity, no matter how grave the situation. Calm yourself then give me your message.'

She knew very well what that message would be. *Here comes the beginning of the charade, the start of deception and dissimulation. The news must finally have arrived.*

'Majesty,' Salcha stammered, doing her best to keep her voice under control, 'two Head Teachers have come asking for an urgent audience. They say they have something terrible to report, but will not tell me what it is.'

'That is only right and proper, Salcha. Please return and tell them I am on my way. Please make them comfortable on the terrace.'

As soon as Salcha had left, she called an elf and sent a message to the Royal Duke requesting him to attend her as soon as he could. Versain would know what the summons meant; they'd prepared their stories in advance. Of course the Emperor still knew nothing.

The two Head Teachers greeted the Empress in the conventional manner, but were clearly extremely agitated. She gave them a moment to regain their composure.

'Domina Scholis, what is it you wish to tell me? Please speak freely; we need not stand on ceremony; this is an informal meeting.'

The Empress had addressed the senior of the teachers by the traditional title for the Head Teacher of a Second School.

'Oh, Majesty, we are so worried!' the teacher burst out. 'As you know, our school won the Jubilee Competition so we were allowed to send two teachers and six pupils to attend the Grand Finale. Naturally, I elected to stay behind to look after the pupils who had not been chosen. The teachers and pupils who were selected were so excited at the prospect of attending the Grand Finale and we were looking forward to hearing their stories on their return.

'We knew that they would be taken on a tour around the moon and so had not expected them to return until yesterday morning. But they did not return. My friend here is Head Teacher of the First School that won in the prize in their category. They were allowed to send one teacher and five pupils. They have not returned either.'

The Empress turned to the junior teacher.

'Primata Scholis, do you confirm what Domina has said?'

'I do, Empress. Whatever can have happened to our teachers and pupils? We waited all day yesterday then discussed the situation together and decided we must come for your guidance. What should we do — we are distraught with worry. What can have happened to them, your Majesty?'

'My dear friends, what a worrying time this must be! I am glad you came to me; it was the right thing to do. I have not received reports of anything else going amiss. The Emperor and I returned straight after the Finale so that the shuttles could return for the prize-winners. I shall ask Lord Versain to find out what has happened; he must report to the Emperor as the shuttle service came under his jurisdiction.

'Perhaps the shuttle assigned to bring your teachers and pupils home got into difficulties and was forced to make an emergency landing, perhaps in a remote place. I am sure they will immediately send out scouts to search for them. If this is the case, we will soon receive news that all are safe and unharmed; let's pray for that anyway.

'Lady Salcha, please find an apartment in the Palace where our guests can rest until we receive news.' She turned back to the teachers, 'I promise to do everything in my power to find out what has happened to our precious teachers and pupils.'

As Salcha was leading the two teachers from the terrace, Lord Versain swept down to land; he bowed courteously but did not speak to the visitors. Approaching his twin he commented under his breath:

'So the first reports have come, Silla? I'd thought angelis would make faster messengers of doom but you were right — your angelas arrived first.'

'Others will be hard on their heels Versain, so we'd better

say everything we need to say before we're besieged. I've suggested the problem probably lies with the shuttle, but as soon as there are reports of other non-returnees that explanation will rapidly founder.'

'We stick to our plan then? I can't see any reason not to.'

'I agree, nothing suggests otherwise.'

'We'll keep Servenken and Council members informed as and when reports come in; some will come to them anyway, but we must seem to be doing everything we can to find out what has happened.'

'Yes. You'd better break the news to Servenken. Tell him I asked you to come here because the teachers had come to tell me the news. Make sure he puts you in charge of the investigation, Versain; we don't want some conscientious diplomat or magistrate poking his nose into things that aren't his business. Shall we walk later, unless you have to leave Cander? By the way, have you heard from Devallian?'

'I have. He tells me the *New Enterprise* set off for Mars without problem; he's following her as we speak and will contact me if there's any sign of trouble; so far, I assume all is well. I shan't leave Cander till I'm absolutely certain there isn't trouble brewing; Gylan will let me know if he needs me in Paradisia, but he can deal with most things himself. So all being well, I'll walk with you at three.'

Over the next few hours the Palace was besieged with reports of prize-winners who'd failed to return from the moon. Bulletins were posted regularly in the city — but there was nothing to report. The shuttles had returned to Verastra to await their passengers but those passengers had never appeared. The shuttle operators had been unsure what they should do so they'd just stayed put and waited.

A few reprimands were issued, though that hardly helped matters. Reporting the passengers' failure to appear any earlier would have made no difference. The spaceship had left Jubilee Park and vanished into thin air. Searches of Verastra and the wilder regions of Stellaster failed to detect any trace of debris.

After five days of searching, the terrible truth had to be faced: the spaceship must have foundered in Space; if so, everyone on board must be presumed lost. After months of joyful celebrations, the entire world was plunged into mourning.

It was a matter of some astonishment when people realised that not one person from Cander Imperia had been amongst those missing. The Paradisia planning team had been careful not to choose anyone based in the capital, since that would allow the *New Enterprise* to put more distance between herself and Stellaster before search parties went scurrying hither and thither looking for her.

Countess Vinchetta and Lady Sibyline were also missing from the Palace but it was assumed they'd accompanied the Chief Seraph to Sriandra. Empress Serenity sent to enquire for their safety and was observed to show unaccustomed emotion on hearing that they were not — and never had been — in Sriandra. Versilla was fast becoming the consummate actor.

Memorial ceremonies were held in the various towns that had lost citizens. In addition, a day of national mourning was declared. The Emperor and Empress led a procession from the Imperial Palace to the ceremonial arena outside the Cander Caves of Eternal Peace and were followed by a great host of mourners.

In recognition of this nationwide tragedy, Chief Seraph Godwinian himself came to officiate at the National Memorial Ceremony.

And that was that.

The trickery had succeeded! The first expedition had been

duly dispatched without the Paradisia community being unmasked. True, Master Tang's reputation was badly dented by the unfortunate outcome of his great endeavour but he wasn't asked to return his ruby sash.

In fact, memories soon faded as other events arose to capture the attention of the small-town tittle-tattlers and the city newshounds and gossip-mongers.

Chapter 9

Disappointing News

In Paradisia, the community spent three days celebrating the successful launch before turning to their next challenge — preparing for the second expedition. On Verastra, the construction crew brought the two half-completed spacecraft back to the assembly area and resumed work under Master Tang's super-critical eye. It was of little concern to them where the vessels might be sent; their task was to complete both vessels on time and to the Master's exacting standards.

Council's plan was to dispatch the second spacecraft, with its carefully chosen complement of passengers, to establish a settlement on one of Jupiter's great moons. Professor Kritten was busy compiling a dossier on these moons for them to make the final selection.

The third spaceship would carry personnel for the Hybrid Project; it would depart two years after the second, heading for Luna. Luna would become the base for the Hybrid Project, though the actual experiments in mind-transfer would have to be carried out on Earth. Devallian would be in command, with Phillestra — by then a thirteen-year-old — accompanying him as trainee and personal assistant.

Versilla now turned her attention to the second expedition; she had assumed that the selection of passengers for this would be easy, since they'd have experience from the first launch to draw on; she now realised it was going to be considerably more difficult. She could not again resort to trickery; no one would voluntarily board another spaceship — not after the first had foundered so disastrously.

Either she'd have to tell those she selected what their selection was for, or she'd have to come up with a new strategy. Yes, but what strategy?

The selection of candidates for the Hybrid Project was proving even more problematic. It was a highly controversial scheme; she couldn't see herself asking potential recruits whether they'd object very much to having their mind extracted by a mind surgeon then transplanted into one of those horrid hominid creatures. After wracking her brains to no avail, Versilla decided she must consult her friend Vyvyan; after all, a problem shared was likely to become a problem solved.

For the past three months, the Empress hadn't left Cander; she had allowed herself no trips to Sriandra during the period of mourning for the lost *New Enterprise*. During her daily audiences, she had made herself available to anyone and everyone wishing to share their distress with her. But now the trauma was beginning to lessen; people were ready to take up the threads of their lives again; at long last she could allow herself a retreat in Sriandra and a long-overdue visit to Paradisia.

'I have to tell you, Vyv,' Versilla said, opening her heart to her friend, 'I'm getting absolutely nowhere with recruiting candidates for the second expedition. I have to confess I'm stymied. I can't think how to invite people to join the expedition without either grossly misleading them, or abducting them — which I will not do. The problem is even worse with the Hybrid Project. I'll have to tell Versain I can't fulfil my assignment.'

'Don't feel bad, Silla; it was always going to be difficult recruiting people for the settlements. You had your brilliant idea for the first expedition but, as you say, we can't pull that trick again. We mustn't put our entire programme at risk by telling potential recruits about it either — especially when it comes to the Hybrid Project.'

'I agree; that's out of the question; in any case, would anyone in their right mind agree to take part in the Hybrid Project once they know what's involved. At least, that's my view.'

'It's mine too and we certainly don't want to transfer crazy minds, do we?'

'So where do we go from here?'

'Let's not throw in the towel just yet, Silla. I believe there is a way — but it also has its drawbacks.'

'What have you in mind?'

'In my opinion, we can only ask for volunteers for the Hybrid Project from the community; we know what mind-transfer involves so we'd be volunteering with our eyes open. The trouble is, we've vowed not to benefit from our work or to abandon our doomed planet before the meteor strikes.'

'Versain told me about that.' Versilla paused, deep in thought. 'But Vyv, since volunteers would be well aware how risky and beastly mind-transfer is, volunteering would actually be a *sacrifice* not a benefit, wouldn't it? It's true your vow presents a problem, but surely not an insuperable one? We should discuss it with Versain. It's certainly a way to make something of all the hard work you've put in.'

'I agree; let's talk it through with Versain; if he agrees, we could put the idea to Council.'

'What about the Seraphim? They've been deeply involved in the Hybrid Project from the outset. Do you think Godwinian would allow us to recruit volunteers from the seraph community? The Seraphim have truly remarkable minds.'

'We can but try, but don't be too optimistic. The Chief

Seraph has always been ambivalent about the Hybrid Project, yet he's given his full support to the seraph he appointed to head the project.' Vyvyan turned to her friend, 'Have you ever met Banderene? He's brilliant; he's an experienced mind-surgeon and the moving force behind the project. I can tell you, Silla, we'd have got precisely nowhere without Banderene's inspiration and guidance.'

'I've met him briefly at Sriandra, but not to talk to; perhaps he'll have a view about your idea, and let's ask Versain to give it his urgent consideration too. What sort of people would we be looking for?'

'We need half a dozen mind-surgeons and the same number of psychologists; they'll come from the seraph community because no angels possess those skills. We'll also need a few Mothers to nurture and supervise the new hybrids till they're able to fend for themselves. The remaining places will be for mind-transfer volunteers.'

'Do you have sufficient Mothers?'

'We need four more to supplement the five already here. By the way, one of those is the Royal Mother we whisked away from the Palace Mother House the day after Versain's marriage. She'd agreed to join us, so Versain had to arrange one of his dramatic escapades to help me get her here.'

'Really? I must say he acted his part very well; I remember he had to reassure Calthea that Phillestra was in no danger from the *mingoloth* thought to have taken the Mother and missing cherubs; he gave no me indication at all that he knew what had really happened to them. Well, well.

'So we need another four Mothers,' Versilla pondered inwardly. 'I wonder who might like to take part in this strange project; at least they won't have to submit to mind surgery!' aloud she said, 'I feel so much happier now we've thought of a way of recruiting people for the Hybrid Project, Vyv. I'll contact Versain as soon as I get back to Cander and arrange a time and place for the three of us to meet.'

'We've still not solved the recruitment problem for the second expedition.'

'No, but we could always switch the order of launchings. Council decided to send the *Hybrid* expedition last to give more time to arrange things. If the problem is solved, there's no reason why we shouldn't dispatch it next.'

'That's true.'

* * * * *

Calthea-Seraphina had now been part of the community for three years; she'd spent five months with the Seraphim following her audience with Oracle and had learnt a great deal more about the nature of mind and the basis of language. She'd also spent time thinking about her assignment and the challenge of capturing vast quantities of complex data within crystal or gemstone.

At present she was working with Maestro Arbrecht Betaline and his team of writers, artists, musicians, mathematicians and scientists as they attempted to codify the entire corpus of angel culture into a simple system that she might be able to immortalise — that is, once she'd developed a technique for accomplishing that awesome task. She was also awaiting a supply of gemstones capable of storing the vast quantities of data involved.

On her return to the valley, Calthea had inherited Girilayne's cave but often preferred to stay overnight in Paradisia; her workroom there had been furnished with everything she could possibly need. She also spent a lot of time with Chrysilla-Flaine; they'd become good friends and found they had a great deal in common. Occasionally she met the Duke but rarely had a chance to talk to him on his brief visits; he always seemed to have matters to discuss with other Council members.

Today, she would get her chance: the Duke had sent a message that he would visit her that morning; then they could fly together to the Council meeting. She had not long been at work when the tall figure of her consort appeared in the doorway; he carried a number of packages; behind him stood Chunka with several more. The Duke advanced into the room, deposited his load on to the bench in front of Calthea then took the other boxes from Chunka and added them to the pile.

'You've been demanding gemstones Calthea, so here they are. I've brought all I could carry; I hope this is enough but I can bring more later if necessary.'

'Goodness, Versain! Have you raided the Royal Treasury?' Calthea exclaimed as she set about opening the largest of the packages, 'Good Heavens, what a fabulous diamond — it's enormous! And it looks virtually flawless. Wherever did you get it?'

'Your guess that it came from the Royal Treasury is correct, but I didn't have to raid the vaults. These beauties were presented to me in full view of the Court by the Empress herself. Others were presented to friends of mine; I retrieved those given to Altrix since they weren't intended for him; they were intended for you.'

'Versain, I have no idea what you're talking about. Can you please explain in simple language what this is all about?'

'You told me your project needed the best gemstones available. I mentioned that to my sister and she had the brilliant notion of presenting us Galliards with gems from the Royal Treasury during the Jubilee celebrations. The State Council bought her idea so she had the pleasure of handing us priceless State treasures in full view of the court.

'It didn't need much to convince Altrix that his gems would

be a hindrance on board — I'm sure you're aware that he commands the *New Enterprise* — so I told him I'd look after them till they could be returned to him loaded with the gems of our culture. Now it's up to you to do just that. How's the project going?'

'Rather slowly I'm afraid but I'm getting a pretty good idea of the scale of the project, of the volume of information to be packed into the recorders. I'm still a long way from working out how to do that. It's a huge challenge.'

'Do you think they'll be ready in time for the second launch?'

'That's little more than a year away; it's difficult to say what can be achieved in that time. This is fundamental research, not just product development. I'll try to have *something* to send with the next launch, though whether it will include anything like a complete record of our culture I can't possibly say.'

'No one expects you to have completed your work by then, Calthea. You're doing your best; no one can ask for more.'

'I realise some recorders will have to be ready for this second expedition; the Jovian moons are much further away than Phobos or Luna; I can't rely on being able to send complete recordings later. Will we be choosing the destination today?'

'I believe we will. The actual question is: which of the moons might prove the least difficult. By the way, did I tell you that I took Phillestra to see the launch of the *New Enterprise*?'

'Did you? How did she enjoy her trip to Verastra?'

'She was extremely excited about the whole thing. I could hardly get a word in edgeways; she gave a running commentary on each and every detail. But I was very proud of her; I asked her to entertain a group of pupils and she showed how much she's learnt from being with Versilla; she proved herself an accomplished diplomat. I believe she's going to be a great asset by the time she leaves with Devallian on the final spaceship.'

'I'm glad you took her, Versain; when the time comes, it won't be an entirely strange experience.'

'If you've finished looking into those packages, Calthea, I think we'd better leave. Are you keeping up with your flying practice?'

'I am so I won't hold you up. Let me stow the last of these boxes — I don't want to find any missing when I return. Thank you for this present; I really am looking forward to working with these fabulous specimens.'

As they left Calthea's workroom, they joined a stream of community members all heading for the meeting of Council in the Crystal Chamber.

'Everyone's going to be there, Versain. Since the launch, morale here has been sky high. Goodness knows how we'll fit everyone in; the gallery won't hold more than fifty but almost double that number are coming to find out where the second spaceship will be sent.'

* * * * *

When Calthea and the Duke arrived, the Council Chamber was buzzing with excitement; the central pillars were occupied by council members and the gallery was full; other observers were packed along the chamber walls behind the pillars. It said a lot for the spirit of those present — all of whom were well aware of the approaching catastrophe — that they could show such enthusiasm and optimism.

As they were about to enter, Professor Kritten plucked the Duke's elbow.

'There's something I need to tell you before we start the meeting, my Lord.'

The two angelis turned away and Calthea pushed through the crowds and took her place next to Chrysilla. A few minutes later the Duke and the astronomer entered and the meeting began. Professor Kritten was invited to present the results of his research. After having commented upon the characteristics of the inner planets and their moons, he turned his attention to the four great moons of Jupiter.

'You must realise that all we know of these moons is what we can see through our telescopes; we know very little of the actual conditions on the surface. There have been no surveys of Jupiter's satellites because no member of the expeditions sent to the Great Planet ever returned.

'That is not our only concern. The Master and I have made a detailed study of the intensity of sunlight the spaceship is likely to receive as it travels away from us. Jupiter is twice our distance from the sun so will receive a quarter of our sunlight; that may be sufficient for interplanetary travel but is not safe for manoeuvring in the vicinity of Jupiter. I believe we must re-think our plans because I cannot recommend that we send the second spaceship to any of these moons.'

There was a murmer of surprise from both gallery and chamber; this elicited a disapproving look from the Duke and silence was rapidly restored.

'I'm afraid this is not my only disappointing news.' The astronomer continued, 'You will know that a group of astronomers and mathematicians have been hard at work trying to calculate as accurately as we can the date the meteor is likely to arrive. The only information we have to go on is the line in the prophecy that tells us that the second meteor will strike *when the solar plane shall cross at square the galaxy again.*

'It is not a simple matter to calculate the average plane of the galaxy or of the Solar System but we have done our best; we estimate that this squaring will probably take place in seven years; in fact, we can be even more precise: our calculations suggest that the squaring will happen during the tenth month of that year.

'That is in line with the timescale we have been working to but in making our calculations we discovered that Mars will be approaching Stellaster at the predicted time of impact. This is very bad news; it means that Mars will also be at serious risk following the collision.

'An impact great enough to shatter a planet into rock and dust will generate a blast zone that could easily extend to the Martian orbit. This means that we cannot consider Phobos a safe refuge for any expedition. I am sorry to have to present such negative results but at least we can make our plans with these facts in mind.'

For a while there was an uncomfortable silence as the implications of this further report were assessed. The Duke then invited the Master to add his comments.

'I must agree with the professor, my Lord; this is very bad news but it does not mean that all our efforts will necessarily be in vain; there's every chance that Earth will escape the blast. In any case, I believe it is wiser to send our pioneers closer to the sun as they will thereby be assured of adequate supplies of sunlight.'

'If Phobos is not a safe refuge Master, ought we to order the *New Enterprise* to change course for Luna?'

'I do not believe that is necessary, my Lord. Phobos will not be at risk for many years and could be a useful stopping-off point for all the expeditions. The passengers can disembark and recuperate there before heading off on their second leg to Luna.'

'May I add a further piece of information, my Lord?' the astronomer asked.

'I hope it's not as discouraging as your earlier contributions.'

The Duke jested.

'I would merely like to remind everyone of something that is already known. Luna orbits Earth with the same hemisphere always facing the planet; Earth then orbits on its own axis; the result is that any spot on Luna is in sunlight for about three hundred and fifty hours and then in darkness for the same period.

'Because angels cannot be deprived of sunlight for such a long time, the Luna Imperial Colony has had to establish two bases and personnel have to up sticks and move before the Earth-facing side is plunged into night, then move back when the outer side begins to enter night.'

'That is a useful reminder, Professor. We must make sure our pioneers organise their lives with this in mind. Now, let's turn to the issue of recruitment for the second expedition. My sister has told me of the difficulties she faces in selecting personnel for the second expedition. It's a tricky matter because, although we know the first launch was a great success, the public believes it was a disaster. But I believe you have a solution to our dilemma, Marima Varenne.'

'I believe we have, my Lord.'

She outlined the plan devised by the Empress and herself to recruit volunteers for the Hybrid Project from the community itself, since community members already knew what volunteering would involve.

'The issue we have to resolve is what to do about the oaths we have taken not to benefit from our various programmes. I believe you have consulted the Chief Seraph on this point, my Lord; perhaps you can tell us what he says.'

'Chief Seraph Godwinian believes that volunteering for the project cannot be thought a *benefit*;' the Duke replied, 'it is his view that, because of the risks involved in mind-transfer, we should regard it as a *sacrifice*. To put one's life at risk from this hazardous procedure and then — if the transfer proves a success — to face life in the body of an alien beast is not a choice any angel should undertake lightly.

'He suggests that if any community member feels willing to come forward, he will hold a special ceremony to release that person from his or her vow. I believe this opinion paves the way for us to consider Marima Varenne's proposal seriously.'

Master Tang caught the Duke's eye. 'I am sure that some construction workers will want to volunteer my Lord, but I will need to vet all applications in advance. We still have two ships to build and equip and all my crew are needed for that. But it's possible that a number could be spared once the second ship is ready.'

'I believe this should apply to all applications,' the Duke responded, 'we can't put other projects at risk by taking away their people for the Hybrid Project.'

'Perhaps I should make clear,' Vyvyan added, 'that for those working for the community, the selection process is simply a matter of ensuring that the volunteer is resilient enough to undergo mind-transfer; that can be done very easily. I ought also to mention that the age limit for volunteers will be the same as for the Jubilee Prize-winners — a cut off at thirty five.

'In brief, we propose sending the Hybrid Project on the next spaceship because we can complete our preparations in good time. That will give the Empress two more years to work out a plan for recruiting personnel for the third spaceship.'

'With that clarification, may I invite comments from members of Council and from any observers wishing to make a contribution?'

There followed a lively discussion then Council voted unanimously in favour of the plan. The Duke closed the meeting immediately after the vote.

For several days the euphoria, which had been momentarily

interrupted by Professor Kritten's disappointing news, returned both in Paradisia and on Verastra. There was widespread support for the plan, and relief that it would leave more time to consider how to select those who would travel on the third and final spaceship.

But then realisation began to dawn of the consequences of this decision: there had been virtually no recruitment to the community in the past few years; there were only a hundred or so community members based in Paradisia and much the same number on Verastra; removing a hundred of them to staff the Hybrid Project would have a major impact on the lives of those left behind.

Many of those working with the Maestro — what he liked to call his *Culture Coding Commune* — were over thirty five and so would not be eligible to volunteer but he was almost certain to lose all the younger members of his elite group. On the other hand, weren't these the ideal candidates for mind-transfer?

Their minds were the very *gems of angel culture* the community had been set up to rescue. In any case, they had almost completed their part in the Recording Project; preserving that work in permanent form was now Calthea's responsibility.

Chapter 10

BIOSPHERES

The morning after the meeting, Calthea and Chrysilla flew to their favourite spot on the northern cliff-face to bask in the early sunlight. Generally they basked in silence but today there was too much to say and only this period before the working day began in which to say it.

'Will you volunteer Chrissy?' Calthea asked, 'The Duke has said I can't because of my assignment but what about you? Are you going to grab a few extra years even if it means lumbering about Earth in a great hairy body?'

'I've thought about little else since the meeting. It's a dilemma, isn't it? On the one hand, they've made clear that if we volunteer we won't be in breach of our vow but then we have to decide whether the project itself is ethical. I have to say that the prof harbours grave doubts on that score.'

'Really? Why, does he consider it unethical?'

'It's a long and complicated argument but centres on the issue of *consent* — not ours, we're free to opt for mind-transfer or to refuse — he's concerned that the poor *recipients* of our wonderful minds might not be quite so happy to be taken over by an alien species for its own ends. They won't have any say in the process because they will be captured, subjected to a procedure they have no capacity to understand and will then have to live with the consequences for the rest of their lives.'

'Hm. I never thought of it like that before... no that's not true. I remember now that, when I was working with Banderene in Sriandra, he had a long argument with the Chief Seraph on this point. I didn't get involved because I'd only recently arrived and was still finding my place in the community.

'I recall that Banderene was vehemently *for* the project, not only because he was its originator, but because he believes the direction of Evolution is always from the simpler to the more sophisticated. He said the hybrids were bound to take Evolution forward on Planet Earth; he also reminded him that Oracle had endorsed the project. Poor Godwinian had no effective answer to that, but he was clearly troubled, as you say Gylan is.'

'The prof's been reluctant speak out against the project in Council but he talks about his concerns to me.'

'What do you think, Chrissy? Are we justified in foisting our minds upon this species of hominids?'

'I suppose it depends on whether we can convince ourselves we're doing it to confer the blessing of our amazing minds on a primitive species, or are simply out to rescue our way of life from extinction. I dare say we shouldn't be over squeamish when it comes to saving our culture before Stellaster is smashed to smithereens.'

'But what about being a volunteer? Would you be prepared to put your life in the hands of a mind-surgeon, knowing you'd be exchanging your lovely angel frame for this hominid's body? Would you be ready to go through the whole process of learning how to walk and talk and everything else, because I'm sure it will be like coming out of the amphora — not that any of us remember that — then having to learn the skills needed to live life as an Earth-bound hominid. Ugh!'

'I suppose we must hope that the settlements work out

and that angels can survive as angels and so keep our heritage alive that way. I have to say the prof has his reservations about that endeavour too. He's not pessimistic by nature but he's not hopeful about the longer-term chances of our brave pioneers, Cal.'

'Why? Does he think Luna will be hit by the blast from the collision? I thought they assured us yesterday that Earth — and therefore Luna — would be safe.'

'It's more fundamental than that. The prof believes that living organisms can only survive in the biosphere in which they evolved. He thinks it's important for us to realise just how complex and delicately balanced a biosphere is. It takes billions of years to create the conditions necessary for Life to emerge and flourish; yet here we are sending our pioneers to Luna, a barren world, in the firm belief that they'll be able to live there as happily as they have lived in the biosphere that gave them life.

'It isn't so obvious in our biosphere but Earth biologists say that every species there plays an important role in a delicately balanced environment. We tend to think of living organisms as independent entities but we should remember that even here, each species is dependent on its habitat. If we send angels to another world without all the elements that make up our biosphere, how will they survive? For example, how will they obtain the bio-silicates needed to replenish their bodies?'

'I'm not a biologist so I don't know the answer. Are you saying it's *impossible* for a species that has evolved in one biosphere to live on another world?'

'That's certainly the prof's view.'

'But for centuries angels have lived on Verastra, Phobos and Luna.'

'They aren't really *living* there, are they? Angelis may spend periods of time on those worlds but then they have to come home to recuperate; angelas can't even visit those worlds and we've never even *tried* bringing cherubs into the amphora on any of those alien worlds.'

'I've never thought of that.'

'It's strange isn't it Cal, that the Immortal Powers should have chosen the three rocky planets in the central zone of our Solar System to develop into biospheres but not the satellites orbiting them?'

'Perhaps they're too small to support biospheres.'

'That may apply to the Martian moons but I wonder why Luna and Verastra weren't thought suitable; they're a reasonable size. The fact is, we don't know why and aren't in any position to question those with any competence to answer.'

'Aha!' Calthea chuckled, 'you refer to the impossibility of asking the denizens of your famous Mentaillion about some of their more questionable schemes.'

'*Precisely so*.' The friends laughed at Chrysilla's mimicry of her mentor.

'Does Gylan believe *all* the projects are doomed to fail then — even the Hybrid Project? Does he believe we should stay put and share Stellaster's fate?'

'He's a *thinker*, Cal; he's only too happy that he doesn't have to make decisions. He's very loyal to the Duke, you know; he won't say any of this in public because it might be seen as criticism of your consort, but he has to be true to himself; he has to tease out these difficult issues as honestly as he can.'

'I see that, but as a Council member it leaves me in the difficult position of sending innocent people to places where they have little or no prospect of surviving. Wouldn't it be better to let them stay here and enjoy their few years remaining in the biosphere in which they evolved?'

'You're beginning to think like a philosopher, Cal. But even the prof realises decisions do have to be made, often without the information necessary to make a good decision. For most of us, it's better to go with the flow, to keep focusing on our goal because that way we spend our days doing things we hope will be for the common good so can sleep easy at night.'

For a while the friends basked in silence, thinking about their conversation. Then a movement on the hillside caught Calthea's eye.

'The Duke is just leaving his cave, Chrissy. I'd better get to my workroom in case he needs to see me. I haven't told you yet, but yesterday Versain brought me some fabulous gifts. If you have a moment during the day, do come to my room; I'd like to show them to you; I can promise you, you're going to be amazed.'

* * * * *

A couple of weeks later, Lord Versain called an informal meeting in his cave — Calthea's previous home. He'd invited members of the community working with the Hybrid Project to meet Balchin, another Galliard he'd appointed to take command of the second spaceship.

Calthea attended as a member of the Paradisia Council and was amazed at the transformation of her training cave; gone was the simplicity and Spartan gloom; all was light and colour. A crystal arch had been set in the entrance to capture sunlight; fibre glass cables carried that light to four crystal chandeliers suspended from the ceiling; for the first time she realised how far back the cave extended into the hillside.

The simple stone couch on which she'd slept was covered with down quilts; a number of pillars had been set up in the centre of the cave, each topped with a down pillow; a carpet of intricate design covered the floor.

'Gracious, Versain!' Calthea couldn't stop herself from

expressing amazement. 'Whatever happened to my prison cell? This looks more like a palace than a cave.'

'It's Chunka's work. Once he realised I'd made this cave my base, he set about turning it into a place he thought fit for the community's leader. I'm told our artists and engineers were inveigled into designing all this then Chunka's dwarves put their designs into effect. It was all done during my tour of duty to the colonies last year — and certainly not by my order. Once Chunka gets an idea into his head, there's no stopping him.'

At this moment Balchin arrived with the rest of the Duke's guests, Banderene amongst them; he left her to make the necessary introductions. Calthea was looking forward to meeting Seraph Banderene again; they'd become good friends during her stay in Sriandra; he'd helped her develop a new recording technique and had told her a great deal about seraph history and culture in the process.

When all were present, the Duke began the meeting.

'Let me introduce Commander Balchin. It needed a great deal of persuasion to get my old friend to agree to take command of our second spaceship; he was hoping to see out his days in the tranquillity of the Sriandra Retreat Centre.' The Duke put a hand on his friend's shoulder as he turned to the others, 'I'm sure you all know that Balchin is one of the Four Galliards.'

The Duke then introduced Seraph Banderene to the commander.

'You'll have met Banderene at Sriandra Balchin, but what you won't know is that he's been working with our community for many years; in fact, he's the leader of the team you'll be carrying to Luna; that team will implement the Hybrid Project. He's the best person to explain the programme.'

'Many years ago,' Banderene began, 'the Seraphim were

asked to co-operate with the Duke's community. I suggested that the technique of mind-transfer might offer a solution to the problem of long-term survival in an alien environment. Mind-transfer is a secret technique, never before discussed with anyone who is not a mind-surgeon, so please understand that what I'm about to tell you must never be repeated without the specific permission of the Chief Seraph.

'I'm authorised to give this account now because you need to know that mind-transfer is a practical proposition and not mere theory; it is the core of the Hybrid Project. Mind-surgeons are authorised to use this procedure in very rare cases where the mind of an individual is regarded as of such over-riding importance that it must be retained in this world at all costs. The mind-surgeon transplants that mind into the body of a younger consenting angel so the valued mind can continue its work.

'The Hybrid Project proposes to use subjects native to Earth. The community's Earth biologists have chosen a creature they hope will prove useful for the purpose. We will transplant angel minds into several of these recipients. After mind-transfer, each hybrid will possess a body well adapted to its environment but that body will come under the control of a conscious angel mind. We expect the resulting hybrid to be able to live a fuller and more cultured life than the hominid ever could.

'I must point out that it is very dangerous to separate a mind from its body,' the seraph continued, 'because doing so usually results in the death of the body and the release of the mind back to its origin. For this reason, the Paradisia Council has decided that the only proper course is to recruit volunteers for the project from well-informed members of its own community. These volunteers will be shedding their angel body and entering the body of this Earth creature.'

'Good gracious! What is this creature you have chosen?' Balchin was clearly astonished.

'We have identified a mammal that biologists call a *hominid*. This hominid is not an attractive creature; it is heavy and hairy; even the female is heavier than a full grown angeli. Nevertheless, the hominid does have a good-sized brain and a flexible hand. Its greatest *disadvantage* is that it possesses no wings so cannot fly; its greatest *advantage* is that it is well adapted for living in Earth's biosphere.

'We propose transferring the minds of our volunteer angels into the bodies of various hominid groups; we will then study each hybrid to establish whether the transplanted mind is able to operate its new body sufficiently well to make use of its pre-existing knowledge of the finer things in life. In other words, we will find out whether our hybrids are able to live a life that is more angel-like than hominid.

'If the mind-transfer is successful, we must then face the next challenge. To tell you about that I will hand over to Marima Varenne.'

Vyvyan took up the narrative.

'That challenge Balchin, is whether our new hybrid species will breed true to type: will breeding produce a hominid body with an angel mind, or will the next generation regress back to pure hominid? To explain, I will need to delve into yet another corpus of secret knowledge — the secrets of Motherhood.'

Vyvyan smiled charmingly at the Commander; she was flirting openly with this old friend of the Duke's, whom she too had known well during their schooldays.

'Are you aware what happens when a proto-cherub enters the amphora?' she asked and without waiting for his response, set about answering her question. 'It's a profound mystery; not even we Mothers fully understand the miracle. All we know is that a powerful force is involved, as anyone who has been a Mother will confirm. A force surges through the body of the Mother before entering the amphora.'

Calthea smiled to herself, reliving in memory that force surging through her own body during the ceremony that brought the spirit of Phillestra into the world. She looked up and caught the Duke's gaze resting on her; obviously he was recalling that same memory.

'Why is it that commoner births require only a Mother?' Balchin asked.

'It's not quite true to say a father isn't necessary; it's just that we keep the male creative force in the National Gene Bank till needed. Not many angelis know this and we don't enlighten them.' Vyvyan laughed, 'We Mothers cherish our secrets, just as the Seraphim do.' she smiled at Banderene before continuing.

'What's crucial is the force that travels through the Mother. What is the origin of this force? We believe it comes from the Inner Heart where Sophia fashions a new soul with its own special characteristics; the new soul travels through the subtle body of the Mother and enters the amphora; this is the ,spirit-light that will eventually develop into the proto-cherub.'

'What do you mean: *Sophia fashions a new soul*? asked Balchin. 'Who is Sophia?'

'Are you not aware of the new cosmology that everyone is talking about? Our highly respected resident philosopher, Professor Bahle has taught us to distinguish between a planet and the biosphere that has evolved on that planet; we are learning to call our planet *Stellaster* and the biosphere that has evolved on it, *Sophia*. It's a useful reminder of the importance and significance of biospheres.

'We *suspect* — such things are beyond proof — that one of the Immortal Powers acts as Guardian of each biosphere. That Guardian directs events in the biosphere, including the dispatch of souls to reside in bodies fashioned from the material of the planet. We call the Guardian of Stellaster's biosphere *Sophia*, the same name as her biosphere; we believe Sophia is creator of all souls that come to live in this world.'

'Vyvyan, you say your project involves the transplantation of an angel's *mind* into this hominid creature's body but now you are talking about *souls*.'

'We believe each soul exists in a casing of mind; it is the combination of mind and soul that is incorporated — literally *enters a corpse* — when it arrives in the amphora. The issue we face in the Hybrid Project is that, whilst we consider Sophia to be Guardian of *Stellaster's* biosphere, it is possible that a different Immortal Power is Guardian of *Earth's* biosphere. The question we face is: which of these Guardians will fashion the souls of our second generation hybrids?'

'You mean, there could be a quarrel between two of the Immortal Powers? How do you propose to prevent that clash?'

'Of course we are powerless. We will have to wait and see what happens when our first-generation hybrids set about reproducing the next generation. Will Sophia put angel souls into the new bodies or will *Geopa* — the Guardian of Earth's biosphere — insist that the souls of Earth's creatures are her responsibility.

'Of course all these beliefs about the Immortal Powers are simply that — *beliefs* — we have no means of knowing how things are organised in the Domain of Mind.'

'How will your hybrids set about reproducing themselves?' Balchin asked.

'It's a pertinent question: the answer is: *we simply don't know*.' Vyvyan raised her hands in a gesture of helplessness. 'We're not even sure how *hominids* reproduce. Studies of their behaviour have been carried out by angelis since angelas cannot fly to Earth. But angelis have no knowledge of *our* reproductive process; as a result, their accounts of hominid reproductive behaviour make very little sense.

'It's why I'm delighted to be part of this expedition; I and my fellow Mothers will be able to make our own studies of hominids and their reproductive habits. We'll then experiment with the first *humans* — as the hybrids will be called — to work out how best to ensure that the next generation breeds true.

'As you'll appreciate, this project draws us into the heart of Life's mystery. In tampering with the natural creative process, we're assuming to ourselves powers that rightly belong to the Immortals. Are we justified in doing so? We simply don't know. All we do know is that we were told to make the attempt. And that, Balchin my friend, is the essence of the Hybrid Project.'

Vyvyan concluded her comments with a flirtatious smile.

'May I add a few comments on the ethics of this strange scheme of ours?' Gylan began tentatively then continued with authority: 'If you are to be in charge of this expedition, Commander, you should be aware of certain issues.'

The professor paused before continuing.

'The essence of an angel is not his or her body but the soul — the spirit-light that has entered the body. During its life in this world, the soul acquires understanding of what it means to live as an angel. But how will the transplanted soul cope with living in the manner an Earth mammal is obliged to live? How will it cope with having to kill other living creatures to obtain nourishment? How will it feel when it finds itself hunted as food by some other creature?

'These are some of the ethical issues we have considered from an angel's point of view. But then, what of the creatures whose bodies we propose to purloin? Here, the questions are different. Are we justified in invading *Geopa's* biosphere? What we are planning to do will result in *Geopan* Evolution taking an entirely new direction; that is inevitable. What will be the consequences of that deviation from its previous trajectory?

'If our experiment succeeds, we will be introducing into *Geopa's* biosphere a way of living markedly different from the way her creatures have lived in the past. What effect will this have on the *Geopan* biosphere as a whole? We angels exploit the natural resources of our planet to a far greater extent than any other known species. What will happen if our new hybrids choose to exploit the resources of their adopted home?

'Perhaps the most important question is this: will our new hybrids take care not to harm or disadvantage *Geopa's* own flora and fauna through their sophisticated mode of living?'

Gylan paused before rounding off his comments.

'It is impossible to answer these questions but they certainly need to be asked because what we are proposing represents a radical deviation from the path that the biospheres of *Geopa* and *Sophia* have taken in the past. We need to think about these issues, Commander. That is all I wish to say on this matter.'

There was an awkward silence as the professor's words sank home. Finally the Duke asked Calthea to describe her project. She gave a brief account of the problems her assignment posed, both in codifying angel culture then in recording that culture in a format that would survive for extended periods of time. She mentioned her need for gemstones of unusual size and purity.

'Commander, I must thank you for allowing such gems to be brought to me.'

'Indeed, Seraphina? How is that so?' Balchin looked bemused.

Calthea still took delight in being addressed by her Oracle-granted title; even after three years she hadn't grown used to the respect that title evoked. She glanced now at the Duke to ensure that she wasn't speaking out of turn.

'I believe Lord Versain relieved you of certain gemstones

recently, did he not?'

Balchin looked even more bemused.

'Yes, he did, but I couldn't make much sense of his reason for doing so.'

'I couldn't explain at the time,' the Duke said, attempting to dispel his friend's confusion, 'because I hadn't yet told you about Paradisia. Calthea is right though: I did relieve you of the gems presented by the Empress because they weren't intended for you, they were intended for her.'

'I see.' Balchin's neutral tone belied his words, but he continued gallantly, 'I'm glad they are of use to you, Seraphina. For myself, I have no interest in fine gems; my preference is for fine books and there are plenty of those in Sriandra's libraries. Do you think your recordings will be available in time for our expedition's departure?'

'There's little likelihood of that I'm afraid, though one or two trial recordings might be ready by then.'

That completed the briefing. The Duke invited his guests to join him outside on the terrace for a couple of hous of conversation and some late afternoon sunlight. They left only when the sun began to sink towards the western horizon.

Chapter 11

Banderene

Banderene and Calthea left the cave together and flew down to Paradisia. Just before reaching the compound, Calthea swerved to her right, signing her companion to follow. She landed on the roof of the west wing.

'Arbrecht uses this roof as this office; he holds meetings here with his team so they can bask as they talk. I prefer to come in the evening as it's the ideal place to watch the sunset. Do you know the *Solema Mortissima*, Banderene?'

'I certainly do; we chant it every evening in Archeo-Angelya; the words have an intrinsic beauty in their original language.'

'Professor Bahle once chanted the morning *Obeisance* in Archeo-Angelya. It's true; I found it quite beautiful but I haven't heard the *Mortissima* in that form — will you chant it for me tonight?'

'Gladly, but it's still some twenty minutes to sunset.'

'Good. That gives me time to ask you something. The professor believes that the birth of a cherub is the creation of something entirely new, something that has never existed before. Doesn't that rather negate the notion of re-incarnation?'

'You believe in re-incarnation?'

'In a way I do, and I know the Duke does, because he believes many of us were sent here specially to deal with this problem of the meteor. He says he has flashes of a previous existence, of a time before he was born. That suggests there's some sort of continuity with an existence *before* we came to this world and surely it also implies some sort of continuity *after* we leave?'

'And you expect to resolve this issue before the sun sets?'

'Well, perhaps not *resolve*, but I'd like to hear what you think. You're from Sriandra so you're more likely to know about things like this than anyone else. After all, it's one of the most fascinating questions one can ask; don't you agree?'

'I do agree; but just because I live in Sriandra doesn't make me an expert in the field, nor does what I believe have any greater relevance or authority than what you believe.'

'But you Seraphim have access to wisdom that's far more profound than even Persinnia peddles to its students. I don't expect you to provide the answer but I feel sure you have a *view* on the topic.'

'And my view would influence you one way or the other?'

'Influence yes, but not *decide*. I know I must come to my own conclusions. But thinking needs a little nourishment; I'm not sure that what Gylan says is particularly nourishing. I'd so very much prefer to believe in re-incarnation than feel there's no continuity after this present life is over.'

'Why should that be the case?'

'Well, if we only come into existence at the instant we enter the amphora, then the implication is that we go *out* of existence when we leave the world.'

'I don't see the logic of that. Just because we *begin* when we take birth need not imply that we *end* when we enter the Caves. Birth could be the start of a process that persists after we die. Why not? Why not think of it as the beginning of a very long journey that might well take us to the Mentaillion when we leave the body at the end of our life here?'

'Are you teasing me or is this what you believe?'

'I don't *believe* in things like that; I think about them and wonder which opinion is the more *useful* for living my life in an authentic and ethical way.'

'That's what Chrissy used to say, but how can one opinion be more *useful* than another?'

'If I think this life is all there is or ever will be, I might not give much thought to the consequences of what I say or do. I mean, I wouldn't be constrained by quite the same moral imperative as if I believed my words, thoughts and actions carried consequences that would persist beyond my death.

'By adopting a philosophy that encourages me to treat this life as a preparation for something that comes afterwards, I'm encouraged to behave in ways that elevate rather than debase me. There's also the point that if I believe that this life is all there is — all there's going to be — that would make me fear the approach of death.'

'Yes, I can see that. But I still don't see how to resolve the issue of whether birth is an absolute beginning, as Gylan maintains, or whether we have had a previous existence, as Versain believes.'

'Does it matter? To my mind what comes *next* is rather more important than what came *before*. We can't remember anything before we entered the amphora, we don't even remember *that*; we only know about our birth because those who were present tell us what happened and we take their word for it. The crucial point for me is to identify this *I* we're talking about. Who is this *I* that began its existence in the amphora or that existed on some other plane before entering the amphora? That's the real issue as far as I'm concerned.'

'I suppose Gylan would say it's the self or the soul.'

'Both are mere words, someone else's view. Who do *you* think this *I* is, Cathea?'

'It's something to do with memory. If I don't *remember* something, that thing doesn't exist for me. If I don't remember being in some other place before I was born, then it isn't part of my current reality.'

'That's a valid point. You could say this *I* is something to do with remembering but I think it's rather more than that. The thing that really matters is *awareness*. It's awareness that powers memory just as it's awareness that initiates intentional action. Of course, I've only succeeded in pushing the question back because now we have to identify what we mean when we talk about *awareness*. But I think we'd better put that discussion on hold if we're going to honour this sunset, Calthea.'

They stood side by side as the sun sank towards the horizon; as soon as the rim touched the horizon, Banderene began chanting the ancient lament to the departing sun. The melody was redolent with sadness, with anguish at the coming absence of the source of all nourishment, all life.

They parted without speaking, each to seek their place of rest for the night.

Next morning, after her start-of-day rituals, Calthea went to her workroom and Banderene joined her there a few minutes later. Like many seraphs, he was naturally reserved but once he had opened his heart in friendship, he loved nothing better than the passionate debate of issues that interested him. Few seraphs were interested in culture; they loved philosophy, not the academic variety, but the natural philosophy of the profound thinker.

'Well Calthea, after what I hope was a good night's sleep, have you resolved your doubts about the journey of the soul before and after death?'

'Certainly not! The topic is going to provide me with plenty of food for thought for a long time. When are you planning to leave?'

'Balchin has some business with the Duke then he and I leave together at noon; I'd hoped to discuss something with Vyvyan but she's engaged. Is there anything we need to discuss — apart from the journey of the soul?'

'There is. Now that I've got the gemstones I need, I wonder if the Chief Seraph might agree to my making recordings of the contents of the Sriandra Library? It's a treasure house of wisdom, so surely one of the *gems* we ought to be preserving for posterity. Don't you agree?'

'It had been our intention to ask but we realise what a challenge you face in recording all the stuff the Maestro has been collating; we thought we'd better wait.'

'Actually, I have the time now. It's true, I could start on the stuff that's already been codified, but I'd rather wait till the entire corpus is available. I've been thinking about the structure I want to use in the recordings; that structure will only work if everything is ready. It would help if I could tackle a smaller project like the Sriandra Library; even then it's an extensive archive. It would help me to perfect the technique you and I began developing when I was in Sriandra.'

'How long would it take? What resources would you need from us?'

'Could you let me have two or three librarians to get the material for me, and to help me to understand difficult sections? I have a couple of flawless diamonds that should prove ideal for the job. As to how long it will take, I can't say with any certainty; my feeling is that three months ought to suffice.'

* * * * *

The recording project in Sriandra went well, in fact, much faster than Calthea's estimate; in just two months she had completed the entire project and was ready to return to Paradisia.

Banderene offered to accompany her as he had work to do there in preparation for the launch of the second spaceship, now only a few months away.

They set off early in the morning and broke their journey four hours later to bask. For a while they leant against a rock in silence. After a time, Banderene turned to Calthea and began to speak hesitantly.

'There's something I want to tell you about mind-transfer that I was reluctant to share before. I'm not authorised to tell you this but these are unusual times and I don't believe the old restrictions and conventions ought to apply in this case.'

'You sound very cagey. If you'd rather not tell me, I shan't hold it against you — how could I?' Calthea smiled.

'I *want* to tell you because, though the Chief Seraph may believe there are some secrets that shouldn't be divulged even in these extreme times, I believe he's wrong. If I don't tell you, it won't get into the archive because I don't know how to add anything myself.'

'So you want me to promise you I won't tell a living soul but that I will make sure your secret is saved for posterity in one of the diamond recorders?'

Banderene laughed. 'Yes, that's about it!' He paused for so long that Calthea wondered if he'd changed his mind, but eventually he continued, 'As I've told you, it is extremely rare for mind-transfer to be authorised; what I didn't say is that it's only ever been authorised in a single circumstance — to ensure the succession of Oracle.'

'I'm not sure I understand what you mean by that.'

'Then let me explain. We know that an Oracle can live for a very long time; it's generally thought that the Oracle who recently left us had lived for over a hundred years. At least, her body had; the soul that lived in that body was far, far older. We have secret archives — records not made available to you during your visit — that hint at the true origin of all modern-era Oracles.'

'You sound very mysterious, Banderene. What is it you are trying to tell me?'

'Magister's disciple, Seraph not only recorded the teachings of Coranda, he also recorded events after Magister and his disciples had settled in Sriandra. In fact, he continued to make recordings to the end of his life. After that, records are patchy; we get some items of information then a long gap. But during the lifetime of Seraph, we have daily accounts of what was going on, as well as what Magister was saying.

'We know, through these records, that one of the angelas who accompanied the leader to Sriandra was the Empress of the day. As in more recent times, the consort of that earlier tyrant didn't share his cruel ways; indeed she did all in her power to protect her people from the terrible things he was doing. Empress Girilayne was …'

'*Girilayne*?' Calthea exclaimed.

'Yes *Empress Girilayne*. I expect your esteemed tutor was named after her — she was a popular heroine in her day. This Empress had been attracted to Magister from very early on; she'd heard rumours of a stranger who was preaching sedition in the city square and sent one of her people to find out what was going on. What she heard pleased her and so on the fourth day she joined the crowd *incognito*.

'Seraph says it was the Empress who warned Magister of the plot to capture him. So it's not surprising she should be chosen as one of the angelas to accompany him when he left Sandolinia.

'Seraph records that both Girilayne and Magister were present at a ceremony to bring a cherub into the world. He doesn't say explicitly that they were the parents of the new arrival but the way the record is worded makes this a distinct possibility; the cherub was given the name *Oracle*. You'll probably guess where this is taking us.'

'Presumably it has something to do with mind-transfer and the succession of Oracle.'

'Indeed it does. Seraph notes the presence of Magister at the birth ceremony then adds the words: *and so our beloved departed*. It's the last reference in his records to Magister being in Sriandra. On the day after the departure, he notes: *we all went to the high caves to mourn the departed and to thank him for the great gift he has left us, a gift that will bring blessings to us and to future generations.*'

'I don't believe I'm reading too much into this report if I interpret the situation as follows: at the birth ceremony Coranda, with the Empress acting as his consort, arranges for a soul to enter the amphora. But it is *Magister's* soul that enters, not a new soul. If that is correct, then of course Coranda's body would die in the process. It would explain the form of words Seraph used: *and so our beloved departed*.

'I believe that the visit to the high caves was to place the sacred body of their leader in a Cave of Eternal Rest. There's a cave in the mountains not very far from Sriandra that's been a place of pilgrimage for a long time though the reason it is held sacred has long been forgotten.

'Did Magister really transfer his soul into the newly born cherub? If he did, *he* would be the origin of our knowledge of mind-transference. The secret records hint rather than tell us that whenever an Oracle has became physically ill or aged, the technique of mind-transfer has been used to transfer the soul living in the aging body into the body of a young seraphina who is happy to sacrifice her life for the purpose — to provide the soul of Oracle with a new lease of life in this world.'

'But Banderene, that's extraordinary! Do I understand you correctly? Are you saying that the being who recently lived in

Srivalian, the being we knew as Oracle, was none other than *Coranda Magister*. Is that really what you're saying?'

'It is. It's a secret very few even in Sriandra are allowed to know, but I think it's too important to die with our world. Surely this fact — if it is a fact — would explain the awesome powers of Oracle and the reason why she was held in such very high esteem, not only by those who met her but by anyone who knew of her existence.'

'If this is true, why did Magister decide to leave at this critical time after almost nineteen hundred years living in the world? I would have expected a being of that order to stay and guide us through the dreadful times ahead.'

'We know very little of the lives of the Great Ones, do we? We don't even know very much about our own lives. We try to guess why we are here, what we are meant to be doing with our lives, but in the end we're left in the dark and can only stumble about and do our best.

'At Sriandra, we've been incredibly fortunate; we've had Oracle to give us guidance on how best to live our lives and moral support to follow that guidance.'

'And you want me to add all this to one of the diamond recorders?'

'Yes. In fact I'd like you to record *all* Seraph's secret records, but only if you can hide this archive in a way that will allow access only to the most advanced thinkers. Cult leaders would dearly love to get their hands on information like this; they'd use it to bind people's minds and entrap their souls. This material must be well hidden from ignorant, ambitious or shallow minds. Can you do that?'

'Yes I can. In fact, it's not as difficult as you might think because of the way the recorders are structured. As a seraph, you use telepathy on a daily basis; most people believe it's nothing but moonshine. I did too until I began my studies with Professor Bahle. He showed me how my prize-winning recorders actually worked. You'd think that, as their inventor I'd know how they worked, but in fact I didn't. I had no idea I was using telepathy when recording and retrieving data. In fact, I strongly rejected such a suggestion from my tutor Girilayne. Now I know better.

'I use telepathy to layer information into the recorder; I *think* systematically through the information and it becomes fixed in the recorder. First I read; then, as I *think* what it means, it gets translated into Metalya — the language of meaning — and the meaning is then recorded. Does that make sense?'

'It's in line with the Theory of Language.'

'I put information into the crystal by telepathy; then it's accessed by telepathy.'

'I was meaning to ask how you extract information from the recorders.'

'The recorders are like libraries — repositories of information. To make use of the information you need to know how to access it; the easiest way is by using a specially programmed reader; I find emerald works best for that. When a recorder is paired with its own reader the user is guided to the information they're looking for; it's like having a librarian available who can locate what you're looking for.

'Even with both the recorder and its reader, you'll learn nothing unless you ask the right questions. In other words, you need to know something about what you're looking for before the reader will unlock the treasures in the archive. But as with any reputable library, there are in-built safeguards that will hide confidential or secret information from those not authorised to access it.'

'I like that — that you've used the model of a library.' Banderene commented.

'Yes; it's like a library with an expert librarian. The reader takes your question then leads you to the appropriate section of the archive. That structure lets me build in filters so that sensitive information can only be accessed by authorised enquirers.

'As far as your secret archive is concerned Banderene, I can store the data so that it will be accessible only to minds of the highest degree of understanding. I can arrange the material so that the enquirer must first demonstrate his or her right to gain access to that information; only then will the recorder unlock the data.'

'Could you explain *right to gain access*? It's rather a crucial issue in relation to what we're discussing.'

'I can program into the recorder and reader combination a set of rules that will determine the level of information an enquirer will be able to access. The reader could ask a question and the answer would determine the layer of the archive made available. For example, the question might be phrased in a way that would elicit a simple answer from a novice; they would be given access only to noviciate levels.

'A person who demonstrated more subtlety of understanding would be given access to deeper layers of the archive — even perhaps to the secret archive we have been discussing. You'll have to help me frame those questions so that the answers will identify those you are happy should have access to your secret archive. Would that work?'

With this satisfactory solution to the problem, they resumed their journey to Paradisia.

Chapter 12

FIRESTONE

It was New Year's Day, an official holiday both for the community and for the outer world. Calthea arrived early and was standing at the edge of the escarpment above the valley, looking down at the place that had become the main focus of her life. As she waited for her friend, she recalled all that had happened in the five years since she'd stood on this very spot with Girilayne and had caught her first glimpse of Paradisia.

She was finding it hard to identify with that person. At that time, she'd burned with resentment at being snatched from a thoroughly enjoyable life. *That* Calthea had thought her new life would be dull in comparison with the social whirl of the city that had caught her up in its vortex, filling every moment with some activity or other so that there'd never been a moment to sense the subtle inner worlds she'd carried around with her all her life. *That* Calthea had thought she'd pine for the excitements of the city. *That* Calthea had thought she'd miss her cherub unbearably.

But not for a moment did she regret the loss of that life; it was sad that she hadn't been around to see her delightful daughter grow and mature; but she knew it had been a price well worth paying for the riches heaped upon her since her arrival in the mountains.

She recalled the day the Duke had done just that — come

into her lab and piled fabulous gemstones on the bench where she was working. She'd been astonished at the perfection and size of those gems. Receiving them, she knew she could complete her assignment by the time the final expedition departed in two years' time.

She'd already completed two recordings of the Seraph Library in Sriandra — only one of which held Banderene's secret archive. Both would be sent with him in the second spaceship that was leaving the day after tomorrow. Her friend Chrysilla would be part of that expedition; they'd arranged to celebrate this New Year's Day together; it would be their last chance to spend time in each other's company.

Just then the figure of her friend rose from the valley.

'Chrissy,' Calthea called, 'I'm here. Come and admire the view.... This is where I had my first sight of Paradisia. I've been thinking about the day Girilayne brought me here. Do you realise, that was *five years* ago? Five years since I was spirited away to the mountains.'

'You sound as if you've still not forgiven the Duke.'

'Nonsense! I've been thinking how fortunate I was to be brought here. I know I made a great fuss at the time but I didn't understand then what this place was all about; now I do. In fact, I'm extremely happy here. What about you, Chrissy?'

'I wouldn't choose to be anywhere else, Cal. Even with this prophecy hanging over our heads there's nowhere I'd rather be and nothing I'd rather have been doing. What a fantastic boon it's been to have something worthwhile to occupy our minds instead of moping about feeling useless and sorry for ourselves, or else terrified out of our wits.'

'I'm going to miss you, Chrissy. I wish we'd spent more time together and now it's too late.'

'No it isn't.'

'What do you mean? In a couple of days you'll be flying off

to Phobos and after that, speeding even further away to Luna.'

'Not so! The prof has changed his mind; he's just asked me to withdraw from the Hybrid Project; he has an assignment for me; it's not actually a cancellation but a deferment of my departure. He says I can always join the project in a couple of years time when the third spaceship leaves — if I still want to. Perhaps we should get to work on the Duke to get him to agree to let you volunteer too.'

'I very much doubt we'd succeed; I asked him if I should volunteer and he said no. Phillestra will be on that spaceship and I don't think it's in his plans that I should spend the future with our cherub.'

'I'm sure his motives aren't that mean, Cal; he only wants to protect you from feeling you ought to volunteer.'

'You don't know my consort very well, Chrissy. People may think he protects those closest to him but the exact opposite is the case. He expects a great deal of himself and just as much of those who have the incredible good fortune to be *his people*; only it isn't always the good fortune people might think.'

'Wasn't it good fortune to be chosen as his consort?' Chrysilla retorted, 'He could have chosen anyone he wanted to be Mother of his cherub, but he chose you, a commoner. I would have thought that the epitome of good fortune.'

'Oh, I was always destined for that role — or so he says. But having been chosen hasn't conferred any great advantages, I do assure you; it's brought obligations, not benefits. My consort regards those close to him as extra limbs provided by a kindly Providence for him to use without the inconvenience of having to ask their consent.'

'Isn't that a little unfair, Cal? I mean, the Duke has put his life on the line more than once for the benefit of the world. He should have been Emperor, yet he's shown no resentment at being passed over by a prince who took no part in the Insurrection.'

'He never wanted to be Emperor. He told me it would have been impossible to set up the community, because he'd always have been in the public eye. Anyway, enough of my esteemed consort. Tell me, what's this assignment you're being given? Has Gylan told you yet?'

'Not yet, but he says it's both important and interesting. Not that that affected my decision; if the Prof asks me to do something, it's not a request, it's an obligation — at least, that's how I see it.'

'You're very fond of Professor Bahle aren't you?'

'I'm just as devoted to him as you were to Girilayne. He's been my mentor for a very long time, so it never crossed my mind not to cancel my plans to travel on the *Amphora of Civilisation*.'

'Is that what they're calling the second ship?'
'It is. In fact, the Empress is coming to name her and send the expedition on its way. I thought you'd be the first to know.'

'I know about the Empress coming. In fact, I shall be there myself — everyone will be there — Banderene has invited me as his special guest. But I didn't know about the ship's name. I like it, don't you? It says the spaceship is an amphora bringing a new civilisation to a new world. I wonder if this hybrid *human* species is going to survive. You'd have been one of the first to find out, Chrissy. Perhaps you still can if you volunteer for the third expedition.'

'Let's wait and see what happens, shall we?'

'OK.' For a moment the friends stood in silence then Calthea asked, 'How shall we spend the day?'

'There's a marvellous crystal chamber very near here that's known only to the dwarves; we're invited to see it. Chunka has got permission from his people to show us this cave. He knows you're an expert on crystals and thought you might like to see this wonder of the world before it gets blasted into tiny fragments.'

'What a great idea! Good old Chunka. I shan't forget the day of the great storm — it was just a couple of days after I'd arrived — after the first part had blown through, there was this cheerful sound of singing. Chunka and a band of dwarves had turned up to sweep the sand from Girilayne's cave. Versain was there as well; we were very amused when Chunka addressed Girilayne as *Highness*. She was tickled pink.'

'I'll bet she was…. We'd better get going, Cal. I'll lead the way.'

They flew eastwards along the valley, over the ceremonial arena where many members of the Paradisia community were celebrating New Year's Day. There were sporting competitions, a fair ground of sorts, bands of various descriptions but most people were hanging about in groups indulging in their favourite pastime — gossip. This was the last time the community would meet together; a great many would be leaving on the *Amphora of Civilisation* as volunteers for the Hybrid Project.

The friends flew towards a dark cave entrance a little way further down the valley. Chunka was waiting to greet them.

'Esteemed angelas,' he welcomed them with a deep bow, 'I am honoured that you have come to see our beautiful Cave of Marvels. It is very rare for my people to let strangers enter our sacred hall but you have been our friends for so long that we cannot think of you as strangers any longer. You are welcome. Please follow.'

The dwarf turned and plunged into the deep darkness of the cave; he stopped almost immediately and turned to ensure that his guests were following.

'It will take your eyes longer than mine to see in this darkness,' he said. 'Please place your right hand on the wall;

there is a groove cut into the rock, it will help you feel your way. When we come to crossings I will lead you to the correct path. The way is complicated but if we stay close you will not become lost.'

It was indeed a complicated route involving several forks and crossings but eventually they noticed a faint glow in the darkness ahead; as they pressed forward the light became stronger. At last the tunnel opened into a great hall that was bathed in sunlight. The Cave of Marvels was far larger than the Crystal Chamber and the light flooding in came through a domed roof formed of clear crystal.

After the darkness of the tunnels, Calthea's eyes were blinded by the brilliance; once her eyes had accommodated, she studied the amazing arena they'd entered. She was impressed not only by the beauty of the cavern but also by the velvet silence that enveloped them as they entered.

'I can see why you call this place the *Cave of Marvels*.' Chrysilla whispered, 'It is extraordinarily beautiful, Chunka. Your people must be very proud of this chamber.'

'We are indeed very proud of it, Angela Doctor. In this cave, our kings were crowned in ancient times.'

'*Kings*? I never knew there were dwarf kings. Why do you have no king now?'

'We have had no king for many thousands of years. In the Age of Giants, our kings were captured and killed and we resolved not to replace them for fear that any new king would also be killed. And so we have become a race governed by the will of the people in preference to being ruled by the will of an alien race.'

Calthea, who had been making a tour of the hall, rejoined her friend.

'You say you're not subject to the will of an alien race Chunka, but you're not really free are you? ' she pointed out,

'You're servants of the Angel Emperor.'

'That may be your understanding, Seraphina Lady, but we dwarves see things differently. We believe that if we willingly accept the work your people give us, then we are free people and not slaves. We love our work and are proud to do it well. In this way we live fulfilling lives.'

'That's a sound philosophy. Can you tell us what the hall is used for, Chunka?' Calthea pointed to the far end of the hall, 'I see some beautiful carvings and statues. Who made them?'

Chunka led his guests to the back wall; it had been deeply incised with strange glyphs into which were set a number of precious stones.

'We can no longer read the language of these inscriptions but our myths tell us stories that we believe are also told here in stone. We believe this panel tells of the destruction of life in the Great Upheaval and how our race came into the world soon afterwards. This next panel tells how dwarves flourished under our kings until the Giants came and tried to make us their slaves.

'This panel records our long association with the elfin people. When first we came across the elves, they lived in separate communities, some in the far South and some in the far North. They knew nothing of each other. We told them of their other cousins and arranged for them to meet in the middle-lands; after that they became a single community again. We are very good friends with the elves for they gave us comfort during the tyranny of the Giants and again in the tyranny of the last Angel Emperor.

'The other panels tell different stories; some may be the same as our spoken legends but we cannot be certain.'

In front of the wall stood a curving line of stone seats. Calthea noticed that they were hewn each from a different semi-precious stone; most were decorated with strange designs, again with precious stones inset. Chunka continued his explanation.

'Our elected dinkars sit on these seats when Dinkarspeak, our Council, holds its meetings. Each dinkar is elected by five hundred dwarves and is responsible for their work and their welfare. Not long ago, in the days of the tyrant Emperor, this hall became our refuge. We had to be careful not to let his agents know of it; that tyrant was very cruel to our people; he treated us with great malice.'

'I have heard Girilayne say as much, Chrysilla.' Calthea remarked to her friend then turned to their host. 'Your people are great experts at rock-cutting, Chunka, and you also know a great deal about stone; what are the names of the stones used for these seats? Some I recognise but some are new to me.'

As the conversation was threatening to turn technical, Chrysilla left them to make her own exploration of the chamber. Calthea pointed to the central seat, which was the largest and most elaborate. It was made of a smooth, amber-coloured stone.

'I haven't met this type of rock before, Chunka. What do you call it?'

'We call it *firestone* because it reminds us of the fire that lives in the heart of a volcano. It is very rare; only our most trusted miners know where it is to be found; only they are authorised to mine it.'

'It's beautiful,' Calthea murmured, drawing her hand over the smooth surface. She jumped back exclaiming, 'But it's *alive*!'

'Yes, it is a magical stone, Seraphina Lady.'

'It has the most extraordinary effect when you touch it Chunka, truly amazing. Might I have a sample to study? I feel sure firestone has some very unusual qualities, which could prove useful in my work.'

'Only Dinkarspeak may approve that request; this stone

is used for the thrones of our kings. Even now, only the Chief Dinkar may sit on that throne. Dinkarspeak will meet in three days, and I will ask then. Will such a delay bring problems, Lady?'

'No it won't. I'll be more than grateful if they agree. I have the strangest feeling when I touch this stone. It's almost as if it wants to say things to me.'

To Calthea's surprise, Chunka came over and placed his hand over the hand she had replaced on the magical stone. It was a serious breach of protocol; dwarves and elves were forbidden to touch any angel unless specifically requested to do so. Chrysilla was also alarmed by their host's shocking action and hurried to her friend's side, but Calthea signalled to her that all was fine.

The dwarf spoke with the deepest respect.

'You have a rare gift, Seraphina. We too know stones by their touch; we know their qualities; their purposes are revealed to us through touch. This stone is reserved for those in high office so it is always given a place of honour. If some is given to you Lady, you will have to promise Dinkarspeak you will treat it with due respect.'

'I will be happy to give that assurance, Chunka. You may tell your Council that I would consider it a very great honour if they would let me study this stone.'

Chunka removed his hand and again bowed deeply.

'Honoured Seraphina, you are the consort of the Great Lord; all dwarves have sworn an oath of loyalty to the Great Lord. He does not know this, but when he rid the world of that cruel tyrant, Dinkarspeak voted him the title, *Honorary King of the Dwarves*. We are sworn to treat any request from the Great Lord as our sacred duty. As his consort, you are also dear to our hearts. I think you need not fear that your request will be refused.'

Chrysilla was standing close by and was deeply moved both by what Chunka had said and by his deferential and affectionate attitude towards Calthea.

'Chunka, are you a dinkar?' she asked.

'I have that honour, Angela Doctor. I was elected more than ten years ago. The Great Lord asked me if we would help him in his secret work, mining for metals in these mountains then helping his people build machines from the metal. Later, when we had built three small machines, he took many of our people in them to build the big machines on the Pink Moon.'

'Do all the dwarves working here and on the Verastra construction site come under you, Chunka?'

'Yes Angela Doctor, they are in my care. Sometimes I am taken to the Moon to see their work and make sure they are well treated but I never need to worry on their account. The Master is strict, but fair to all his staff, angels and dwarves alike.'

'Is Dorka a dinkar too?' Calthea asked, recalling the day she was held hostage by that particular dwarf.

'He is, Lady; Dorka cares for the dwarves working in the university, the city and the Palace. He is one of our most senior Dinkars and held in the highest esteem.'

'And I suppose he is also under an obligation to obey any and every request of the Royal Duke,' Calthea muttered under her breath but was overheard.

'It is no obligation because of our oath, Seraphina Lady; it is something we do joyfully and out of respect for the Great Lord. He is our honorary King.'

After an awkward pause Chrysilla changed the subject.

'Are your people aware of the real purpose of the community, Chunka? Do you know why the Duke has set up Paradisia in such secrecy?'

'We have always known, Angela Doctor. When the Great

Lord first asked for our help, he told me of the ancient prophecy. He also invited Dinkarspeak to choose fifty of our community to send on the first ship to save our race from destruction.'

'But you didn't send them! Did the Duke change his mind?'

'The Great Lord would never go back on his word, Seraphina. No, it was our decision to refuse his invitation. We love our world; we love the mountains and the sand dunes, we love the sun and the wind, above all we love the rocks and the caves of our home. We could never live on any other world and would only take up places that angels could use, so we declined the Great Lord's offer.

'When destruction comes, our people will gather here in this cave system to share the fate of our Mother. We shall end our days in the caves we were born in.'

After a few moments of silence as each thought of the terrible fate in store for their world, Chunka led his guests silently out of the hall, through the same maze of tunnels and out into the bright noonday sunshine.

With profuse thanks for the great honour that had been granted them, Calthea and Chrysilla flew back to Paradisia and then up to the escarpment where they'd met a couple of hours before; they spent the next hour basking in silence.

'Would you like to spend the night in Girilayne's cave, Chrissy? There's a west-facing plateau nearby from which we can watch the sunset and I know of no better place than Girilayne's terrace to perform the *Obeisance*.'

'Will we be back in time for the morning briefing?'

'Easily. It takes only an hour and the briefing isn't scheduled till mid-morning. You always said you wanted to visit Girilayne's cave and I doubt there'll be a better chance than today.'

This agreed, the friends set off towards the south.

* * * * *

Two days later they were together again, this time as passengers in the shuttle taking them up to Verastra for the launch of the second spacecraft. Also on board were some members of the Paradisia Choir.

'Are you relieved you're not actually leaving today, Chrissy?'

'I admit I'm pleased to have another couple of years working in the community but I haven't changed my mind; I'll volunteer next time round. I hope by then the first contingent will have smoothed out any teething problems.... What's in the box?'

'It's the Sriandra Archives; they're for Banderene. He'll act as Guardian in his lifetime then appoint a successor to take over before he departs. He'll be the first in a long line of Guardians — at least, I hope it'll be a long line.'

'But the archives are intended to be used, aren't they?'

'Yes of course, but the seraphs travelling today will have their work cut out in establishing the Hybrid Project; only when the new species is fully functional and no longer in need of their constant attention will the seraphs be able to establish their own community; then my recorders will come into their own; they'll be a resource for teachers as they seek to re-establish the traditional Seraphim way of life.'

'I see. And who carries the recorders for the Hybrid Project?'

'They aren't ready yet. That's a much more complex undertaking; I've not even begun recording yet. But they'll be ready, never fear; they'll have to be ready by the time you set off in a couple of years, won't they?'

'About that red stone you were discussing with Chunka, did they let you have any, Cal?'

'I should hear tomorrow; if they agree, I'll receive some in a week or two. Authorised miners have to be sent to a secret location to collect samples as they don't keep any in store.'

Calthea moved closer and whispered.

'Have you been given your new assignment yet, Chrissy?'

'Yes, but this isn't the place to discuss it.' she replied softly, 'We'll talk later.'

They turned to watch the world rapidly disappearing below them then stood for a long time in silence.

'This is the first time I've been in Space, Cal — the first time I've seen our planet from this perspective. It's a stunning sight but also rather unsettling.'

'Why unsettling?'

'I mean, to see the world we take for granted as a mere object in the sky. It's beautiful but somehow also rather vulnerable. It's not easy to explain: it seems quite likely that a rogue meteor could come and blast that golden ball down there into a myriad fragments. But when I'm standing on the ground with the horizon a great distance away in every direction, it seems quite impossible that a single object could do anything more than make a big dent in the ground.'

'I know what you mean. But it's a stunning sight, don't you agree? As Stellaster turns we'll see the Vale of Cander coming into view and our mountains disappearing beneath the rim. Then, when she has turned full circle, we'll see Paradisia come back into view; from that distance, the mountains will look like a deep gash stretching from pole to pole; then it will look as if the globe could easily break into two — even without this prophesied meteor.

'The Duke brought me to Verastra soon after I returned from Sriandra and I saw it then, saw how fragile our world really is. He brought me to see the spacecraft under construction; there were three then but after today, there'll be only one left, the one that'll take you and Phillestra to a new life and I shan't see either of you again.'

The journey was uneventful; in due course they disembarked. In the course of the next few hours, other shuttles brought members of the community who would be travelling on the spaceship, plus colleagues come to bid the travellers *farewell*. The royal twins arrived from the Imperial Palace on the final shuttle.

This was a very different scene from the Jubilee launch: the grandstand and ceremonial flags were gone, trumpet voluntaries and formal speeches forgotten. The only people here who'd been present at the first launch were Master Chorton-Tang, the Empress and the Duke. No community members or dwarves had attended that jubilant Finale, for it had been essential to keep Paradisia a secret.

The atmosphere now was both less formal and more emotional. Those present knew full well that these partings would be final. The community was being torn in two, one half facing a future of total uncertainty, the other a future of total certainty — the coming annihilation of their world. It was difficult to tell who was comforting whom as colleagues and friends embraced each other for the last time.

Also present were a few seraphs — the psychotherapists and mind-surgeons who would carry out the mind-transfer procedure — and their friends from Sriandra who had come to see them off. In all, there must have been two hundred people milling around beside the vast spaceship.

At the centre of the throng, the Empress, the Royal Duke, the Chief Seraph, Commander Balchin, and Marima Varenne formed the focus. Master Tang and his assistants were still on board making their final checks. Seraph Banderene stood to one side talking to a small group of friends. From his stance, no one would guess that he was the real leader of the Hybrid Project for he preferred to avoid the limelight; he was happy for others with less important roles to be presented to the Empress and to receive her formal blessings for their mission.

Calthea walked over to Banderene and handed him the recorders he'd helped her to make. It was the last time she'd see the quiet, impressive mind-surgeon who'd become such a close and valued friend.

But there was no time to express her sorrow at this parting for at that moment Maestro Arbrecht struck a bronze gong: it was time for the formal ceremony to begin. He collected the choir and they sang the opening anthem. An hour-long programme included many of the community's favourite songs and everyone was invited to sing along. The nostalgic mood was rapidly replaced by one of joyful celebration.

Finally the Empress stepped forward to name the second spaceship *Amphora of Civilisation*. Then it was time for those who were leaving to embark; last minute hugs were reluctantly released and those travelling bowed to the Empress before flying up to the open panel; many did not actually board but would fly alongside until the ship was well clear of the ground. Four shuttles were accompanying the spaceship to act as ferries between Luna and the surface of Earth when the Hybrid Project team was ready to start work.

As Vyvyan embraced the Empress, her long-time friend, she whispered; 'At least I've been able to say a proper *goodbye* this time, Silla. Versain has promised to keep me informed of how things are going here — until it's no longer possible for him to do so. He will visit Phobos before we leave for Luna; send me a message with him if you can.'

Once the spaceship had cleared the ground, the Maestro collected the remnants of his choir to close the programme. They chanted a beautiful hymn often performed at Farewell Ceremonies; this again invoked a mood of sadness and separation that perfectly expressed the heart-break of those who remained behind.

Finally, the Maestro took up his lute and played the haunting melody that had come to be known as *Girilayne's Farewell*. Even when the last notes faded into silence no one stirred; no one wanted to break the fragile bubble of bittersweet nostalgia.

Chapter 13

DEVASTATION

For a long time, those who'd come to watch the launching of the *Amphora of Civilisation* stood in silence, rooted to the spot; eventually a communal sigh broke the silence and people drifted towards the shuttles waiting to take them to Paradisia.

Chrysilla took Calthea's arm and began walking away from the crowd, hoping for a private talk, but Professor Bahle came hurrying after them.

'My dear angelas, please don't rush away. I need a word, Chrysilla. Do forgive me for interrupting your conversation.'

Chrysilla turned to Calthea.

'Shall we meet when I'm free?' then she asked the professor: 'Do you think I will be able to travel home with the Seraphina, Professor?'

'Certainly, certainly. I shall not detain you for more than a few minutes.'

But Calthea was not to be allowed any solitude either; the Duke was making his way through the crowds towards her.

'Ah, Calthea, will you walk with me? There's something I want to ask you.'

They walked in silence for a while; finally the Duke asked:

'Have you seen Kinver's new observatory?'

'No, I haven't; I thought it was being built in the southern mountains.'

'Not so, it's here; it's that structure over there. The telescope's lenses are ready at last so our dwarves are putting all their energies into completing the observatory that will house them. Kinver will soon have the most powerful telescope ever built, in the best equipped observatory in the world, then he can start scanning the skies for our rogue meteor.'

'And that's what you wanted to ask me, Versain?' Calthea asked laughing.

'No, but I thought we'd walk in that direction as we talk; I'll show you the observatory before we return home.'

They fell into step. Calthea recalled the many times they'd walked like this in the Palace gardens but she didn't share her musings with her companion; he didn't like it when she harked back to the old days. Nevertheless, she was happy to be with her consort now — to be in his company and to relish her old memories.

They walked without speaking for a while; Calthea was reluctant to break the silence knowing the Duke had something to say. But why was it taking him so long to say it? At last he began in an uncharacteristically hesitant tone.

'You asked if you should volunteer for the Hybrid Project but I refused chiefly because your assignment isn't complete, but also because I don't believe you really wanted to go — you asked because you thought it was expected of you.'

Calthea was puzzled: *Where is this taking us*? Aloud she said: 'Are you saying I *should* volunteer for the next spaceship, Versain?'

'No, not at all. What I'm asking is: what would you *like* to do when the time comes? To my mind there are several options; I want you to think about them and let me know if one appeals to you, or if you have some other notion of what you'd like to do before the meteor finally makes its appearance.'

Calthea was astonished. Could it be that what she'd told

Chrysilla was wrong and that the Duke really *was* concerned about her future; could it be that he actually *wanted* to know her views before he told her what she was going to do?

'What options have you in mind?' she asked cautiously.

'Well, once the third expedition leaves, your project will be over but there'll still be a few years before the meteor arrives — we hope — and during that time we'll have to tell the authorities about the prophecy. My sister has agreed to organise that stage of our mission; you might like to offer her your help; I'm sure she'd welcome it.

'On the other hand, you might wish to spend those years at Sriandra. Oracle arranged for you to study with the Seraphim and I'm sure there's still a lot you could learn once you're released from your commitments in Paradisia. You could volunteer for the Hybrid Project, though I don't think that really appeals to you.

'If you would like to go to Luna without being part of the Hybrid Project, I could arrange for you to join the seraph community there; you could become their Custodian of Archives. There's a good case for that, if it would appeal to you. Or you could opt for early retirement to the Caves. I think that will be the choice of many when their work in Paradisia is complete, especially those of advancing years.'

'I'm not sure that going to Luna without taking part in the Hybrid Project is an entirely honourable option, Versain. Like everyone else — including you — I've vowed not to benefit from what the community has been doing. I agree that waiving that vow was the only practical way of getting subjects for the Hybrid Project, but I don't think waiving my vow to join the seraph settlement has quite the same justification.'

'I rather thought you'd say that, Calthea; it's what I'd have felt in your place. Anyway, you don't need to decide now; let's hope there's still plenty of time.'

The Duke stopped, placing his hand over his ruby responder.

'It's an urgent message from Devallian. Will you forgive me if I take this, Calthea?'

He listened for a while then slipped the pendant back under his sash.

'I'm afraid our tour of the observatory will have to wait. I must return to Paradisia immediately, and so must you. I'm afraid it's bad news, bad news that affects your work.'

The Duke said no more but took to the air, making straight for the shuttle pad, signalling Calthea to follow as quickly as she could. On arrival he dispatched a dwarf to find Chunka, who had attended the launch; he drew the dwarf to one side to brief him. Calthea wondered what could have happened to cause the Duke such obvious anxiety; she'd find out when he was ready and not a moment sooner.

As the shuttle was approaching Paradisia, the Duke made an announcement.

'I'm sorry to report that while we've been away, a miscreant has broken into our buildings and caused a great deal of damage. Fortunately, a member of my staff was on hand and has told me of it. Please remain outside the buildings until I've had a chance to assess the situation; I need to find out what I can about the intruder and his motives. Chunka will accompany me, as will the Seraphina.'

As the shuttle landed, Devallian was there waiting. Calthea thought of all her precious gems; she hoped the thief hadn't discovered the boxes but her hopes were dashed when she, the Duke, Devallian and Chunka entered her workroom and she saw the devastation. The intruder had opened every box and attacked the contents with considerable force, smashing every gemstone into tiny fragments.

She was appalled at the ferocity evident in this act of wanton destruction. The Duke's face was set in a rigid mask and she suspected he was also struggling to contain his anger.

'Did you catch the intruder, Captain?' he snapped 'Did you see who did this?'

'I saw him, my Lord but couldn't identify him. I was on the terrace of your cave and had a good view of the valley, but he was too far away to identify; I only saw him as he entered the sunlit courtyard. He came from an easterly direction, keeping to the shadows of the southern cliffs. He must have worn a dark cloak as it was only when he crossed the courtyard that I spotted him.

'I flew down immediately to get assistance from the guards; they weren't in the guard house, so I came straight to the courtyard. I heard smashing glass and came in here to find this mess. He must have heard me coming because I saw a dark shadow streaking away from the eastern side of the building. I gave chase. He flew east, down the valley and I followed.

'He made for the deep shadow of the southern cliffs and must have entered a cave; I couldn't tell which as there are many caves in the area. I remained outside and contacted you from there; when I saw the shuttle arriving I came to meet you. The thief hadn't emerged before I left, so he must be hiding there still.'

'Unless he escaped after you left.'

'He couldn't; I got a couple of guards to keep watch before I left; they'll let me know if he tries to escape. They've promised to keep watch through the night so he'll have to stay put or be caught. Dwarves have far better night vision than angels so he's effectively trapped.'

'Good; but dwarves won't be able to keep up with him if he does try to escape. You'd better send some angelis to supplement your dwarves; all the shuttles should have returned by now. Set up a rota of two good fliers plus a messenger who can bring us news. Chunka, can you get your people to search the caves in the area the captain has indicated? I want this fellow found and I want him in a fit state to be questioned.'

Chunka bowed low to the Duke then stopped in front of Calthea and made a further deep bow.

'Seraphina Lady, please do not worry about these gemstones. Dinkarspeak will vote you all the firestone you need for your work; I give you my word on this.'

He reached for her hand and the Duke and Devallian gasped; they were about to lunge forward to stop the dwarf from touching Calthea, but she countered their intention by deliberately stepping towards Chunka and holding out both her hands. He bowed low over them with deep reverence and left.

'My Lord, you need not fear for my honour with Chunka, or indeed with any dwarf. Dwarves are as devoted to me as they are to you — well, almost as devoted.'

'And how do you know that? You seem on very intimate terms with Chunka all of a sudden.'

Calthea was amused at the Duke's tone. Did it hold a touch of jealousy?

'Yes, I've come to know and trust Chunka. He's arranging to send me samples of a rare gemstone for my recordings. It may serve my purpose very well, perhaps even better than these poor destroyed gemstones.' She gently touched the shards.

'How did you come to know of this new stone; what is it?'

'The dwarves call it *firestone*; they've promised to let me have a sample. Now that all my other gems have been destroyed, this will be my last hope. Chunka has just assured me that his Council will vote me all the firestone I need if it turns out to be suitable.'

'What is this firestone? Have you seen it?'

'I have, but I'd rather not say where — that is Chunka's secret, not mine. It looks like molten red glass but it's nothing like any glass I've encountered before. It has a strange feel, quite unlike normal glass. I won't know its chemical structure until I've had a chance to study a sample but I feel that it's going to be very special indeed.'

'I see. Well, Calthea, there are clearly mysteries involved but this isn't the time to go into them. Captain, you'd better leave to organise your surveillance team. I want this fellow alive; he has a lot of explaining to do. I want to make sure he's a lone agent, not part of some gang or expeditionary force.'

'My Lord, I didn't want to say so in front of Chunka but I have a shrewd idea who the intruder might be.'

'*Who?*' Calthea and Lord Versain burst out together.

'There was something in the way he moved that reminded me of the missing engineer, Davrinka-Danyetta.'

'So you were right! You never accepted that he'd died. Well done, Devallian.'

'I'm not saying it is Danyetta, my Lord, but there's a strong possibility. We'll only find out if and when we can catch the fellow.'

Devallian left to carry out his orders.

'Why was Devallian here, Versain? Did you suspect that something like this was going to happen?'

'Actually it was Devallian's idea. He offered to come and supervise the guards so that everyone could attend the launch. I don't think he was consciously expecting trouble but he has good instincts in such matters; I've grown to trust his judgement. On this occasion his instincts seem to have been only too reliable.'

'I seem to remember you told Girilayne that he was the most *intuitive* person you knew; was it instinct or intuition that roused his suspicions, do you suppose?'

'I'm not sure I understand the fine distinction.'

'Gylan calls instinct *intelligence of the body*, cognition *intelligence of the mind* and intuition *intelligence of the soul.*'

'You've become quite a philosopher since coming here, Calthea.'

'Well that's your fault!' Calthea laughed, taking delight in teasing her consort, 'You told me I should listen to Gylan so I took your advice seriously.'

The Duke was pacing round the room, inspecting the damage. He stopped and swept the shattered remnants of a large diamond together with his hands.

'Some of these gems have been in the Royal Treasury for hundreds of years.' he mused, as much to himself as to Calthea, 'They're irreplaceable. Versilla took a great deal of trouble to get them to me and now they're destroyed. How can I tell Council what has become of our royal treasures? They trusted me to keep these gems safe, and now they're just a pile of dust.'

'You aren't responsible for this devastation, Versain. In any case, the gems weren't ever going to return to the Royal Treasury, were they? They were going to travel to worlds a very long way from the Palace; indeed, four are already speeding on their way to Phobos in the care of Banderene.'

'Did you use the largest of the diamonds, Calthea?'

'No, I think that's the one you've swept up; I recognise the box. It was the finest diamond I've ever seen, incredibly large and completely flawless.'

'It is — or rather *was* — the second largest ever mined; fortunately, the largest still lies safe in the Treasury vaults; even Versilla couldn't liberate that treasure — it's used in the coronation of emperors and empresses. This one, this pile of shards, was called *Amphithon*. Didn't you recognise it? It was often used as a focusing lens for royal births; in fact, it was this diamond that drew the spirit of Phillestra into her amphora.

'We must preserve these precious fragments, Calthea; Godwinian will know what should be done with them.'

'I don't remember any diamond being used during our marriage ceremony.'

'Don't you? When first we held hands, don't you remember a seraph holding a diamond — this diamond — above our hands?'

'All I remember is that I almost fainted; it was only because you tightened your grip on my hands that I didn't fall to the ground.'

'Yes, I remember thinking that Versilla couldn't have warned you of the power of these focusing lenses. You almost lost consciousness, so it isn't surprising perhaps that you don't remember every detail of that evening — but I do.'

'I remember a lot of the ceremony but obviously not everything. I often relive my memories of that extraordinary evening. Only my audience with Oracle is more deeply etched on my soul.'

'Yes, powerful emotions do leave their mark on the soul; some record times of intense pleasure, but many are scars left by overwhelming fear — or final separation.'

The Duke was suddenly in the grip of some strong emotion, as on the day after Girilayne's departure. Calthea looked at him in surprise; he was usually so reserved, so self-contained. Then she remembered and felt again a surge of empathy — only a few hours earlier one of his oldest and closest friends, Vyvyan-Varenne had left the world for good. He must know he'd never see her again and this wretched intruder had chosen this time of personal sadness to attack the Duke's beloved community.

To lighten his mood she steered the conversation to a less personal topic.

'I didn't use *Amphithon* for the Sriandra Archives; I didn't need its full capacity. I was reserving it for the Musical Archives; they demand a flawless gem with a large recording capacity. Now I'll have to trust to firestone to do the job instead.'

'How many gems did you send with the expedition, did you say?'

'Two large diamonds and two cabochon emeralds, the latter as readers. So not all the Empress's efforts have gone to waste.'

'Why did you send separate readers? Quartz crystals serve as both recorders and readers.'

'Quartz recorders hold only a fragment of information. Recordings of an entire culture require the layering of information. Each diamond recorder I made holds the entire Sriandra archive; it's organised like a library with information stored by topic and by level of sophistication.'

'And what does that mean?'

'It means that students begin with basic texts; then, as they become more knowledgeable, they're given access to more advanced material. The emerald readers serve as librarians; they guide students to the information appropriate to their level of understanding. In the case of the Seraphim Archives, seekers will be given access to the teachings and practices prescribed by the sages that are appropriate to their stage of progress along the spiritual path.'

'Ah, so the recorders won't be sufficient on their own; practice is also necessary if the wisdom of the Seraphim is to be preserved?'

'*Precisely so*, as Professor Bahle would say. The new cosmology would never have made sense to me if I'd simply read it. I could only understand what Chrysilla was describing because the professor showed me how to test what she said through meditation and contemplation.'

'I'm told you've become good friends with Doctor Flaine.'

'I have; it's revealed a whole new world. I've always wanted a friend to whom I could open my soul as an equal — someone who'd also open their soul to me. I'm so glad Chrysilla didn't have to leave today.' then she added tentatively, 'So many of our friends have left, Paradisia is going to feel very empty.'

'Yes, we're going to miss our friends a great deal.'

Calthea, still feeling her way carefully, said diffidently:

'Why did Vyvyan have to leave, Versain? Surely someone else could have been found to supervise the breeding programme of these hybrids.'

'Vyvyan is by far the best qualified Mother for the task. She won't have to swap her beautiful form for an ugly hominid body; she's going because she's the person most likely to find a way of getting the hybrids to breed, because unless they breed successfully the whole project will be a failure.'

'Yes, I see that. I wonder what it's going to be like here without all our friends. Still, there's plenty left for me to do.'

'You feel you'll still be able to complete your assignment without these gems?'

'I'd like to see what firestone is like before I answer that question.'

'You were very mysterious about that. Where did you see it?'

'I suggest you ask Chunka, my Lord. It's not my secret; as I told you, it's his.'

'Yes, I'll do that.'

The Duke seemed reluctant to leave the scene of the crime and Calthea was only too happy to prolong their conversation.

'Coming back to Devallian's suspicions Versain, do you think he might have suspected that Danyetta would try to cause mischief at a time when Paradisia was virtually deserted? He must have been spying on us all these years waiting for his opportunity.'

'Devallian never really accepted that the fellow had died; he was always on the look-out for any sign that Danyetta was still around. I believe our young friend is unusual in having more than the average of all three of your categories; he's intelligent, intuitive and today he's shown his instincts are also reliable; which all augers well for the future.

'Now that all three expeditions will be heading for Luna, Altrix and Balchin will govern the settlements initially. They'll work together to perfection; they've been friends for a long time and have complementary personalities. Altrix is very much an action angel, Balchin a thinker. It will seem as if Altrix is in command, but he will invariably act on Balchin's advice.

'In those early years, Devallian will be their junior but I expect they'll give him a great deal of responsibility to prepare him for taking over in due course; then he'll govern in his own right. When that time comes, our friend will need all three of your categories of intelligence.

'Now, we must get some rest, Calthea. Devallian can deal with catching this intruder. Please let me know if this firestone proves useful. If not, we'll have to find a way to liberate a few more of our national treasures.'

The Duke might think he was competent to decide the future of his aide; but Devallian's future lay not in his hands but in the hands of the Immortal Powers; only time would tell whether Lord Versain's plans for his protégé would come to fruition.

Chapter 14

Retribution

Paradisia seemed deserted on the morning following the launch; the east wing was empty; the Mothers and geneticists, who'd been based there, were on their way to prepare for the implementation of the Hybrid Project. The only people in the west wing were older members of Arbrecht's *culture coding commune*; the remainder were on board the *Amphora of Civilisation* as volunteers, as were the younger engineers and scientists of the Spaceship Design Team, who'd been based in the north wing.

Of its previous complement of a hundred, only thirty Paradisia staff remained; the rest had embarked the previous day to join ten seraphs and twenty construction workers, ten of whom would serve as crew members during their journey to Luna. Even Chrysilla had vanished, no doubt despatched by Professor Bahle on her secret mission; they'd had no chance to talk because she'd gone before Calthea returned to Paradisia with the Duke.

Only Calthea, it seemed, had work to take her mind off the emptiness of her surroundings; Chunka had brought her samples of *firestone* to analyse and test. He promised to bring just as much as she thought she would need to complete her assignment — always supposing that this magical substance proved suitable.

With her attention fully focused on this fascinating task, Calthea had little time to follow the unfolding drama of Danyetta's arrest and interrogation.

His trial would prove a deeply traumatic experience for all those remaining in the community. The Duke asked Professor Bahle to organise the trial and appointed him as judge. The trial itself took place in the Crystal Chamber barely two weeks after the capture of the dissident engineer.

* * * * *

Judge Bahle stood at the central pillar, Devallian to his right and Master Tang to his left. An additional pillar had been set up in the centre of the fixed circle and Davrinka-Danyetta stood hunched over it, head bowed, resting forward on his arms. Although the manacles had been removed from his wrists, a heavy iron chain still constrained his feet and the tether remained around his wings.

In the crowded gallery, the Duke was a passive and inscrutable observer. Once silence had descended Judge Bahle opened the trial.

'This court is convened under the Paradisia Constitution;' he began, 'it will follow the procedures for investigating serious breaches of community regulations. We are here today to consider evidence that Engineer Davrinka-Danyetta acted in breach of the oath he took on joining the community; it is also alleged that by his actions he has put the community and its vital work at risk. He is further accused of causing wilful damage to priceless community property.

'I have asked Captain Devallian to act as Prosecutor and Master Tang to serve as Defence Council for the accused.'

The Judge paused before addressing the prisoner.

'Engineer Danyetta, do you agree to Master Tang speaking

on your behalf?'

There was a mumble from the accused but no actual words could be discerned.

'Stand up straight and speak clearly,' thundered the judge. 'This is a Court of Law. You will conduct yourself with due respect for the Court.'

In common with everyone else, Calthea was astonished; she'd never heard the professor speak in such tones. Then she recalled how, on the evening of her arrival in Paradisia, the professor had morphed from friendly mentor to stern disciplinarian in the space of a few sentences. Gylan-Bahle was obviously a chameleon with hidden talents; he would have made a fine actor, she thought.

At his pillar, Danyetta made an effort to straighten up. As he did so, what had appeared as a gesture of defiance was seen for what it was — extreme exhaustion of spirit. The pathetic figure, with plumage unkempt, face gaunt and eyes haunted, had clearly been living in hell. When he spoke, his words were weak but much clearer.

'I don't mind if the Master speaks for me; *I* have nothing to say.'

Captain Devallian was invited to present his case and did so succinctly, setting out the facts of the matter in the manner of an officer reporting to his commander. He called a number of witnesses, including Calthea, to support his case. After giving her testimony, Calthea joined the spectators in the gallery to watch the drama unfold; and drama it certainly turned out to be.

Master Tang then spoke; he reminded the court of the valuable ideas Danyetta had contributed to the design of the spaceships; he asked the Court's permission to question his client in court as he'd been unable to get any response from him during several private interviews.

'Davrinka, can you not explain to the Court why you left Verastra so suddenly? Did I not treat you well when you were working with me on the construction site? I believe I'm a fair employer and I thought we enjoyed a good, trusting relationship, yet you never contacted me to explain what had gone wrong. I'd have helped in any way I could; I'll do what I can now but you have to help me; you must tell us why you felt unhappy, why you chose to leave your post in the way you did.'

There was a long silence then Danyetta took a deep breath and launched into a tirade that rocked everyone back on their heels.

'Yes, *you're* fair, but not everyone here is.'

He turned, scanning the empty pillars behind him, then raised his eyes to the gallery; seeing the Duke, he swung round and pointed a finger up at him.

'Look at him! He thinks himself so high and mighty; he's far too arrogant to speak to an insignificant commoner like me. He's happy enough, pressing people to join his projects but try to talk to him and either he sends his sidekick to do his work, or he cuts you down with his sharp sarcastic tongue.

'He gets us to swear we won't leave on the spaceships he makes us build, but then sends his paramour to safety on one of them.' This deliberately cruel reference to the Duke's close friend, Vyvyan-Varenne, drew an angry hiss from the gallery. 'He's a hypocrite and a liar and I can't see why everyone bows and scrapes to him. You're nothing but a bunch of timid time-serving *elves*.'

'Stop this immediately!' the judge exploded, 'If you cannot speak with respect to the Duke at least show respect to this Court. We're trying to be fair to you, though the case made against you is very strong. If you wish to present any objections to the *facts* as presented by Captain Devallian, then do so; but do not abuse the privilege given you of addressing this Court to spread your wicked slanders.'

Judge Bahle paused to let the muttering in the gallery quieten down then spoke in a calm judicial voice.

'Engineer Danyetta, are there any errors of *fact* in the case you have just heard?'

Danyetta remained silent, his posture now openly defiant, not defeated.

'Very well. Since you do not wish to challenge the facts, I must interpret that as an admission of guilt. I therefore find the charges — Breach of Oath and Criminal Damage — to be proved. I will consider the best way to deal with your crimes. What you have done to harm the community permits me to pass a very severe sentence; I wish to take time to consider all the circumstances before deciding upon so drastic a step. This hearing is adjourned; the Court will re-convene in three days.'

The Judge turned to the guards at the back of the chamber.

'The prisoner is to remain in custody in the Paradisia guard-house until I pass sentence. Please take him away.'

Professor Bahle turned to Master Tang to express his concern, assuring him that no blame could be placed at his door for the disgraceful conduct of his erstwhile assistant. Then he made his way out of the Crystal Chamber, followed by Master Tang and Devallian.

The disgraced engineer might have thought to turn the hearts of members of the community against their leader, but his attack had quite the opposite effect. In the gallery, respect for the Duke ignited spontaneously into devotion and everyone wanted to show that devotion, yet no one moved; they saw the frozen expression on his face. Calthea pushed her way through the crowd and took her consort's arm.

'Let's go for a walk, Versain. The air in here has become very stuffy.'

She was shocked at his passive response; he seemed to have lost all volition; he followed her meekly like an obedient cherub. People stood back to let them pass and she led the Duke into the sunlight. Avoiding a group of people who clearly wanted to speak to him, she took to the air. The Duke followed submissively. She landed when they were well clear of the Crystal Chamber.

'There's a place in the high peaks not far from here, Versain; you probably know it. Let's bask there in this lovely sunshine; I feel in need of wholesome air.'

They flew to the place where she and Girilayne had basked with Devallian after her first Council meeting; it was the only time before the trial that she'd set eyes on Davrinka-Danyetta. They rested without speaking against the rock; when she felt her companion might have recovered a little she spoke, in a light neutral tone.

'It was in this very place that Devallian told Girilayne and me that you were training him to be a wizard. Do you remember that time, Versain? I believe...'

Hearing nothing of the content of her remarks, the Duke burst out:

'I'm not a tyrant am I, Calthea? It would be disgraceful if I was what that fellow implied. Am I really so arrogant? You once told me I was, but I thought that was because I'd handled things badly when I brought you here. Have I been misled all this time? Do people actually think of me as a tyrant and a hypocrite?'

'Of *course* they don't, Versain! Didn't you see the reaction of those around you in the gallery? They were *furious* at what that wretch said; they wanted to assure you of their love and support but held back because they could see how deeply shocked you were. Please believe me; you are *loved* by your people; respected always, but I believe you are now also loved;

we all know that whatever you do is for our mission, to save what can be saved from our poor doomed world.

'Please don't give a second thought to what Danyetta said; he wanted to hurt you for some slight — imagined or real — and letting him succeed will only feed into his distorted view. It's one thing to take on board criticism that's intended to help you become a better person — I learnt that during my training with Gylan — but to let yourself be affected by something so intentionally hurtful and so patently untrue is the height of stupidity; and one thing you are not is stupid.'

'You think I should ignore what he said? How can I? He said those dreadful things in front of all our people; how can I ever look any of them in the face again with his words resonating between us?'

'Versain, you have to wash that vitriol out of your mind. It wasn't the truth speaking, it was malice and envy. He knew he'd done wrong and would have to pay for his wrong-doing, so he lashed out at you, the person who represented authority in the community. Can't you see that?'

She stopped and studied his face. 'You don't look convinced. Do you have any reason to think his accusations were justified? Do you know of anything that might have triggered such deep burning hatred?'

The Duke told her of the time he'd rebuffed Danyetta at Girilayne's Farewell, and how it might have led to his disaffection and disappearance. She smiled.

'Well there you are! It's a simple case of *pique*; he has an inflated Ego and a thin skin so was hurt when you rebuffed him, especially because it was in front of people he knew. It just goes to show what a shallow mind the fellow has — and a complete lack of empathy. You have done nothing to criticise yourself for; anyone would have reacted the way you did in those circumstances.'

For a while there was silence, but a more comfortable silence and she felt able to admonish him:

'Why did you let such a silly accusation hurt you so, Versain? In your position, you must be the butt of a great deal of envy and pettiness.'

'I don't know, Calthea; I simply don't know why his words got under my skin. I agree, it is foolish to let them affect me so much.... Oh, it's so good to be in good clean mountain sunlight.' The Duke stretched his arms and wings wide. 'I begin to feel better already.'

After a time, he added: 'You know, you're a more sympathetic person than I gave you credit for, my dear Calthea. Some very heavy clouds are beginning to lift. I feel clearer in mind — indeed almost serene — for the first time in a very long while.'

Calthea, scarcely breathing, said nothing lest she shatter this unexpected sense of closeness. She was aware that her present ability to empathise with her consort was the fruit of her stay with the Seraphim; before that, she would never have had such insight into the heart of another being.

In fact, ever since their conversation following the second launch, she'd had to revise her assessment of the Duke's character. He was more caring and sensitive than she'd suspected. But he was also proud — not surprising in a prince of the Alphaline — and that made him vulnerable to criticism, well founded or not. It also made him more approachable; but she knew it would be a serious error to take advantage of his present fragile state of mind.

For a long time they basked in the warm sunshine.

'It's almost sunset, Versain. Shall we stay to watch Sol retreat to his nightly abode before we fly home? I'm not as nervous of flying in the dark as I used to be.'

'If we do, will you sing the lovely hymn you chanted the

evening I abducted you?'

'Of course I will; it's one of my last memories of Phillestra; we'd chanted the *Solema Mortissima* together the evening before.'

Calthea turned to face the Duke.

'May I ask a favour, Versain? Will you bring Phillestra to see me before she boards the spaceship? I would dearly love to see how she's turned out. It's six years since I saw her — a long time in the life of a cherub.'

'Yes I will. I promise to bring her to spend time with you. It would be a good idea for her to see Paradisia and learn about the work we've been doing. She should also find out how the recorders she'll be taking with her have been made and how they work.'

'Thank you. I'll make a special recorder just for her; I can put into it everything I'd have wanted to say as she grows up; it can be her guide and mentor, a substitute for what Girilayne was for both of us — a source of wisdom, love and guidance.'

'That sounds an excellent idea.'

For a while they again basked in silence.

'When I've escorted you home tonight, I shall fly on to Sriandra. I need a long rest after these difficult days. I feel a great deal better for our talk, Calthea — but also very, very tired.'

'But Versain, I'm not returning to Paradisia tonight; I plan to stay in Girilayne's cave. That cave used to be your home-in-the-mountains. I'd like it very much if you would consider it your home again. I never use the inner room; it's your room; I've never even put my nose inside. If you escort me there tonight, it'll make no sense to fly to Sriandra; it's in the opposite direction and you're exhausted.

'Why not stay the night; in fact, why not stay as long as you like in your old room and leave for Sriandra when you feel fully restored. No one will trouble you; I'll leave in the morning straight after the *Obeisance*.'

To Calthea's relief her plan was approved.

* * * * *

The sky was paling; dawn could not be far off. Calthea stood on the terrace of her home waiting to chant the *Obeisance*. To her delight, she sensed the Duke come to stand beside her. She loved to watch the dawn miracle flashing across the eastern horizon when the sky was clear; it was the signal for her to begin chanting.

On cue it came, that fine brilliant arc of light heralding the sunrise. Calthea began chanting the familiar words that welcomed Sol back to his daytime kingdom. Beside her, the Duke was silent; he was not a follower of the State religion so it must be a complement to *her* that he had taken the trouble to rise early and join her.

The chant over, they found themselves places against the rock-face to bask in the strong morning sunlight.

'I wonder how they're doing on the *Amphora of Civilisation*.' Calthea mused.

'Yes; it will seem strange not to have sunrise and sunset to regulate their days and nights. Time feels very different in Space; you have to discipline yourself to rest at regular intervals. Flying to the colonies, we have to adjust to conditions very fast. There's no problem with basking; we're in full sunlight even when flying away from the sun; we get sustenance from sunlight falling on our wings and back plumage.'

'How will they manage inside the spaceship?'

'There are windows; they'll have to set up a rota so everyone gets their share at windows facing the sun. The stronger angelis can fly alongside the spaceship at times thus getting both nourishment and exercise.'

'It'll be a long journey, first to Phobos then to Luna, and then the much shorter journey to Earth. I wonder when they'll be able to start work on the Hybrid Project in earnest. I imagine it will be several years.'

'Yes, and then many years before they can tell whether it's been a success.'

'I wonder whether these hybrids will turn out to be people.'

'*People*?'

'Yes, all Stellaster's species can be described as *people* — dwarves, elves, seraphs and angels are all *people* — but, from what I've heard, none of the species on Earth can be described as people; they're animals or insects or plants or whatever.'

'You've omitted to mention my favourite species.'

'Did I? Who did I miss out?'

'You didn't mention the harbingers of dawn. Not many angels know about these delightful creatures but I have to admit they support your thesis: harbingers are definitely people; they have their own unique form of culture.'

'I thought the *harbingers of dawn* was a poetic way of talking about the dawn miracle. Do you remember the song everyone sings at school?

'Towards the east I turn my eyes to paling skies
A shimmering skein of golden light avails my sight
The joyful harbingers of dawn proclaim the miracle newly born
Each blessed day, each blessed morn
When Sol doth rise to grace our eyes.'

'Yes, I do recall the song. But, these creatures aren't mythical, Calthea; they're the most delicate beings you could possibly imagine. You're a devotee of sunset, but I've always preferred the dawn because of the dawn miracle.'

'Yes, but what is that miracle? Do you mean sunrise itself?'

'Sunrise is certainly one of the miracles of Nature but no, I mean the arc of light that flashes just before the sun appears over the horizon. Have you never noticed it?'

'I saw it this morning, and you must have done so too.'

'Have you never wondered what it is, what the song's line, *a shimmering skein of golden light*, really means?'

'I thought that flashing arc was an artefact due to sunlight striking the high, night-cold atmosphere.'

'Not so. One day I'll take you to meet the harbingers, but you'll have to fly under your own power — to visit them in a shuttle would frighten them to death. They live at the margin where the atmosphere meets Space. I visit them whenever I can and have even learnt to understand a little of their strange language.'

'Well, there you are; your harbingers obviously prove my point: *Sophia* has produced beings whose way of life is different from the life-threatening competition and general mayhem that seems to characterise life on Earth.'

'It's true; there are fundamental differences between our life-forms and those of Earth; the Hybrid Project is named to reflect that fact. It combines the best of both worlds — both evolutionary systems. Just think: the hybrids will be able to experience the richness of Earth's diversity with angel-awareness. They'll live in the vastly more varied landscapes of Earth and will survive when our own world has ceased to exist. Surely that's justification enough to make the attempt?'

'I harbour grave doubts as to the ethics of the scheme, I'm with Professor Bahle on this, but we've been through that already.'

'You'd rather see all we represent — all we've achieved — blasted to sand and dust? You'd rather see the end of intelligent awareness as a basis for life and living?'

'That's what it comes down to, isn't it? It's about believing our way of life is superior to *Geopa's* way.'

'Yes it does; and it's why Oracle told us to set up the community in the first place. Do you consider she was wrong?'

'Of course not!' Calthea exclaimed in exasperation. 'But it's the same issue as believing in her prophecy; either we place our trust in that remarkable being — and having met her I do place my trust in her — or we reject her and what she has asked us to do. Oh, it's just so *complicated*, Versain. I just worry deep in my heart that we're putting something in motion that will have consequences we cannot predict.'

'We're all pawns in a game we don't understand, Calthea. We're required to do things that will change the world. I do understand your concern; I've been through this same agonising process myself. We're trained to be obedient and expected to be discriminating — to act on our orders but also to take responsibility for those actions.

'It all comes down to trust. First we have to satisfy ourselves that the person or principle we're putting our trust in is right. Then we have to do what that person or principle expects of us. It's why that fellow upset me so yesterday: the community has placed its trust in me; if people feel that trust has been misplaced, they'll question what they're doing here. It's not a trivial matter, Calthea. Our people simply have to trust me, and I must know deep within myself that their trust is well founded.'

'Surely you've discounted everything that liar said, Versain; you can't let the poison of his hatred divert you from your work. Why do you mind what he said?'

'How can I not mind? I must talk this over with Godwinian — and with Versilla, if she's still in Sriandra. You've been a great help, Calthea; I can't tell you how much I appreciate your support. But I think I'll leave now; you'll be leaving for Paradisia, so let's fly to the valley together then I'll head on to Sriandra.

'Please tell Gylan where I've gone — he can always contact me in an emergency — I shall spend a few days in silent retreat to clear my mind, so ask him not to call unless it's urgent.'

Chapter 15

Planning the End Game

Since returning to Paradisia, Calthea hadn't left her workroom except to sleep — she even basked at a window whilst working rather than lose a moment in trying to understand the nature and qualities of firestone. Yet despite all her best endeavours — and those of a chemist and a geologist she'd recruited to help her — she was making little progress.

They could find no reference to firestone in the literature — she'd assumed that someone somewhere must have come across this material, perhaps under a different name, but it wasn't so. It seemed that firestone, so precious to dwarves, was totally unknown to angels. So Calthea and her colleagues had to start from scratch.

They carefully measured its physical and chemical properties but that provided no insight; firestone was like no other rock or crystal any of them had encountered before. It appeared to be homogenous, without markings or blemishes of any kind; it wasn't particularly hard as rocks went — it could be easily worked — but that was all they could say about it.

After many days of intense scrutiny, firestone remained an enigma. So Calthea thanked her colleagues for their help and switched her attention to investigating the material's potential for storing data. With her mind focused on this task, she was totally unaware of the malaise that had crept over the community.

Everyone had heard the terrible accusations hurled at the Duke by Danyetta, they'd seen their leader wounded deeply; they'd seen the Seraphina lead him from the Courtroom in a state near to somnabulance; since when he'd vanished and no one had had sight or sound of him.

The malaise affected everyone in the valley; even Maestro Arbrecht, generally the epitome of jovial good humour, had fallen victim to its spell; the aging remnants of his *culture-coding-commune*, having completed their work, were left wondering how they were to spend the rest of their days till the meteor arrived, bringing a final coup de grace to their existence.

On Verastra, Master Tang's crew were still hard at work on the final spaceship and Professor Kritten on his new observatory, so there at least morale remained high.

The deteriorating atmosphere in Paradisia worried Gylan; he'd heard nothing from the Duke since the trial. He knew he didn't have the Duke's charismatic charm; he could deputise for him in many ways but couldn't replace him as the inspirational leader of the community.

The professor was torn between sympathy for the Duke and deep concern at the deteriorating morale of his colleagues. He decided to consult his erstwhile pupil; Calthea was apparently the only person still in the Duke's confidence. He found her at a window holding a sample of firestone to her forehead and focusing deeply.

'Seraphina, may I claim your attention for a moment?' he advanced towards her, 'I need to contact Versain; he is badly needed here; yet I know how seldom he is able to enjoy any peace and quiet. But before telling him of my concerns, I thought I might seek your guidance: am I justified in disturbing the Duke's retreat?'

'What is concerning you, Professor? Has that wretch, Danyetta escaped?'

'No, no my dear Seraphina, he is safe under lock and key. But his trial has had a disastrous effect on the community — have you not noticed? I have never seen my colleagues so down-hearted. Even when they were waving off our many friends on the *Amphora of Civilisation* they weren't as dispirited as they are now. The wanton destruction of your gems then that terrible trial came as a great shock to us all.

'We need Versain here, Calthea; we need to assure him of our love and support. We saw him deeply hurt by those scurrilous accusations and need to show him how little those insults matter.'

'Oh dear! I'm afraid I hadn't noticed.' Calthea looked guiltily at the professor, 'Since the trial, I've been preoccupied with testing firestone. You do realise don't you Gylan, that the Recording Project is now completely in my court? Maestro Arbrecht's team has completed its work and given everything to me. But firestone is proving a real puzzle; I don't yet know if it's going to be up to the job but I do have an intuition it's going to turn out even better than the gemstones Versain brought me.'

'Well, that's good news, Seraphina. You at least have work to keep you busy. But what of those who have completed theirs? What are they meant to do? Many are near or past their Due Departure Dates and are wondering what comes next. We need the Duke here to help us plan for these remaining years. You do understand?'

'Yes I do. I've been so focused on my own work that I didn't notice what was happening to my friends.' She paused for a long time in thought, 'You know Gylan, it might be a very good thing to tell Versain what you've just told me — that he's badly needed here; I'm sure he'll rise to the occasion.

'Danyetta's accusations hit him hard and he told me why: he felt that those accusations would destroy our faith in him and thus destroy our faith in his mission. He went to Sriandra as much to avoid people here as to get some rest; he felt sure he'd lost their trust and respect. I tried to convince him otherwise but I don't think I succeeded.'

'But might he not resent being called away from his retreat?'

'He might *regret* it but he certainly won't *resent* it — and he won't refuse to come either. He'll get over his doubts far more rapidly if he has a crisis to deal with; he'll discover how essential his leadership still is. I was surprised at the extent to which it worried him to think of facing people who'd heard that nonsense. I never thought he cared a button for what people thought of him — but on that occasion, he did.'

'Yes, it's strange and quite out of character.'

'It is, Gylan. But you know something? I think we'll get to know our respected leader a lot better as a result of this crisis. We've always regarded him as invincible and infallible — the Galliard who rescued the world from that awful tyrant. Perhaps we *needed* him to be infallible. But Versain is not one of the Immortal Powers; he's an ordinary mortal who's carried a heavy load of responsibility ever since Girilayne decided to leave.

'During that ghastly trial we were able to witness his feelings; usually he keeps them hidden behind that mask of lordly reserve; but we saw that he can be hurt like anyone else. That will help us to treat him as a person no different from us, someone we love and respect, perhaps a little more than we love and respect most others.'

'Precisely so, dear Seraphina; this trouble could well have a positive outcome. Very well; I will contact the Duke and ask him to convene one of his famous briefing conferences; we need to discuss what the community ought to be doing during these remaining years.'

* * * * *

The Duke responded immediately to Gylan's plea; it was just what he needed — a crisis requiring his urgent presence. With his customary efficiency, he organised a meeting in the Crystal Chamber so that everyone remaining in Paradisia could come; only Chrysilla was absent; Calthea assumed she was still away on her secret mission.

Firstly, the Duke invited suggestions as to who might join the final expedition; he also invited ideas for projects for the years before the meteor struck. Several proposals were put forward; some were for the immediate future, some for longer-term projects. The Duke suggested that everyone should go away and discuss these ideas; they could decide which to take forward at a further conference in four days time. This proposal was met with enthusiastic approval.

All in all, the meeting achieved its main goal of restoring a sense of optimism in the community and not least in its leader. Everyone agreed how much better the Duke looked by the close of proceedings. The next four days witnessed a resurgence of excitement in the community and the creeping malaise was halted in its tracks.

The meeting was also a success for the Duke: facing his demons, he discovered they weren't demons at all but wraiths that melted away when challenged. In fact, he discovered that his colleagues had retained all their old trust in him; in fact he felt a degree of affection for him he hadn't sensed before.

At the conference four days later, some important issues were resolved. With Luna now the destination for all three expeditions, it wasn't necessary to select a self-supporting community for the final spaceship. Devallian would be its commander with Phillestra as his trainee and assistant; the ship's complement would be chosen either to strengthen the initial community or to provide additional volunteers for mind-transfer and further staff to support the Hybrid Project. This resolution had just been formally approved when the Duke looked up and, turning to Professor Bahle, exclaimed:

'I believe our ambassador has just arrived, Gylan. We'll be able to consider our proposal after all. You may wish to have a private word before she joins us.'

All heads followed the professor as he walked to the entrance of the Crystal Chamber. Who was this ambassador that no one had heard of? There was a frisson of surprise, not least from Calthea, when that ambassador turned out to be Chrysilla. The professor spent a few moments talking to his protégé before escorting her to the empty pillar beside his own. The Duke welcomed her.

'We are delighted you were able to join us at such short notice, Doctor Flaine. May I ask, were you able to conclude your negotiations successfully?'

'I was, my Lord. In fact, your invitation to attend this conference helped a great deal. Do you wish me to report on the outcome?'

'If you have completed your work, the need for secrecy has passed. No one here but you, the professor and I know anything of your mission, so please begin by outlining what that mission was.'

'My Lord, as you know I wasn't in at the beginning of these negotiations; I was asked to take over when Seraph Banderene left on the *Amphora of Civilisation*. Some years ago, you asked Seraph Banderene to approach the Council of Elves, to discover whether they might like to send a contingent of their people on the final spaceship to establish a new community of elves and so perpetuate their race after the disaster.

'You will all be aware that relations between elves and angels have not always been cordial;' this comment was greeted with a murmur of agreement, 'elves have long been exploited by our race and sometimes even treated as slaves. Elves are an ancient and proud people so it required great diplomacy to ensure that your offer was seen for what it was — an altruistic desire to help their race survive, not a callous attempt to acquire slaves for our new angel settlements.

'The Seraphim have always been trusted by the Elfin community, so Seraph Banderene was accepted as an ambassador; he established a basis of trust that I have been able to build on. It helped that our community has always treated elves with respect; the fact that our Empress has re-instated the ancient position of Queen of the Elves was, perhaps, the most significant reason for their change of heart towards us.

'Nevertheless, I had to proceed with care so that the delicate bond established by Banderene would not be strained through putting undue pressure on the Queen to give a reply any earlier than she wished. Your invitation to attend this conference meant that I was obliged to inform Queen Scintilla that her options might be closing; decisions might well be made today that assigned all places on the final spaceship.'

'Do you know, my Lord,' Chrysilla's voice expressed amazement, 'the Queen actually laughed when I told her this. She said she'd been prevaricating because she enjoyed having me at her court; she had already made up her mind to accept your invitation, but she knew that telling me so would result in my departure.

'My Lord,' Chrysilla went on, slipping a heavy pouch from around her neck, 'the Queen has asked me to present this pouch to you as a token of her acceptance and of her gratitude on behalf of the Elfin people.'

Chrysilla gave the pouch to the professor, who carefully examined the delicate but weighty object before passing it to the Duke.

'This is an extraordinary gesture on the part of the Queen,' commented Gylan. 'This pouch is down-work of the very highest quality. I have never known such a precious object being presented to an angel — it's a gesture of great significance. This is a peace offering; it tells us that past atrocities have been forgiven and forgotten.'

The Duke examined the pouch then opened the cord around its neck. From it he let fall into his palm a green gemstone that flashed in the sunlit chamber.

'Good heavens!' he exclaimed, 'How very beautiful! Seraphina, can you tell us what it is?'

Calthea took the stone from the Duke and held it up to the light.

'It's a rare type of emerald found only on Meon but I've never seen one more beautifully cut; it is domed on the under side to enhance refraction and has at least a hundred tiny facets. It's quite exquisite, an excellent example of gem-cutting; but then elves have long been renowned for their gem-cutting skills.'

'Excellent! Now, I believe we can finalise numbers for the third spaceship.'

It took only a few minutes to assign forty places to the elves and the remainder to those who'd supplement the first expedition and the Hybrid Project. The Duke then invited discussion on the projects that might occupy their remaining years.

'If Professor Kritten's estimate is correct, we probably have another five years before the meteor appears — that's too long for the public to know about the pending catastrophe. In the Empress's view, the prophecy should not be revealed till a year or so before the meteor is due. How shall we occupy ourselves between now and then? Who will start the ball rolling?'

Discussion was lively and productive; several ideas were approved for taking forward and the Duke asked Professor Bahle to co-ordinate their implementation. Before leaving for Cander Imperia, the Duke made a point of talking to community members; one person he did not contact was Calthea and it did not escape her notice.

Calthea was thrilled to have her friend back and begged to hear all about her secret assignment. Chrysilla had left for Senton Elftown directly after the launching of the *Amphora of Civilisation* so didn't know anything of the destruction of Calthea's gemstones or of Danyetta's capture and trial. Calthea described to her the effect that trial had had on the Duke.

But why had her consort deliberately avoided her after the meeting? True, she'd been in conversation with Chrysilla, but surely that shouldn't have prevented him from greeting her. She was worried and hurt but her fears of an estrangement from the Duke were put to rest next morning by the appearance of a visitor.

Chunka knocked at the door of her workroom and was invited to enter.

'Seraphina Lady,' he bowed with his customary respect, 'yesterday, the Great Lord asked me to show you where firestone is mined. He says if you see for yourself where it is found it may help you in your work. Dinkarspeak has given consent for me to take you to this place; it is known to only a few of our people.'

Calthea was amazed that Dinkarspeak should have agreed to this request and that it had been made in the first place. It certainly made up for the Duke's avoidance of her. She feared the trip might involve a long journey, but it turned out that the secret mine was in the Quartz Mountains close to the cave she now called home.

They entered a cleft in the rock high on a west-facing slope and followed a tunnel diving steeply into the heart of the mountain; Chunka had fluorescent torches to light their way. The tunnel ended in a large cavern where a number of niches lined the walls; Chunka led her to one of the niches.

'Our people came across this cave in ancient times, Seraphina Lady; we believe the giants used it as a final resting place for their dead.'

'So these niches house the bodies of dead giants, Chunka? Are you telling me these are the Caves of Eternal Peace used by the giants of old?'

'We do not believe that giants went into the caves when they were alive, like angels do. Our ancient myths say that giants brought their dead to these caves.'

'How astonishing! But where does firestone come into the picture?'

'Put your torch into the hollow, Seraphina Lady. See what is there.'

Calthea leant into the niche and saw a smooth substance at its base. She placed her hand on the reddish rock and immediately felt the unique *buzz* of firestone.

'Goodness! Are you saying that firestone is the deposit left by the decomposing bodies of dead giants? Is firestone *organic* Chunka; was it once living flesh and bone?'

'All I can tell you Lady, is that only in this system of caves have we ever come across this material; it is a magical stone and must be kept secret from…. Oh!'

The dwarf stopped looking embarrassed. Calthea laughed.

'You were going to say, from *angels*, weren't you, Chunka? We angels must not be allowed to discover this miraculous material. Don't worry, I understand very well why that was so, and it's all the more of a complement that I've been brought here today to be shown this wonderful treasure.'

'You treat firestone with respect Lady, so we are happy to give it to you.'

'Having seen this, I have a far better idea of what I am dealing with; I can now understand why I haven't made much progress to date. You suggested that this cave is one of several?'

'There are five intact caves like this one, but one tunnel was blocked by a land-quake in ancient times. Our miners have recently cut a tunnel through the fallen rock and broken through into a cave. The landquake crushed the hollows where firestone would have been, but we have managed to mine a few pieces. This rock is different; it has been lying under heavy rock ever since the landquake, and that seems to have damaged it.'

'Are there samples of this damaged firestone, Chunka?'

'There are, Lady, but we didn't send you any because we believe it may have lost its magical powers.'

'I'd like to study this new firestone. After being subjected to such high pressure, it may have different properties. Would Dinkarspeak let me have samples, Chunka?'

The answer to that question came a couple of days later when blocks of the new substance were delivered to Calthea's workroom. They were black and crystalline, not at all like regular firestone, which was russet red, smooth and opaque.

Calthea referred to her new samples as *fire-crystal*. To her amazement, these samples began to change colour after being exposed to sunlight for a couple of hours; they began to turn ruby red.

* * * * *

For the next year and a half, everything was once more hustle and bustle, both on the Verastra construction site and in Paradisia. Preparations were advancing well for the completion of the final spacecraft and for recruiting and training those who would travel in her. The Empress was responsible for selecting twenty Mothers for the Hybrid Project, then extracting them from their present posts. Devallian would, in due course, select his crew and those who would supplement the first expedition.

Various projects kept community staff fully occupied and motivated. Morale-raising celebrations were planned and held every few months and certainly achieved their aim. The most significant project to emerge from the Duke's conference was a proposal put forward by Maestro Arbrecht.

'Friends,' he'd told the conference, 'there are some very cultured people here, some of the most creative and talented angels in the world. Our younger members have departed with the Hybrid Project leaving us older folk hanging about with little to do yet much still to offer. An idea has been simmering at the back of my mind for some time and is now taking shape.

'I'd like to compose an opera about a meteor and the impact on the world of its predicted arrival. Opera is the most comprehensive of all the performing arts: it can help us probe to the deepest roots of our emotions; it can encourage us to pursue our highest aspirations. There is great power in opera: it opens our hearts and minds to novel experiences and feelings. Attending an opera, we identify with the characters — ordinary people like ourselves — as they face extraordinary situations; having done so can help us if and when we encounter similar situations in our own lives.

'If we portray the coming of this meteor as a story, we can provide insight into the ways different people respond in a crisis; we can give ourselves and our audience a chance to prepare for an event that is, in fact, going to happen. A catastrophe of this magnitude is bound to overwhelm us and perhaps freeze our responses — unless we have prepared and protected ourselves well in advance.'

'The creation of an opera demands considerable resources and a great deal of time,' the Duke had commented. 'Do you have these at your disposal, Maestro?'

'I believe I do, my Lord. As I say, we have some highly creative people with us who have little to occupy them at present. We need, let us say, three or four years to create the opera, which will leave us a year or two to perform it. If the work is to serve its purpose, it needs to become part of the national repertoire well before we announce the coming of the actual meteor.'

'You see this opera as part of our programme for preparing the public?'

'I do, my Lord. The opera will provide a conceptual framework so that when we announce the coming crisis, people will have something to help them deal with their inevitable fear.'

'Have you thought of the story the opera will tell, Maestro?' Calthea had asked.

'I have Seraphina; the outline of the plot is already taking shape in my mind; I believe we should tell the tale of our own community, but set it in a historical context so that no one draws parallels before we want them to. We should portray our own emotions and reactions when first we heard of the prophecy; in that way, the story will be authentic and will carry conviction.

'This opera will also allow us to express our deep affection for our beautiful world, which has supported and nurtured living beings for so many aeons. I hope it will encourage us to delve deep into our hearts and so learn to express our deepest feelings in a way that music, art and drama encourage us to do. If successful, this opera will be a final vindication of all that is best in our culture and civilisation — a gem among Stellaster's many gems.

'If anyone would like to contribute, I'd be delighted to include their story in the script. If the idea is approved today, I can begin briefing my colleagues and we can get down to work without delay.'

'It's a brilliant idea, Maestro,' the Duke had commented. 'And you believe you have all you need for this ambitious venture?'

'I believe we do.'

'Can anyone contribute to this project, Maestro?' Calthea had asked.

'There's a part for anyone who wants one, Seraphina. Some of my colleagues are seasoned performers; they can take the lead roles; others may want to join the chorus or create the scenery or the costumes; we need writers for the plot and lyrics, and musicians to assist with the composition. One of opera's greatest strengths is that it requires people with many different skills and aptitudes.'

'Where might you stage your opera, Maestro?'

'You're well ahead of the game there, my Lord. To create the opera will take at least three years; we'll then need to rehearse and put on trial performances for our own community. Only when we've polished the work can we present it in public. There's much to be done before we reach that stage.'

'Would you put on performances in Cander Imperia?'

'If the opera is to play its intended role, it must be seen by as many people as possible around the world. We can portray the coming of a meteor as fiction — opera plots are usually based on fiction or myth — so when the world is finally told of the coming disaster, it won't be a totally unimaginable horror.

'Our opera will have displayed a range of reactions to the fictional meteor; that should help people in coming to terms with their own reactions when they hear that disaster is on its way. If I'm right, the opera will play an important role in preventing mindless panic or universal paralysis.'

After that conference, anyone not directly involved in preparations for the third launch found themselves caught up in the creation of the Maestro's opera.

Chapter 16

PREPARING TO LEAVE

The Duke kept his word: six months before the launch of the final spaceship, he took Phillestra out of school and brought her to spend time with her Mother; he felt it appropriate that his daughter should embark on this journey — the first stage of a far longer journey — at New Year. It was exactly seven years since he'd carried Calthea to the mountains but on this occasion they took off from the roof of his palace.

Devallian came to see his future protégé set out on an adventure he'd share with her in due course. He promised to visit her often in Paradisia as he flew there often these days in preparation for the launch. Phillestra slept the entire journey strapped securely into the harness her father wore; they landed on the same terrace to which he'd brought Calthea all those years before.

Her parents made that day special, a wonderful memory to treasure all her long life. Phillestra hadn't seen Calthea since the day she'd vanished so mysteriously. Although that day was now fading in memory, it had left her with a love of twilight when the magical stars would appear as daylight faded. She recognised her Mother immediately but was at first uncharacteristically shy; that reserve was soon dispelled as they leant against the rock-wall outside Calthea's cave, saturating themselves in the clear mountain sunlight as they talked.

Later, her parents took her on a tour of the local area; she saw the Great Sand Ocean to the east lapping against the sheer thousand-foot high escarpment and the convoluted badlands to the west. She was also shown the extraordinary crystalline rocks that gave this section of the range its name, the Quartz Mountains. Then they landed and Calthea led her companions on foot to a nearby site.

'See that cleft in the rocks, Phillestra? That's the entrance to deep caves where a wonderful material called *firestone* is mined. It's a secret place so you must never talk about it or show it to anyone else.'

Turning to her consort she said:

'Versain, I've never thanked you for getting Chunka to show me these mines. It was the breakthrough I needed to unlock the secrets of firestone and fire-crystal.'

'What are firestone and fire-crystal, Ma?'

'You'll find out soon enough, Phillestra. Very soon you'll start training for your adventure; you'll learn all about these magical materials and what I've been able to do with them. But today is New Year's Day and a holiday. Today, we want to show you something of this beautiful world before you fly off with Devallian to explore other distant worlds.'

That evening, with Phillestra safely tucked up in the inner room, her parents could talk in private. Calthea had a question.

'Have you told Phillestra *why* she's setting off on this adventure with Devallian, Versain? Does she know about the prophecy?'

'No. I thought I should discuss with you first how much she's told and when. In my view she should *not* be told about the meteor until what is going to happen has happened. Devallian will be with her; she has complete trust in him — as have I — so I'm sure he'll explain the situation in a sensitive and supportive way.'

'I need to know how much she knows so I don't go blurting things out that would alert her to the real reason you're sending her away. I'll also need to warn my colleagues to be careful what they say in front of her.'

'About firestone Calthea, you said that seeing the mines made all the difference to your work. Can you explain that?'

'Having seen firestone *in situ*, I realised it was an organic fossilised substance and not natural rock.'

'Really?'

'Yes. Firestone is the fossilised remains of the giants of old.'

'Good gracious! What does that mean?'

'It means that firestone is the residue left after piling vast numbers of bodies on top of each other over vast periods of time, then leaving them to decompose. Those bodies were left undisturbed for millions of years so that the residue metamorphosed into the rock-like material that dwarves call firestone; they call it that because it's the colour of hot volcanic lava. Chunka told me that they've recently excavated a sixth cave in which the approach tunnel had been blocked by an ancient landquake.

'The firestone in that cave has been subjected to extraordinarily high pressures and temperatures, which has changed it into a crystallised form — fire-crystal — with very different properties. In fact, I am using fire-crystal for the archive recorders.'

'How do you make recordings, Calthea? It seems miraculous to me that you can take a piece of crystal and record our culture into it. What's the secret?'

'Aha! So you want to know my secrets, do you, Versain?' Calthea teased, 'Well, just as Vyvyan jealously guarded the secrets of Motherhood and Banderene jealously guarded the secrets of mind-transfer, I believe I'm entitled to guard my secret of recording into crystal too.'

She continued more seriously, 'The truth is, I really don't know how it works. I do know that I must use a material that resonates with my mind but how the process works is a total mystery. It was Gylan who explained that I used telepathy in my original recorders — I'd not realised that till I did my training.'

'Can others do it — record into fire-crystal?'

'No one else who's tried has succeeded… as yet. It seems that anyone can use my quartz recorders and ruby responders but even Gylan couldn't get information to register in the fire-crystal globes. I hope Phillestra will succeed; anyway, I'll show her how it's done.'

'What do you propose calling your archive globes?'

'I haven't thought of a name yet. What do you suggest?'

'What about *encyclopaedia*? Or perhaps, since they're a compendium of our culture, why not call them *compendia*?'

'What about *parapendia*? It would indicate that they're *super* compendia?'

'A new word for a new device! I like it, Calthea.'

'Then *parapendia* it is.'

* * * * *

The following morning, Phillestra flew by gentle stages to Paradisia with her parents. The Duke left them in Calthea's workroom then went in search of Professor Bahle. He returned a couple of hours later.

'Calthea, having talked to Gylan, I believe we *should* tell Phillestra why she's really here.'

'I thought I was here to prepare for my visit to Phobos with Captain Devallian, Royal Father. You said it would be an adventure I'd remember all my life.'

'That's true Phillestra; but you won't be visiting Phobos only; you'll travel on to Luna and will probably stay there for a very long time.'

'But I've still five more years at Second School and then college. Isn't that what everyone is expected to do?'

'In normal times yes, but these are far from normal times.'

In carefully chosen words, Versain and Calthea told their daughter about the prophecy and the reason for setting up the Paradisia community.

Her mother explained, 'Your father was told to plan for a future that most of your friends will not live to see, Phillestra. We....'

'Who told him, Marima?'

'There was a great being who lived at the North Pole, a being called Oracle. She was able to see into the future, which is not something most people can do. She could see a terrible disaster coming that would spell the end of this world; she asked your father to set up this community so we could do something to save our species.'

'And how will you do that, Royal Father? How will you save our people when this terrible catastrophe comes?'

'It won't be possible to save *everyone*, Phillestra; what we've done is to build spaceships....'

'You mean like the one I saw being launched at the Finale of the Jubilee; the one that came to rather a sticky end?'

'No more interruptions, please till we've told you the whole story.'

The Duke recounted the facts concerning that spaceship; he told her there'd been a second successful launch but said nothing of the Hybrid Project — that was rather too controversial a topic for a twelve-year-old. Phillestra then learned that, though she and Devallian would board the final spacecraft, her parents would not.

'You won't be alone,' Calthea reassured her. 'Devallian will be commander of the spaceship and he'll also be your guardian. You feel safe with him, won't you?'

'But why can't you and my royal father come too? If he's in charge Ma, surely he can make sure you both escape on the spaceship.'

That prompted a lecture from the Duke on the moral obligations of leadership. He emphasised that being assigned a place on the last spaceship was not a favour he'd wangled to save his precious daughter from disaster but a tough assignment that would severely tax her courage and endurance. Her visit to Paradisia was not actually a holiday; it was a period of intense training for her life's work.

Phillestra needed time to absorb all this; to help her do so, Calthea suggested a visit to the Duke's cave in the cliff-face; Phillestra would be staying there and Calthea would stay with her whenever her father was away.

At noon, the Duke departed for Cander Imperia but before leaving he had some private advice for his consort.

'Don't get emotionally involved, Calthea; remember, I abducted you to prevent you becoming attached. Phillestra is a charming child and it would be all too easy to form bonds that will cause great hurt to you both when they have to be severed. Far better to keep a distance between you; let our daughter create precious memories of your time together but don't break her heart — or yours.'

*****

Mother and daughter found great delight in this time together. For the first few days Phillestra was on holiday and spent her time exploring the Paradisia valley with Calthea and sometimes with Chrysilla too.

On the sixth day, Calthea announced that the holiday was now over. Instead of returning to school, she would continue her education under Calthea's supervision. Various members of the Maestro's commune coached her in Maths, Music, Science and Literature; Chrysilla gave her a basic course in Thinking and Malgan-Mandow, the Earth biologist taught her about that planet's amazing bio-diversity.

She attended a course in astronomy and was then taken by shuttle to Verastra to meet Professor Kritten. Earth was close at the time so, through the professor's powerful new telescope, she was able to see amazing detail both of the planet and its moon, Luna. She was fascinated to have close sight of a world that would become her home in the not-too-distant future.

Mars was not visible but would be approaching in six months time when the third spaceship would take off, heading for the Martian satellite, Phobos. Devallian happened to be on Verastra during her visit; his spaceship was in the final stages of preparation and he'd come to select the crew that would run the ship under his command. For that, he needed the help of Master Tang. Devallian took her on a tour of the spaceship.

Back in Paradisia, Phillestra became Calthea's eager assistant; she learnt a great deal about crystallography and her Mother's unusual talent for turning crystal and gemstone into a range of useful devices. Best of all, she helped her Mother to turn the great globes of fire-crystal into magical parapendia, archives of angel culture.

Calthea had arranged for chunks of flawless fire-crystal to be sent to Senton Elftown to be fashioned into perfect spheres of a specific size; an entire team of elves had been assigned to the task and were kept busy for many months. Shortly before Phillestra's arrival, she'd received five large globes and one smaller one. Calthea's task was to load the five large globes with all the information codified by the Maestro's team. The small globe was a special gift for her daughter; they decided to call it her *mentori* — her personal mentor.

* * * * *

One morning, a month after Phillestra's visit to Verastra, Devallian knocked at the door of Calthea's workroom.
'Is Professor Bahle here by any chance, Seraphina?'
'Captain Devallian! How lovely to see you. He is, so if you're looking for him, you've found him.'
'Didn't you know Calthea; Devallian is no longer a captain?' Gylan chided her.
'Really? Has Versain finally given him his marching orders?'
'Indeed not! May I inform you that you are addressing Colonel Devallian; I'm surprised you didn't know. I thought you'd be first to hear.'
'It seems not. Congratulations, Devallian. If I might say so, this promotion is long over-due. How long were you a major? A week?'
'The Emperor gave me my commission as Colonel on my return from Verastra. It was a total surprise because the Duke had said nothing. He did explain that he'd blocked my promotion in the past as he needed to keep me as his ADC so I could run errands here and help him with other community business. He said that now I was fully occupied with preparations for the launch, promotion was appropriate.
'I'm to create a new regiment — it will be called the *Emperor's Elite Guard* — and I'm being allowed to select soldiers from any of the other regiments. Of course, this is just cover for selecting those who will accompany me on the *Brave Endeavour*; that's the name the Empress has chosen for the final spaceship.'
'But surely there won't be room for an entire regiment on

board, especially as some of the places have been assigned to Mothers and elves.' Calthea objected.

'I won't need to choose the entire complement, just the forty I want to take to Luna. In fact, the reason I'm here today is that I need Professor Bahle's advice on that selection. All the community's geneticists have left with the Hybrid Project, but the Duke says I shall do very well if I consult the professor.'

'I shall be happy to help. We know only too well how dangerous it is to choose the wrong person in a small community. We made that mistake with Danyetta; he was perfectly competent to do the job he was recruited for; it was his personality that was at fault. We must identify the qualities you should look for and those you must avoid at all costs.'

'I agree. We must weed out evil, not give it any chance to cause trouble.'

'In fact, I've come to the conclusion that evil as such doesn't exist. It may be relevant to ask what constitutes a good *action* or an evil *action* but a better question is to ask is what *motivates* someone to perform a so-called evil action and whether that motive can be regarded as evil from all points of view.

'It's all a matter of perspective, of the stance from which you ask the question; by which I mean that an action seen from, let's say, the actor's viewpoint may seem both appropriate and justified — in other words, it's a *good* action. That same action seen from the victim's perspective may seem inappropriate and unjustified — it's an *evil* action. That's because the motive of the actor isn't apparent, is misunderstood or isn't accepted as valid by the victim.'

Calthea smiled; she loved to sit back and listen when Gylan took some casual remark and set about analysing its roots. She recalled how bewildered Devallian had been when she'd launched into a philosophical debate all those years ago when he'd held her prisoner in the cave. She wondered if he'd become glassy-eyed now but he rallied bravely and asked if Danyetta's actions could be seen in this way.

'I believe they can. There's no doubt he possesses an over-sensitive nature; he's extremely vulnerable to criticism or to any perceived slight; these are a result of his up-bringing. I happen to know that in First School he came under the influence of a sadistic schoolmaster; that experience badly damaged his personality. But he was doing well under Master Tang because the Master understood Dannyetta's delicate personality and made due allowances.

'The Duke didn't know him at all; the fellow must have felt slighted when you were sent to answer the issue Danyetta had brought to Council. It was singularly unfortunate that their second encounter should have reinforced his earlier opinion, that the Duke was uncaring and arrogant.

'It seems he approached the Duke when he was leading Girilayne to her final rest; he lacked the social skills that would have told him this wasn't the moment to ask his question. The Duke told him to get lost or words to that effect; Danyetta saw this as confirmation of his previous opinion. He decided to punish the Duke for this second public snub by doing exactly what he'd told him to do — get lost.

'It was childish but it didn't start out as an intention to do evil. Things soon got out of hand and before long the unfortunate fellow found he was doing things that only made his situation a great deal worse. Soon he could see no way out of the mess he'd got himself into. The real problem is that Danyetta lacks insight — many people lack insight, it's not a crime — that led him to do things that took him further and further from any chance of a favourable outcome.

'Go and talk to him Devallian, and when you do, bear in mind what I've said. I think you'll find him a pathetic figure, not the epitome of evil most people think him. Without the gift of insight, the poor fellow faces a bleak future because he cannot accept that his present situation is the direct consequence of his own actions and not a conspiracy against him by people he once thought his friends and colleagues.'

'Do you visit him, Gylan?' Calthea asked.

'I try to see him every week. After all, I sentenced him to his present lonely existence so I take responsibility for making sure he is coping.'

'You make me feel very guilty. I shall also visit him from time to time. When next you visit, may I come with you? However much he tried to hurt us, he's still a member of the community; we shouldn't leave everything to his guards.'

Before leaving, Devallian assured the professor that he would visit the prisoner then enquired where he could find Phillestra.

'She's at her Maths class; it'll be over in ten minutes. You'd better not leave without seeing her Devallian; I don't want her sulking all afternoon.' He promised.

Devallian kept both his promises; he spent an hour with Phillestra then later he visited Danyetta. The engineer refused to speak to him at first — after all he'd acted as prosecutor — but when Devallian told him he wanted to understand why he'd disappeared in the first place since that had been the cause of all his troubles, the prisoner began to open up and they had a useful conversation. Devallian was able to convince him that the Duke had never wished him harm, indeed, that their leader had the highest regard for everyone who served his mission.

*****

Three weeks before the launch, the Duke visited Paradisia and quizzed Calthea on Phillestra's progress.

'She's been helping me make recordings in the parapendia,' Calthea reported, 'her *mentori* is also nearly ready; it's working out very well. I've layered the contents so she'll receive guidance appropriate to her stage of development.'

'How will that work?'

'Do you remember what I told you about the way parapendia work? In each parapendium, I've layered the information so novices get access to basic information and those who are more advanced gain access to more advanced information; the way a question is phrased determines the level of the archive that can be accessed. I've used the same principle in programming Phillestra's *mentori*; it will keep track of her questions and thus know the stage she's reached in her development; having done so, it will give her guidance appropriate to that stage.'

'Wouldn't it be simpler to keep track of time?'

'No, because her experience of time is going to be distorted as she travels in Space — you must know that having travelled extensively yourself. Anyway, I'm not competent to do the Maths necessary for keeping accurate track of time; what I've done should work well enough.

'It does seem Phillestra's visit has turned out very well. Everyone I've talked to says she's bright and an enthusiastic pupil. I wasn't sure it was a sensible idea for you to spend time together, but she has certainly matured during this time with you. I hope you haven't formed too close a bond; I hope you won't be deeply hurt when you have to say *goodbye* to each other.'

'I'll certainly miss Phillestra; she's fun to be with and endlessly stimulating, but I won't die of a broken heart — and neither will she. It's good that Devallian visits her here; they're very close and that will spare her much anguish when parting from her parents and her friends.

'By the way Versain, she often asks after the Empress; we haven't seen Her Majesty here since the second launch. With Vyvyan no longer in Paradisia, I realise there's less reason for her to visit, but Phillestra would dearly like to spend time with her before the launch; I know the Empress will be there but it'll be a public event.'

'It's a good point, Calthea. Versilla has been recruiting the twenty Mothers for the Hybrid Project, a difficult task at the best of times; but she's decided to combine it with a rather dangerous scheme. She....'

'*Dangerous*? Whatever is she up to?'

'She'll certainly be in deep trouble if things go wrong. She's worried that we're still bringing new cherubs into a world on the verge of destruction — as indeed am I. Do you remember the cherubs abducted on the day after our marriage?'

'How could I forget that terrible morning? I was worried for Phillestra's safety.'

'Vyvyan and I had ensured that those particular cherubs didn't survive to enter a world due to become stardust in a few years time. Of course we couldn't prevent *all* births without announcing the coming of the meteor. Versilla is planning something similar to coincide with her recruitment of the Mothers.'

'What's her plan?'

'She has identified the twenty Mothers she wants to send but she's going to have to tell them why they're being asked to vanish from the world, so she has to be able to trust them. She wants each of them to destroy the Gene Bank at their Mother House before leaving; that should prevent any further births until the banks can be re-supplied. They must all be destroyed simultaneously to prevent counter measures being taken, which means that her chosen Mothers must also vanish simultaneously.

'As Empress, she will insist on investigating the situation herself — she doesn't entirely trust the present Motherhood Supremo. She's playing a tricky game Calthea, but it should prevent a great many births till we're ready to announce the coming of the meteor and can ban all future births.'

'Oh, I do hope she takes care, Versain. I suppose, as Monarch, she can keep control over things.'

'She can, but it will take only one slip-up or one disaffected person and she could find herself in a lot of trouble very rapidly.'

'When you see her, will you give her my love? And please say I'll be praying for her safety and the success of her mission.'

Chapter 17

The Third Expedition

For Calthea, time seemed to be flying by at a terrifying rate; it was going to be a rush to complete all her projects before the last spaceship's departure and there was still a great deal she needed to tell her daughter.

'I want say something about firestone and fire-crystal, Phillestra. You've seen how good fire-crystal is at storing large quantities of data in an organised way but that's not all these magical materials can do. They are both excellent communications media but they work in different ways.'

'What does *communications media* mean?' Phillestra loved to ask questions.

'Something that lets people talk to each other at a distance, and even over vast distances. You're familiar with my ruby responders — you now have one of your own — but they only transmit short messages over comparatively short distances; firestone facilitates communication over very great distances.'

'Do you have to shout very loud for your message to carry?'

'Don't be flippant Phillestra, this is important, so please pay attention.'

'Sorry, Ma.'

'How do the ruby responders work; how do they transmit your message?'

'You told me about that when I first came, but I'm not sure

I remember.'

'Then you had better try harder.'

'Hmm… it was to do with sending your *thoughts* to the other person; that's right isn't it? You have to *think* into the ruby then the other person with a tuned ruby must focus their thoughts on the sender. That's it, isn't it?'

'And do you remember what that process is called.'

'It's called *telepathy*; most people think it doesn't exist because it doesn't depend on sound waves or any other sort of radiation; they think it's a load of moonshine.'

'And do you think telepathy is a load of moonshine, Phillestra?'

'How can I when I've seen you and my royal father talking to each other when he's in Cander — or some other place — and you're in Paradisia? But how is firestone better at doing that than a ruby responder?'

'It's a lot more sensitive and more… *comprehensive* in its ability to transmit not only messages but also non-verbal thought.'

'And what does that mean? How is it more comprehensive?'

'It means that if your father was on Phobos say, which is a very long way away, he'd get my message as fast and as clearly as if he was here. He'd not only hear my words but see anything I was seeing and hear anything I was hearing. In other words, with firestone, conversing is like standing next to the person you're talking to — it's better in a way, because you also know what they're thinking and feeling.'

'How do you know, Ma? Have you sent one of your new devices to Phobos?'

'Not to Phobos, but I did try some experiments with Devallian when he was on Verastra; it was as if he was here. Physical distance isn't relevant because firestone mediates communication in *mental* space; it transmits messages directly from mind to mind. No matter how far apart you are, conversation will be immediate — no having to wait while your message travels through Space and the reply comes back to you.'

'I remember you told me that you had to tune ruby responders to each other so they could be used in pairs or sets. Do you also have to tune firestone?'

'No I don't; it's a good question, Phillestra. It seems that firestone is already tuned to itself. Fire-crystal isn't as good for communicating as firestone but it has other properties; it's as if bits of fire-crystal know where other bits of fire-crystal are even if those bits have been apart for some time. I was given a piece of fire-crystal to experiment on; later, I received other samples. I was astonished to find that, if I held one piece in my hand, I knew without looking where all the other pieces were.

'It's hard to explain so perhaps I'd better show you. Close your eyes and hold your *mentori* in your hand. Now, tell me where the parapendia are at this moment.'

'How do I do that, Ma? Oh! I see what you mean... I can't describe it but I just know they're in the cupboard behind where you're standing.'

Phillestra opened her eyes.

'It was very strange; I could tell where they were but how did I know? I didn't feel any vibration or anything, I just *knew*.'

'You knew because you had a question in your mind: *where are the parapendia*? It's as if fire-crystal is intelligent; it seems able to read our minds. Maybe that's why I was able to organise the data stored in them; fire-crystal seems to understand how questions and answers work. The truth is. I don't really know what happens. It's a mystery, but it's something you should remember. It might prove useful.'

'Ma, I've been wondering if I can use my *mentori* to record my own thoughts. It would be lovely if I could tell you what's going on in my life. You'll be talking to me as I grow older so I'd like to be able to talk to you as well. I know you won't actually hear what I say, but it would be like having you there — though at a distance — to tell you how I'm getting along. Does that sound silly?'

'It doesn't sound silly at all; in fact, I think it's a great idea, darling. I'll show you how you can do that. You can use your *mentori* as your personal diary; you can record important events as well as your ideas.'

'Did you know Ma, Marima Serenity keeps *two* diaries? One is for her official engagements and the thoughts and opinions she doesn't mind posterity knowing about; that diary will be put in the State Archives when she enters the Caves; that's what she says. But she keeps another secret diary for her personal thoughts, which certainly won't be sent to the Archives.

'In fact, now I come to think of it, she asked me not to mention it to anyone in case they tried to steal it. I shouldn't have told you Ma, so please forget I did. I don't want to disappoint Marima Serenity by breaking my promise.'

'If you make a promise like that, Phillestra, it is a matter of honour to keep it. I shall certainly not mention it to anyone. The Empress is right to be cautious; if that diary should fall into the wrong hands it could put her life at risk.'

'Gosh! How awful. But why would it put her life at risk just because someone reads her private journal?'

'Just think about it, Phillestra. She's bound to mention her work for your father but that work is very secret; if the wrong people found out, your father could be at risk too. The Empress might also mention Paradisia….'

'Why would she write about a place she's never been to?'

'Because she *has* been here — many times. The Empress has been working for us for many years. That shouldn't come as a surprise now that you know your father is our leader. I hope this lapse of yours will teach you that when you promise to keep something secret Phillestra, you absolutely must not break that promise — unless it is morally wrong to keep silent.'

'When would it be morally *right* to break a promise? Would it be OK if the secret referred to something illegal?'

'Not necessarily. Strictly speaking, this community is illegal. Sometimes what is *strictly* illegal may be *morally* justified. I'll ask Professor Bahle to talk to you about this, because you're clearly able to understand the issues involved. Now I'd like to explain more about how the fire-crystal globes work. Take out one of the parapendia, hold it to your forehead using both hands and tell me what happens.'

'Nothing happens. It just feels very heavy and a bit hot.'

'Now, ask a question, something you don't know but would like to know.'

'Oh! How astonishing! It's told me something very odd.'

'Tell me what you asked and what the parapendium answered.'

Phillestra carefully replaced the globe on the bench and turned to her Mother.

'I asked about Oracle, the person you said told my royal father to set up the community. I asked why she had left the world before the meteor came because that seemed wrong. If this Oracle person could see the future, why didn't she stay and warn people that the meteor was about to arrive so they'd be able to escape in time?'

'Your father has told you it won't be possible to save everyone because there's only one spaceship left — the *Brave Endeavour* — and there's no possibility of building more spaceships in the time remaining. What answer did the parapendium give?'

Calthea was intrigued; she hadn't covered this issue when

loading the device.

'It said some things were too mysterious for me to understand. It said a being like Oracle didn't need to comply with ordinary standards of behaviour, because she was guided by the Immortal Powers. That's odd, don't you agree, Ma? I thought the Immortal Powers would take not the slightest notice of what angels did or didn't do. I thought they would be too concerned with more important matters.'

'I agree, it's a pretty mysterious answer but then Oracle is — or was — a pretty mysterious person. I only met her twice, but if there's one word to describe her it would be *mysterious*. Anyway, this gives you some idea of how the parapendia work. Ask the same question in a year or two and it will probably give a different answer.'

I'd dearly like to know what that answer would be Calthea mused but she kept that thought to herself. 'You've felt how heavy a parapendium is;' she continued, 'that's why I've made separate readers. I find emerald best for extracting information.

'Take this emerald and put it to your forehead just above your eyes. This is the *third eye*; it's where the eye of your mind talks to your brain. Focus your attention on the emerald and ask the parapendium another question, perhaps something you've studied at school.'

'I've been given an answer… but it keeps on going… Goodness! It's amazing.'

'Put the emerald down; tell me what happened. What was your question?'

'I asked what sort of event could possibly destroy an entire world and it came up with a whole list of possibilities. It said that the centre of the world could become unstable and set off a great many volcanoes that would split the world into bits. Do you think that could happen, Ma? Could something like that destroy the world?'

'It's possible. What other suggestions did it have?'

'It said a comet or a meteor could crash on to the surface, or cause one of our moons to become unstable in its orbit and fall out of the sky. Perhaps horrid dark Meon will fall out of the sky; after all, everyone calls it the *evil moon*.'

'We've already told you about the prophecy — that a meteor is coming — it could be that its arrival will unsettle one of the moons and make it collide with the planet before the meteor does. What else did it say?'

'Oh, it went on and on. It quoted probabilities for the different disasters; most of which were *extremely* remote.'

'Enough of such gruesome things! Was it easier when you used the emerald?'

'It was much lighter and I think it was better at moving around.'

'I know what you mean: the reader is quicker and more thorough at locating answers than the parapendium on its own.' Calthea held the parapendium up to the light, 'It's so beautiful and so very intelligent.' she mused more to herself than to her daughter. 'The dwarves only let me have samples of firestone and fire-crystal as a great favour; before that, they'd been a closely guarded secret.

'Dwarves treat these materials with great reverence Phillestra, and I was asked to respect them too. I want you to promise you will also treat the parapendia, your *mentori* and the firestone pebbles with respect, in honour of the dwarves' generosity.'

'I promise, Marima; *and* I'll remember what you said about keeping promises.'

'Good. The globes will be safe during your long journey; our dwarves have made special obsidian boxes for them and our elves have polished and carved those boxes and will pack the globes and their readers into them with soft cherub-down.

'Now, I'd like to tell you about the firestone pebbles; they're simpler devices than the parapendia but they're much better at aiding communication. I love holding them; they're alive.' She gave Phillestra a pebble, 'Do you feel it too?'

'There's something you should remember about these pebbles: if you want to talk to a person who speaks another language, remember that telepathy uses Metalya to communicate. What might be the significance of that? Do you remember what I told you about Metalya?'

'Hmm.... You said language uses Metalya to assign meaning when choosing the words you want to say or when understanding what's being said to you. Right?'

'Right. Give one of the pebbles to Devallian and to anyone else you might want to contact at a distance. I'll keep one too; so for a while we can stay in touch. What shall we call the pebbles?

'What about *peblos*?'

'That'll do nicely. I'll give you a box of *peblos* to take with you.'

'I shall give one to my royal father; then I can talk to him as well as to you till… till you know when!'

'Wear your *peblo* round your neck, Phillestra — I'll have them all made up as pendants — then you'll know when someone wants to speak to you.'

'Do they vibrate, like the ruby responders?'

'No, it's more subtle, more like when you held your *mentori* to your head and asked where the parapendia were.'

'Thank you Ma, these are wonderful, wonderful presents. I'm very lucky.'

* * * * *

All too soon the day of the launch was upon them and Calthea had to prepare for the coming separation. Empress Serenity had come to Paradisia early to spend a full day with Phillestra. She also told Calthea that the Mothers she'd chosen for the expedition had destroyed their Gene Banks before leaving, fortunately without any suspicion falling upon her; she'd already started her sham-investigation.

The Empress travelled with Calthea and Phillestra by shuttle to Verastra; they joined the group gathering beside the spaceship. Some days previously, Calthea had given the Duke the five boxes containing the parapendia and their emerald readers plus a box of *peblos*; presumably they were now safely on board. Phillestra wouldn't part with her *mentori* even for those few days; she clutched it close to her chest.

Master Tang was still on board giving the crew its final briefing. Devallian was deep in conversation with the Duke; his recently recruited soldiers, proudly sporting new regimental sashes, formed a guard of honour round the ship. Empress Serenity was talking to the Mothers she'd chosen for the Hybrid Project and introducing them to various community members.

In fact, all Paradisia had come to speed the expedition on its way; only two members were actually leaving on the *Brave Endeavour* this time round. Calthea was relieved that Chrysilla wasn't one of them; she was being sent on another assignment and that had saved her from having to volunteer again.

Queen Scintilla was surrounded by a cluster of elves; most would be leaving to found an elfin colony on Luna. The Queen had appointed Princess Fragilaine as their leader; she looked too young and too delicate to be faced with such a responsible mission. Laughter and excited chatter came from this group; elves, when free from oppression, were a naturally fun-loving people.

The Third Expedition

The construction site, scene of frenzied activity for so many years, was virtually deserted; the crew's dwarves had left to join their fellows on Stellaster. Most of the younger crew members had either departed as crew on one of the first two spacecraft or would be joining this final one; the older workers had stayed to watch their ship take to the skies; they would then return to Paradisia for a long and well-earned rest.

Maestro Arbrecht struck a bronze gong to open the proceedings; the Duke told the assembled company that the two earlier expeditions had left Phobos, heading for Luna. They should have established settlements there by the time *Brave Endeavour* joined them. The last spaceship would still head for Phobos where the company would rest until Earth was in a favourable position for them to set off for Luna.

Eight of the community's ten shuttles would accompany the expedition; they'd provide transport between Luna and Earth once the Hybrid Project was ready to start work. That meant that only two shuttles remained to take the spectators home; that was no problem, there would be very few of them now left.

The Duke invited members of the third expedition to board the ship; as soon as the elves and Mothers were on board, Devallian went over to Calthea who gave her daughter a final hug. Phillestra made dutiful curtsies to the Duke and the Empress then took Devallian's arm, in clear excitement at the adventure about to unfold.

Calthea heard her daughter ask: 'Do I have to address you as *Commander* on board, Devallian? My royal father says I must as you're such an important person.'

She laughed happily, dancing along at her new guardian's side. Calthea did not catch his reply.

They boarded and the door-panel closed behind them; immediately the vessel began to rise majestically from the ground with its escort of soldiers flying alongside; when the ship was clear of the moon's gravity, the soldiers embarked and the space-ship continued its ascent. During the ascent, the Maestro played Girilayne's Lament on his lute as a final farewell.

The escorting shuttles kept formation as her trajectory took the *Brave Endeavour* over the horizon and she vanished from sight. For long, those left behind stared in numb dismay at the empty sky. Calthea now realised how clever the Duke had been to separate her and her cherub all those years before; she was sad but not over-whelmed by this parting.

She recalled what the Duke had said the previous evening when he'd called in to see her on his way up to Verastra:

You will have a greater part to play in Phillestra's future than I will, Calthea. You will continue to educate and guide her for many years to come through the mentori you've given her. My influence will be less direct; I have trained and guided Devallian and he will be her living mentor as she grows to adulthood. I suppose we've each done the best any responsible parent could be expected to do.

He'd shown her the *peblo* Phillestra had just given him.

I'm so grateful to have this. It means I can keep in touch with her and with Devallian until.... I gather that you have kept one too. He'd chuckled as he asked: *Do you remember how angry you were when I tore you away from your life in the city to come here to make these miraculous devices? I know you've long forgiven me but I'd like to know that it has been worthwhile — that bringing you here has given you a fulfilling life.*

She'd told him how very much richer her life in Paradisia had been compared to anything she could have expected as an academic. He'd taken her hands in his but abruptly dropped them as if he was in danger of showing too much emotion; then he'd left immediately to board his shuttle for Verastra.

Now, as she stood beside the Duke savouring the historic

moment, Calthea was aware of a deep sense of peace percolating through her being. They'd done what Oracle had told them to do: they'd sent Stellaster's precious gems to another world for safe-keeping; surely one of the most precious was this child she and Versain had called down into the world — the delightful Phillestra.

What became of their efforts was no longer in their hands — now others must take up the baton. Deep within her being, she prayed to the Immortal Powers, asking that they take good care of all those precious gems and especially of her daughter.

After what seemed an age and without saying a word, the Duke turned to offer his arm to the elfin queen; he led the group of elves to the shuttle waiting to take them to Senton Elftown. He then boarded the other shuttle, which carried the few remaining spectators back to Paradisia, each wrapped in stunned silence.

Chapter 18

A Twist in the Tale

Still Sol's acolytes orbit in faithful attendance: Mercury in the hot seat; Venus swathed in her dense shawl; ice-capped Earth, her continents lathed by vast oceans and circling above, scarred Luna. Then Mars with her two satellites, her ocean tinged lilac by its red bedrock; next dark Meon and rosy Verastra contrasting with Stellaster's golden sands; then Jupiter, greatest of the Gas Giants, those ponderous worlds each a sun-system with its own attendant acolytes; and all these worlds, great and small, moving around Sol in a courtly quadrille, as they have done for billions of years.

And the meteor — massive, dark and dense — scything its solitary path through the empty reaches of Space towards its ever-nearing target; invisible to the telescopes that nightly scan the skies in fruitless search.

Destiny closes; the established order in Sol's bailiwick will not remain so for long.

A Great Being once said; 'You wish me to give you assurances Empress, that the universe will not continue to move in accordance with its Destiny; that the Immortal Powers will intervene to save this one small world of the myriad worlds that crowd the heavens.'

But the plans of the Immortal Powers are not revealed to mere mortals: that which they will to happen will happen, no matter the hopes of the denizens of that one small world, or the consequences for those they have sent away so trustfully to safety.

* * * * *

With the final spaceship safely on its way to Luna, the few members remaining in Paradisia now turned their attention to the final phase of their mission — preparing the planet's population for the destruction of their world. Once more the Duke called a conference in his cave and this time he invited his sister to join them since she was on retreat at Sriandra.

Kinver-Kritten began by confirming that there had been, as yet, no sighting of the meteor. His team of astronomers kept constant vigil from the observatory on Verastra, scanning the skies for the least clue. It meant they could not yet inform the State Council of the coming catastrophe.

'But we must say something to the authorities very soon,' the Empress argued. 'Perhaps we could reveal things to carefully-chosen officials a little at a time so they can begin making plans.'

'But, Majesty,' Malgan-Mandow protested, 'why would anyone believe what we say? There is still no tangible proof; nothing has changed; we still face what we have always faced — a lack of any concrete evidence to support the prophecy.'

'But I feel less and less inclined to wait for that proof, Professor. If we tell them that all of us at this meeting endorse the prediction — even if it means revealing that we are in breach of certain laws — then surely our warning must be taken seriously. I suggest we prepare a confidential report for the State Council, endorsed by all of us here — that is, if everyone is willing to be quoted — telling them about the prophecy.'

'I see the merits of your plan, Versilla.' The Duke paused in thought. 'It would certainly give those in authority more time to make practical arrangements.'

'And Versain, we really must tell the Emperor; I'm sure

he'll prove a valuable ally. I see no reason to keep the prophecy from him any longer; don't you agree? He will be invaluable in helping people to prepare for the turbulent times ahead.'

'I agree; there's a lot to be gained by bringing Wellbeloved on board. Persuade the Emperor to take the prophecy seriously and we're halfway there.'

'Fine!' The Empress now spoke directly to her twin, 'So we tell Council about the prophecy, but then what? We must have advice ready to help them deal with the situation. But try as I might, I simply cannot think of a way of preparing the millions who are going to lose their lives in the coming catastrophe.'

'I agree, Your Majesty.' Malgan added. 'The total destruction of our planet and the extinction of all living beings is a terrible prospect for anyone to take on board.'

'I'm not sure I feel quite so pessimistic.' Everyone was surprised at Chrysilla's intervention; this was her first attendance as a Council member. She went on; 'Perhaps we're approaching the situation in the wrong way. It's true, this will be a *global* catastrophe, but its impact will definitely be felt *personally*. After all, each of us is a centre of awareness and must face our approaching demise in our own unique way. Therein lies our opportunity to help.'

There was a puzzled silence as everyone sought to grasp the point the young philosopher was trying to make. Finally, light dawned upon her mentor.

'It is as you say, Chrysilla.' Professor Bahle was beaming with approval. 'We must adopt a different perspective; we must put the individual at the centre of our thinking rather than trying to make plans for the world as a whole. I am glad you have made this important point.'

The Empress, still looking dazed, asked, 'Could you elaborate, Professor? I'd like to understand how a change in perspective will help us in our present dilemma.'

'Your Majesty, Chrysilla is reminding us that we must put the individual at the centre of our planning; we need to establish what each person will need to help him or her face death with courage and optimism, rather than in terror and anguish. Most people don't consider death as something that will happen to them until just before their Due Departure Date; then death becomes a highly significant matter. But people are always offered support as they prepare for entering the Caves.

'For example, farewell ceremonies are held that not only help those who will be left behind, but also support the person who is about to leave by instilling feelings of gratitude and appreciation for the life they have lived. Great consolation comes also through music, poetry and the sharing of precious memories. Why do we not adopt these same principles? We must devise programmes that help individuals rather than planning for populations. Chrysilla's suggestion gives us plenty to think about.'

The professor was still beaming at his protégé. He continued, 'I do commend my young friend for reminding us of the real issue. We need to consult the Seraphim; the Seraphim help us to prepare before entering the Caves, and they help us design our farewell ceremonies.'

'I endorse Chrysilla's point,' Calthea grinned broadly at her friend. 'I believe we should follow Professor Bahle's suggestion and consult the Seraphim; we should invite them to work with us in this final phase of our mission. At Sriandra, I came to appreciate the depth of wisdom the Seraphim possess, but they won't come to us, they wait to be asked before offering advice. I believe we should make that approach.

The Empress nodded, 'I agree, we must ask the Seraphim; the Seraphina is right to remind us how much wisdom there is in Sriandra. Let's ask for their help and guidance. It's a monumental undertaking: a million people needing support and only a handful of us to provide it, especially if we have to wait for confirmation that the meteor really is on its way.'

'Your Majesty, may I make a suggestion?' Chrysilla was gaining confidence from the ready acceptance of her earlier contribution. 'We members of the Duke's community have felt it an honour to serve his mission. I'm sure that many who are *not* members of the community would feel the same. Once they know of the coming crisis, people will want to help in any way they can; in fact, we could well face an avalanche of volunteers.

'May I add, Your Majesty, that having work to do has kept our minds busy so that we have not had time to be worrying constantly about things beyond our power to control or change. Should it not be part of our plan to give that same advantage to members of the public — to give them something to do that helps their fellow angels face the crisis? All of us here are well aware that *service* gives meaning and value to our lives.'

There was a general nodding of heads so the Duke closed the discussion:

'We agree? Good. In my view, the Empress is the best person to deliver our invitation to the Seraphim; she represents both the community and the State Council. Agreed?... Good. And let's make Chrysilla's further suggestion the basis for our planning.... Now, Arbrecht, how are things progressing with your opera project?'

'I'm very happy to report that....'

As he spoke, a figure appeared in the entrance; all heads turned in surprise; who'd have the effrontery to interrupt the Duke's conference? Versain recognised the visitor as Captain Mandavine who had replaced Devallian as his ADC.

'I hope this is important, Captain.' The Duke spoke in his

most authoritarian tones, 'I did not give you leave to come here.'

'I come from the Palace with an urgent message, my Lord. May I speak to you in private?'

The Duke left the cave and joined his aide on the terrace outside.

'Who sent you, Captain?' The Duke demanded.

'It was the Emperor himself, my Lord. He asked if I knew where I could find you and, as it was an emergency, I felt you would expect me to use my initiative.'

'Very well. Make your report.'

'My Lord, the Emperor asks you to return to Cander immediately. A grave emergency has arisen. Late last night, a badly injured officer staggered to the palace gates and told the guard that there was mutiny in Cavalin Barracks. He could only mutter the name of the ring-leader before he succumbed to his injuries and died.'

'Good Heavens! What was the name?'

'He was out of breath and extremely weak, but the guard said it sounded like Captain Morgan Trixon.'

'What regiments are based at Cavalin at present?'

'The Fourth Palace Guard, and the Surveillance Corps.'

'Could the name have been Turven Chixon?'

'I couldn't say sir; I didn't see the messenger. Could this Turven Chixon be behind the mutiny?'

'We shall see. You did well in coming, Captain; I will return to the Palace immediately. Did you tell the Emperor where I was?'

'No my Lord, His Majesty didn't ask; he asked if I knew where you could be reached and, if so, to request you to return immediately to deal with this crisis.'

'Good. I wish to remind you that this place is not to be mentioned under any circumstances, unless or until I tell you otherwise. You must not mention that you have seen the Empress here; as far as you know, Empress Serenity is on retreat at Sriandra.'

'Return to the Palace; tell His Majesty I am following with all haste. Tell him also that I have instructed you to proceed to Cavalin with a troop of experienced trackers. Select the best scouts available; find out anything you can without risking capture or injury. There's a cave near the barracks used by the local dwarves as their base. Do you know this cave?'

'I do, Commander.'

'Good. Meet me there tomorrow at noon to report what you have been able to discover. Tell Manika, the local dwarf chief, that you are acting on my instructions and request the assistance of his dwarves in discovering the cause of this mutiny. Please make clear, I am *requesting* his help, not demanding it; dwarves are our loyal allies. And Captain, when addressing the dwarf chief, please address him with the respect you would accord any senior officer. Do you understand?'

'I do my Lord. I have noted the respect with which you treat all dwarves, and will follow your example in this as in all things.'

'I intensely dislike flattery, Captain. I thought you would know that by now.'

'I would not presume to use flattery, my Lord; I simply wished to show that I appreciate the importance of your order.'

'Well, well! You'd better be off. This is a chance to demonstrate your military skills. I'll meet you at noon tomorrow and will then decide what's best to so.'

The ADC saluted and vanished westwards to Cander. The Duke re-entered the cave to an atmosphere of intense curiosity.

'This couldn't be more irritating,' he burst out in frustration. 'It seems an old wound is still festering and has come to a head at this most inconvenient of times. There's mutiny in the Cavalin Barracks. Does the name *Captain Turven Chixon* ring any bells, Versilla?'

'Wasn't that the name of the officer who was trying to sir up trouble in the Palace some years ago? You were worried because he was dropping hints about a secret construction site on Verastra. Am I right?'

'You are; this captain is at the root of the mutiny at Cavalin.'

'Is that the old wound you refer to, Versain?'

'It is, Calthea; Chixon was the pawn of our old friend Danyetta.'

'But I thought Danyetta acted alone when he destroyed my gemstones.'

'He did, on that occasion; but when he disappeared he tried to stir up trouble by persuading this Chixon fellow to turn scandal-monger. But Danyetta can't be involved in this present affair; he's here, safely behind bars. I suspect Chixon is resentful because he didn't get a promotion half-promised by Devallian.

'Many years ago, Devallian effectively silenced this troublesome officer by dispatching him on a wild-goose-chase after non-existent terrorists; he dangled a possible promotion as reward for success, but of course that wasn't going to happen. I dare say when Devallian was promoted to colonel, Chixon thought he'd put a spoke in his wheel; perhaps he hopes to embarrass Devallian through this mutiny. If so, he's going to be disappointed; Devallian isn't here to answer for that deception; he's far away commanding a spaceship.'

'How serious is this threat, Versain?'

'Now that we know about it, Silla, we should be able to crush it easily. But the timing is unfortunate to say the least. Here we are considering how best to inform the State Council about the meteor and this situation blows up to spike our guns.'

'I don't follow your logic, Versain. Why should this affect our plans?'

'Because if we now get Council to announce a State of Emergency, citing an unconfirmed meteor strike, everyone will assume I'm only diverting attention from this disaffection in the ranks; it would be a crude strategy but people will believe it's my real motive.'

'I really do despair!' The Duke continued passionately, 'There's obviously a deep flaw in our psyche. Here we are, priding ourselves on having saved our unique culture for posterity, dispatching spacecraft to another world, when this destructive tendency has to rear its ugly head and put a spoke in our wheels.'

'For more than twenty years, there's been peace — no wars, not even a minor skirmish. But it seems we don't want peace! Something drives us to destroy what we've striven so hard to attain. It's as though there's a demon gnawing away at our souls, driving us to disrupt any enduring peace out of a trivial desire for excitement or perhaps through sheer boredom. And I simply cannot *bear* it.'

For a time everyone stared at the Duke, stunned by his uncharacteristic out-burst of anger. The Empress went to his side and put a hand on his arm.

'You can't blame our entire species for the silliness of a bunch of soldiers, Versain. Soldiers are chosen for their willingness and ability to fight. Of course they want to display those talents from time to time. But surely military discipline should have stepped in and nipped this trouble in the bud. Was discipline at the Cavalin barracks deficient in some regard — was it too harsh or too lax?'

'I agree, Versain,' the Maestro added, seeking to pacify his friend. 'Let's not tar our entire species with the shortcomings of a bunch of squaddies. Perhaps this will cause us to delay a little before we approach Council but there's still plenty of time. You'd better go and stamp out this mutiny as quickly as you can so we can get on with more important matters.'

'I dare say you're right, Arbrecht. But I wonder whether Oracle might not have made a grave mistake in getting us to preserve our culture, when it carries buried within it this self-destructive canker. Perhaps the gods are right to send this meteor to wipe out our race once and for all — and here we are doing our very best to counter their intention.'

'Please keep faith in your mission, Versain,' Gylan pleaded. 'There's good and bad in each of us, surely that's part of our strength. Without it, where's the merit in striving for good? Deal with this mutiny then we can get on with our work.'

'I'll return to Cander immediately, but I hope we can make progress with our plans while I'm away. We should go ahead and consult the Seraphim; Versilla, you must return to Sriandra today; take Calthea and Chrysilla with you. If there's trouble brewing, I'd like to know all three of you are safe in the care of the Seraphim.'

* * * * *

Gylan was examining a scroll he'd just received from Sriandra when his ruby responder began to vibrate. It was the Duke.

'Gylan, there's some very distressing news that I want you to share with our colleagues in Paradisia; Calthea, as you're listening too, please pass this news to the Empress and to Chief Seraph Godwinian. Mandavine is on his way to Paradisia and will give you a full account. I'm sorry to report, the Emperor has been assassinated.'

In Paradisia Gylan exclaimed, *'What!'* and in Sriandra

Calthea simultaneously enquired, '*What* did you say?'

'It was an unfortunate accident but technically an assassination; the Emperor was killed by an arrow loosed by a mutineer. I'll leave Mandavine to recount the full story; the mutiny is over but its aftermath certainly isn't. Calthea, you and Chrysilla had better return to Paradisia. Please ask the Empress to return to Cander as soon as she can; all is safe, she's in no danger, but she's needed here and there are things we have to discuss.'

The Duke ended the call but Calthea and Gylan remained in contact.

'This is terrible news, Gylan. We'll return as soon as I can find Chrissy.'

'Yes, yes please do; I'm glad the Duke is safe and the mutiny quashed. I do hope Captain Mandavine arrives soon.'

'... and that Chrissy and I arrive before him; we'll want to hear his story too. I must go and find the Empress. It'll come as a terrible shock; she was very fond of the Emperor and will miss him greatly. I'd better say goodbye.'

'Have a safe journey, Seraphina.'

The disastrous news created shockwaves in both Paradisia and Sriandra, everyone wanted to know the full story. Late that evening, an exhausted Mandavine presented himself at the entrance to the Paradisia compound. He was detained by a suspicious guard who, unwilling to admit a complete stranger to the headquarters of the Duke's secret community, sent a colleague in search of Professor Bahle. Gylan came personally to welcome the Duke's ADC; he escorted him to his own room.

'My dear fellow,' he exclaimed, 'you look done in. I insist you rest for at least an hour before you even try to talk. Please lie on my couch; I shall arrange for a room to be placed at your disposal while you are here.'

To prevent further conversation Gylan left in search of

Calthea and Chrysilla, who had returned only an hour before. He found them in Chrysilla's room.

'Gylan, has Captain Mandavine arrived?' Calthea demanded as soon as his head appeared around the door.

'He's in my room but far too exhausted to talk. He probably had much to do before setting out on his journey. Please join me in my room in an hour to hear what he has to report, I'm on my way to invite the Maestro and Malgan to join us. The Master is returning from Verastra tomorrow and will hear the news then.'

The professor's room was lit only by a couple of fluorescent rocks; even in the dim light Calthea and Chrysilla could see how gaunt the young ADC looked. Gylan told them that their visitor had slept only two hours the previous night and wished to get his briefing over so he could have a long sleep before returning to Cander.

'We'll dispense with introductions, Captain.' Gylan said, 'Please tell us what happened. All we know is that one of the mutineers has managed to assassinate our very much loved Emperor Wellbeloved.'

'I'll begin at the beginning. I was sent by the Emperor to ask the Commander-in-Chief to return to Cander because there'd been an incident at the Cavalin barracks; an officer had been badly injured in that incident but escaped; he managed to get to the Palace to report the mutiny but succumbed to his injuries at the gates.

'The C-in-C asked me to return immediately and tell the Emperor he was on his way; he also told me to initiate enquiries at Cavalin to establish what had been going on. When I got to the palace, I found that the Emperor had set out for Cavalin to try and resolve the situation himself. He believed the soldiers would respond to a personal appeal from their Emperor.

'He took only a dozen of his personal guards with him;

those guards aren't soldiers Professor, they're aristocrats chosen for their social graces not their martial skills. The Emperor's unarmed escort came under attack as it entered a narrow defile guarding the entrance to Cavalin barracks; the ambushers didn't know they were attacking their own Monarch. By the worst possible misfortune, a stray arrow struck the Emperor in the heart; the archer certainly hadn't intended to kill anyone; he only wanted to prevent the party from entering the barracks.

'It was only when the Emperor's escort cried out: *Stop! You are attacking the Emperor of Stellaster* that the ambushers realised the trouble they were in. Then the escort saw that their Emperor had been hit and lay dying. The mutineers were appalled at what they'd done; they threw down their arms and were marched into Cavalin Barracks by this band of brave but totally untrained guards, escorting a litter on which lay the now-deceased body of their Emperor.

'I learned all this when I arrived at Cavalin an hour later. The Royal Duke had told me to recruit a team of scouts; instead I took a company of soldiers from my own regiment as it was clear the Emperor might be in grave danger — I had little idea how grave. We arrived at the barracks an hour after the late Emperor's own cortege. By then things there were in a state of total confusion.

'I sent my troops to find the senior officers; they found them imprisoned in the strong-room. The brigadier in charge at Cavalin told me that a group of junior officers had taken control of the barracks, sent out patrols and had obviously set up ambushes on all approach roads. The brigadier arrested the dissident officers and restored order in no time.

'Those junior officers are the real culprits in this tragedy and will certainly be held to account; the ambushers were just ordinary soldiers carrying out the orders of their immediate superiors. One could argue that they should have refused to obey orders from mutinous officers but they weren't themselves actually in breach of military discipline.

'I left my soldiers to assist the brigadier in any way they could and set out to meet the C-in-C on his way to our rendezvous. When I told him what had happened, he was incandescent with rage at *this senseless outcome to a senseless mutiny* — those were his words.

'He told me he knew the officer suspected of having initiated the mutiny and would ensure that he paid the full penalty for his treason. He said I was to take an hour to rest, then I was to report to the State Council; he wanted them to hear my report at first hand. After that he sent me here to report to you, Professor.'

Captain Mandavine paused; he looked exhausted and deeply affected by the situation he'd had to cope with. He was young, barely out of the Academy, yet he'd had to take charge in one of the gravest crises to hit the Empire in a very long time. Calthea wondered whether the Duke had made due acknowledgement of his efforts.

She'd seen how tough Versain could be with Devallian in his early years as ADC, but Devallian had been mentally and emotionally strong. She wondered if the Duke's new *aide* possessed the requisite resilience for the job. She hoped so; he seemed both competent and intelligent, someone she'd like to get to know better.

'Rest now, Captain,' the professor told him. 'Calthea and Chrysilla have also come a long way today. We should all take our rest now; let's meet again at noon. Please sleep as long as you wish, Captain. You probably haven't had much chance to sleep during this terrible crisis.'

Chapter 19

A New Emperor

The assassination of a reigning Monarch in time of peace was unprecedented in the modern history of the Empire. Emperor Wellbeloved had been one of the most popular Monarchs of recent times so news of his death was met with disbelief at first and then with an outpouring of genuine grief. Not only angelis but angelas, dwarves and elves were deeply shocked by the untimely death of this gentle, compassionate and greatly loved ruler.

The Duke was also in shock at the loss of a friend and Monarch. He'd known Servenken, both at school and at the Academy and had been instrumental in getting him proclaimed Emperor after the insurrection. In return, the Emperor had accorded his friend considerable leeway in conducting his official duties; this had allowed the Duke to set up and run his clandestine community in the mountains.

Wellbeloved hadn't known about Paradisia — at least, the Duke assumed he hadn't — but Mandavine's account of what the Emperor had asked *and what he had not asked* when summoning him to deal with the mutiny, led the Duke now to doubt that assumption. Wellbeloved had been highly intuitive, so Versain would not have been surprised to learn that his Monarch had begun to suspect that his Commander-in-Chief was leading a double life.

A New Emperor

What *was* surprising was that the Emperor's pointless death had not sparked a general uprising; fortunately, the immediate reaction of the people had been grief and not anger. Those responsible were now under lock and key and would be held accountable for their wickedness at a public trial. People might not be baying for revenge but they were certainly deeply shocked and confused.

What would happen now?

The morning after the Duke's return from the Cavalin Barracks, he received a visitor. He was delighted, but also surprised, to see his friend Councillor Taitaillin, the lawyer who had defended the Galliards so brilliantly at their trial.

'Versain,' the lawyer was clearly worried as he greeted the Duke, 'I wonder if you realise what this crisis means for you, and more especially for your sister?'

'What crisis, my friend? We've quashed the mutiny and re-established the rule of law. What's your concern?'

'Let me remind you what the Constitution dictates must happen when a Monarch dies before the end of his or her term: the State Council must assume the role of interim Monarch and will rule in partnership with the consort of the deceased Monarch until a replacement is proclaimed. If it is the Empress who has departed early, the surviving Emperor is permitted to choose an Interim Empress to reign as his consort for the remainder of his term; but if it is the Emperor who dies, the Empress must relinquish her crown as soon as the new Emperor is proclaimed; she must then retire to the Caves and the new Emperor will choose his Empress.'

The Duke stared at the lawyer in dismay.

'Taitaillin, I had no knowledge of this. I haven't had a moment to think about the consequences of this pointless assassination but it sounds as though they're likely to be extremely... inconvenient, to say the least.'

For a time there was silence; the Duke was contemplating the implications of this bombshell for his mission. He'd only been able to achieve what he had because of his position as Commander-in-Chief and brother of the Empress. A new Emperor would choose not only his Empress but also his Commander-in-Chief. As soon as the new Emperor was proclaimed, Versilla would have to enter the Caves and he might be in no position to arrange one of his spectacular rescues.

The timing of the crisis was atrocious. Here they were at the very last stage of his mission, about to launch a programme to prepare people for the annihilation of their world and this crisis had to come along and scupper all their hopes and plans. There was still no proof of the truth of the prophecy, so how was he to persuade a new Emperor that his community just *had* to be allowed to continue with its crucial work — and that Versilla was an essential part of that work?

He wondered if his sister was aware of her precarious position and whether she might have ideas of her own about what could be done. He knew she'd returned from Sriandra, so he must go and consult her without delay. He was about to make his apologies to Taitaillin when Versilla swept into the room.

'Councillor Taitaillin, I was told you'd come to see the Royal Duke; I assume you have informed him that he will shortly be the *ex*-Royal Duke. He looks in a state of shock so I dare say I am right.'

'Indeed Majesty, that is the case. I also wished to find out what ideas he might have for securing the succession. My own view is that Council would be very happy if he would agree to his name being put forward. It's usual for eligible candidates to be princes in their twenties but there's good reason to waive that convention in the present circumstances.'

'Your proposal is exactly in line with my own thinking,' the Empress came over to the lawyer and gave him her hand to kiss. 'But I have a question, Councillor: is there anything in the constitution to bar Versain from choosing the *present* Empress as his consort? Is there anything to bar him from choosing his full sister — in other words *me* — as his consort?'

'One moment, *if* you please!' The Duke protested laughing, 'Before you stitch me up as your new tame Emperor, might I be allowed to offer my own opinion?'

'Only if you agree, Versain.'

'Well I don't — and you know why not, Silla. It would be torture for me to be Emperor. You might think it an honour but I'd find it tantamount to imprisonment. I can't be tied down by all that protocol and procedure; I'd feel like a puppet, always at the beck and call of courtiers and petty bureaucrats. It would *kill* me, Silla.'

'I wish you wouldn't fly off the handle without thinking things through, Versain. If you were Emperor you could….'

She stopped; she'd been on the brink of mentioning secrets she had no right to reveal in the presence of a member of the State Council. She looked guilty, which only added to the lawyer's curiosity.

'What could Lord Versain do as Emperor that he cannot do as Royal Duke, Majesty?'

'My sister is referring to a secret, but it's about time you were made party to that secret, Taitaillin. We are dismayed at the timing of this ridiculous constitutional crisis because it affects secret work we have both been engaged in for many years. You have a more flexible view of what is right and what is wrong than most lawyers but what I am about to tell you may swing even your moral compass further than you will find comfortable.'

Briefly, the Duke told the lawyer about the prophecy, the establishment of the community, the successful dispatch of three spacecraft to Luna and their plans for the final years before the arrival of the meteor. He did not mention the elders who still offered their valuable knowledge and experience for the benefit of Angelkind.

'Our problem has always been that, without a definite sighting of this meteor, the prophecy cannot be revealed to the public; there've been many false predictions of doom and all turned out to be either deliberate hoaxes or ill-founded imaginings. On the other hand, we couldn't wait for a sighting before making plans and putting those plans into effect. Our astronomers tell us that we might well have as little as a month from a first sighting to the moment of impact and the end of our world.'

'I see.' Taitaillin considered this information. 'And what persuaded you that this particular prophecy was not a hoax or an imagining, Versain?'

'Because it came from a strange being called Oracle.'

'Oh, if *Oracle* was the origin of the prophecy then I can well see why you had to take it seriously. But surely you could have told the State Council that? We'd have given you every support; I'm sure I can speak for my colleagues on that point.'

'There are very good reasons why I could not. Oracle specifically forbade me to tell anyone that she was in any way involved; a few other members of our group know of her existence, but not everyone. And now Oracle has left so cannot confirm or deny what I have told you — told you in deliberate breach of my undertaking to her, I should add. Anyway, how do *you* know about Oracle?'

'Perhaps you were not aware that Liberelli and I were....'

'Liberelli? You mean the prosecutor at our trial?'

'Yes, my mentor, the legal brain behind the arguments put forward in court. He and I were summoned to Srivalian immediately after your arrest and briefed on how we were to get you out of the sticky mess you were in.'

'I knew Oracle had had something to do with our trial — Versilla told me the old Empress sent Girilayne to consult her when we were arrested — but I didn't know she'd orchestrated the trial itself. It doesn't surprise me though; I've been finding out the many ways in which Oracle was guiding events without ever appearing in the picture herself.

'I should also point out that not all members of Council know about Oracle, Taitaillin; I know at least one who would be extremely dismissive were we to suggest that such a being was a dependable source of prophecy. No, we must proceed with caution as far as the State Council is concerned. But let's deal with this crisis then we'll know better how to protect the community and its work.'

'That's all very well Versain, but if you refuse to agree to our brilliant idea to have *you* proclaimed as Emperor, I don't see how we're going to rescue the situation.'

'*And* rescue your sister from having to enter the Caves.' The lawyer added.

'If you believe Council would accept an older prince, I would like to suggest a different Galliard, my old friend Hugorin; he's especially popular since the Jubilee; remember how he wowed the crowds at the Jubilee parade? He may possess great presence but Hugorin has the common touch; he'd be the ideal choice. The public would welcome his proclamation with far greater enthusiasm than if I were chosen; they may trust me to keep them safe — though I've let them down badly over this mutiny — but they don't *love* me as they loved Wellbeloved. I believe they'd soon come to love Hugorin.

'If there's no legal bar to our present Empress being chosen, I'm sure Hugorin would be delighted to appoint Versilla as his consort. He'd be a fool not to want her experience and wisdom to guide him, especially with this prophecy hanging over our heads.'

This plan was discussed with Hugorin who agreed to his name being put to Council; it was agreed that this experienced soldier and diplomat was the ideal choice at this time of political uncertainty and so two days later, the proclamation was made: Prince Hugorin of the Alphaline would be the next — and final — Emperor of Stellaster with Empress Serenity continuing to reign as his consort.

Lord Versain could retain his title of Royal Duke and would also remain in post as Commander-in-Chief.

* * * * *

Hugorin was a couple of years older than the other Galliards and the last to join the Duke's community. Altrix and Balchin were far away commanding the first and second expeditions; now the last Galliard would join Versain's secret service but, like Versain, he'd remain on Stellaster until the meteor arrived to wreak its havoc.

Hugorin had been as horrified as everyone else by the senseless assassination of the Emperor, who he'd known well — they were the same age and had shared their education and military training. Hugorin had left Stellaster on a long posting to Luna immediately after Servenken's coronation. Returning fifteen years later, he'd seen an astonishing transformation from a world traumatised by a tyrant into a realm where people lived in freedom and contentment; he appreciated the role Wellbeloved had played in that transformation.

Under the tyrant, people had lived in constant fear of arrest on some trumped-up charge; public entertainment had been banned, sporting events were ill-attended as only the tyrant's favourites were supposed to win. It had been a grey, depressing world where even the sunshine seemed tainted

A New Emperor

by the general atmosphere of fear and suppression. Now Hugorin would inherit a happy, flourishing empire.

But his empire faced an even greater threat than a tyrant, one that could not be dispelled by a group of brave young cadets. The challenges he would have to face would be different from those Servenken had faced; he'd have to shield the Duke's secret community until a definite sighting of the meteor made it necessary to inform the public of the coming disaster. Then he would be in a position to support the Paradisia community in the final phase of their work as they implemented their programmes for helping people prepare for the terrors to come.

* * * * *

Month tumbled upon month in a veritable cascade of Time and suddenly a year had flown by since the interrupted conference in the Duke's cave. He had made no visits to Paradisia in the interim; he'd been in constant demand by many people to deal with many problems. The year had seen the public trial and execution of the ring-leaders of the mutiny; then there had been a coronation to organise — Hugorin chose the name *Constant* as his Imperial title — and a ceremony to re-instate Serenity as Hugorin's Empress Consort.

There had followed a series of triumphal pageants and parades to establish the new Emperor in the hearts of his people. All in all it had been an exhausting year but well worth the efforts made by the Royal Duke to secure peace and harmony in the realm. At last things had returned to normal in Cander Imperia and in the provinces; the Duke could escape for a few days to resume his community duties. To catch up on events in Paradisia, he re-convened his interrupted conference.

'Let's hope we have no unexpected visitors,' he joked,

welcoming colleagues to his cliff-side cave. 'Arbrecht, I believe you were about to give us a progress report on your opera when you were interrupted by Captain Mandevine.'

'I was Versain, but we've made considerable progress since then. In fact, you're invited to attend our final rehearsal this evening — we've been waiting for you to join us before staging this important event. I have to say, I'm delighted with the opera. It's been a fascinating challenge to produce a work of this magnitude with only the people we have here, but we've met — perhaps even exceeded — my original hopes.'

'And then what, Arbrecht?'

'We must correct any defects that emerge from this evening's performance; if all goes well, we'll be ready to send our protégé out into the wide, wide world.'

'But how can you present a brand new opera without revealing its true origin, its composer?'

'There we've had a stroke of luck. Of course, *I* can't claim to be the composer; I've been dead for far too long.' the Maestro's laugh boomed round the cave and everyone joined in. 'But one of your sister's secret supporters is a composer of some repute; he is prepared to pass off the work as his own. He was reluctant at first; he regarded that as tantamount to theft; but he's been persuaded to do me this favour.'

'Is he in a position to put the opera on at the National Opera House?'

'He is — he's the Musical Director. To prepare the ground, he's been dropping hints that he's about to reveal a new opera to the world. If all goes well tonight, the Gala Performance could be announced within days. We must rely on you to ensure that Emperor Constant and the Empress come; their attendance will give the opera the seal of royal approval and thus a fashionable cachet.'

'I very much look forward to seeing… have you chosen a

title?'

'We call the opera *Armageddon*. The first act recounts the stories of some of our colleagues and their reactions on learning of the prophecy; the second act follows the dispatch of three expeditions to other worlds to establish settlements. The final act covers events after the meteor is sighted. We have explored the many ways in which people might react to the sight of a meteor blazing across the sky, becoming larger and brighter each night. It's a good dramatic plot.'

'And do you think it will achieve its intention?'

'After tonight Versain, you'll be in a better position to answer that than I am. I've been too close for too long.'

'Good, well *that* project seems nicely on course. What about plans for when the meteor is finally sighted? Who's in a position to report on that?'

Gylan-Bahle accepted the invitation.

'We have not been idle this past year. You asked the Empress to approach the Seraphim and they have been helping us to design a range of programmes that can be rolled out at short notice. Chrysilla set us off in the right direction; she urged us to focus on the needs of individuals and that is the line we have taken. You might wish to invite her to describe some of these programmes?'

'Indeed I would. Doctor Flaine?'

'We've been working with the Seraphim to adapt existing farewell ceremonies to suit large groups of individuals, all of whom will be preparing to face their death at the same time. We have also been given access to many of the Empress's secret supporters and that has proved immensely useful. Some of these supporters work in the Motherhood Programme; they have helped us design strategies for the Mother Houses; others are teachers and they have helped us design strategies for First and Second Schools. We've tried to identify different ways of helping different people to face a situation that will soon be facing us all.

'Most of our programmes are ready to be discussed with leaders of institutions the moment the meteor is sighted. The Seraphim have promised to help us run the farewell ceremonies until five days before impact; they will then travel to Srivalian — Oracle invited the Seraphim to spend their final hours in the crystal pyramid.'

'What about the dwarf and elfin communities, Chrysilla? Will they be making their own arrangements?'

'Queen Scintilla invited me to take part in her consultations at Senton Elftown. Perhaps you should ask the Seraphina about the dwarves, my Lord.'

'Ah, I'd forgotten that Chunka is a particular friend of yours, Calthea. Do you know what the dwarves are planning?'

'I do. They'll congregate at their ancestral meeting place, which Chrysilla and I visited some years ago. I can't reveal where it is but I do know they'd welcome a visit from you Versain, because all dwarves hold you in high esteem. I could ask Chunka to arrange a visit, if you agree.'

'Why would they want me to visit, Calthea? I'm sure they hold most angels in contempt — and with good cause.'

'Dwarves do *not* hold you in contempt, Versain; quite the reverse. They'd be greatly honoured if you would visit them once they've assembled; they'll set out for this meeting place only when the meteor has been sighted.'

'I'd certainly like to see this mysterious meeting place.' The Duke turned to his deputy: 'Gylan, we appointed Doctor Flaine to be our ambassador to the elves; why don't we appoint the Seraphina as ambassador to the dwarves? What do you think?'

'I think it's an excellent idea. In the past, the Empress has been our official link with Sriandra, shouldn't we now appoint

A New Emperor

her as our official ambassador? But maybe she still has too many other matters on her plate.'

'I'll ask her on my return but I believe she now has more time to give to her community duties once again. I'm sure she'll also want to discuss the programmes Doctor Flaine she has been working on.' The Duke glanced round the group, 'Does that complete our review? Then may I introduce a topic of my own? The Emperor has told me he would like to be involved in our work. Firstly, he would like to visit Paradisia to meet you all, and he'd like to visit your observatory on Verastra, Kinver. May I extend those invitations on your behalf?'

It was agreed; everyone was excited that their efforts would soon receive the support of their new Emperor.

* * * * *

Emperor Constant visited Paradisia two months later. The Duke had arranged for the entire community, now numbering less than thirty souls, to assemble in the Crystal Chamber. First, the Emperor visited the Verastra observatory, then Professor Kritten escorted him by shuttle to the Crystal Chamber. When their guest had been shown to the central pillar, the Duke invited him to address the assembly.

'My friends,' the Emperor turned to acknowledge each Council member at the circle of pillars then glanced up at those watching from the gallery, 'you may be surprised to learn that for quite some time now I have known all about you and the important work you have been doing in the Duke's secret community. Many years ago, Lord Versain invited me to assume command of your first spaceship but at that time my body was in bad shape so I had to decline his invitation; I knew I would not long survive so early a return to Luna.

'I know very well the problems our pioneers will be facing

as they seek to set up their settlements on that world; I lived there for many years. I also know that sending them there was not a miscalculation; they have not been exiled without good cause. I now *know* that our world faces certain annihilation and that we have only a short time left to prepare for this terrible catastrophe.'

There was a gasp of surprise as the implications of the Emperor's words sank home. The Duke looked questioningly at Professor Kritten and the astronomer nodded significantly. The Emperor continued.

'I have just come from your observatory on Verastra where I spent the moon's night in the company of your distinguished astronomer and his colleagues. Versain, I believe the professor should now take over.'

The Duke signalled the astronomer to comply.

'My dear colleagues, we have been waiting for this moment for a long time; I can hardly believe I'm reporting the first conclusive evidence that the prophesied meteor actually exists, that we now have the first definite sign of this alien intruder. Emperor Constant could not have chosen a better time for his visit — we first detected this object only five nights ago but did not report it till we had confirmation. Even now, the meteor is not visible through our telescope, but we have a highly sensitive device linked to the telescope, which has picked up faint traces of intense radiation coming from a source not previously detected in that region of the skies.

'For five successive nights we have tracked this source of radiation and can only explain the signals we are receiving as emanating from an extremely dense object, possibly a chunk of collapsed matter ejected during a supernova.'

'Might this supernova have been seen from here, Kinver?'

'I very much doubt it my Lord, there's no reason to believe that this object has not been speeding through Space for millions of years. Its position and trajectory indicate an origin outside our own galaxy, so it is probably very, very old. I cannot yet *absolutely* confirm that the radiation comes from a meteor, or even that this object is on a direct collision course with Stellaster.

'What I can say is that there is something very dark and very dense speeding towards our Solar System. It may be a little time before we can confirm its precise composition and trajectory, or estimate its approximate date of arrival. These things will become clearer in due course. For the present, all I can say is that this evidence tends to confirm the prophecy.'

This report was received with excited chatter; many people signalled a desire to speak; Gylan was first to catch the Duke's eye and was introduced.

'Hugorin, I'm sure you will have heard of our eminent philosopher, Professor Gylan-Bahle. He is my deputy here and keeps me abreast of affairs when I'm away. Gylan, you have the floor.'

'Your Majesty, it may seem strange to you that we should welcome this news with relief. We have gambled much on the prophecy proving true and not merely the latest in a string of false predictions. We now know we were justified in abducting a hundred innocent citizens, winners of the Jubilee Prizes, and sending them to live as virtual prisoners on an alien world; we now know we were justified in dispatching many of our friends and colleagues, plus a contingent of elves, to face hardship and uncertainty in Luna's inhospitable environment.

'As soon as we have final confirmation, we'll begin preparing people for the premature ending of their lives. It is a relief to know that our Emperor appreciates and supports our work; in this I am sure I speak for everyone present.'

There was a rumble of approval from the gallery.

'I have promised the Duke my full support, Professor,'

Hugorin responded, 'I know that Empress Serenity has long been a member of your community; now your Emperor has also joined. I am here to familiarise myself with what you are doing here in the mountains so that I can offer my help in the most appropriate way.'

An informal discussion followed then the Duke concluded the meeting.

'Let us all return to Paradisia. The Emperor has told me he would like to visit our magnificent headquarters; if everyone would go to their own office or workplace, I'm sure he will be happy to meet you there and discuss with you what you have been doing these past few years.'

Chapter 20

Armageddon

For three months Paradisia had been deserted. There was no longer any need to keep the community secret, or to keep secret the prophecy that had been the reason for its existence. Every night the advancing meteor glowed a little brighter; it was a hazy ball in the sky rising four hours after sunset and approaching at a tangent to the plane of the solar system.

The erstwhile inhabitants of Paradisia were now scattered around the globe, in pursuit of their final assignments. Many were helping the Maestro to present the final performances of his prophetic opera, *Armageddon*. Even before the arrival of the meteor in the night sky, the opera had caused a considerable stir with its graphic portrayal of a world doomed to annihilation. Now, it was the only event anyone wanted to attend. Each performance was followed by an open discussion with its composer and performers, all part of the process of encouraging people to come to terms with their deepest feelings and fears.

For some time, Chrysilla and Gylan, had been conducting courses for staff and students at various universities and colleges. Calthea, after special training with the Seraphim, was conducting similar courses for members of the public in Cander and provincial towns and settlements. After taking the course, people were encouraged to discuss with their friends the option they would choose: early retirement to the Caves, or to remain and witness the coming of the meteor.

Emperor Constant had taken responsibility for organising farewell ceremonies; these were held for those choosing retirement to the Caves. Most ceremonies were held in Cander where the bulk of the population lived. Already, many thousands had entered the Caves rather than await the coming of *Armageddon*, the name given to the meteor.

Serenity, as Monarch of Mother Houses and schools, had taken up residence in the southern sandlands. Hers was the hardest task; every day she had to bid farewell to cherubs and proto-cherubs as they entered the Caves, escorted by their inwardly distraught but outwardly calm Mothers and teachers. She could do little to lighten the burden of these devoted angelas; none of the cherubs they had nurtured so well and loved so deeply would live to enter adulthood. Versilla was finding it hard to retain her faith in the Immortal Powers; how could they inflict such suffering on these innocent children? It was all such a dreadful, dreadful *waste*.

Five days before the calculated date of impact, all seraphs, having honoured their commitment to the angel community, returned to Sriandra; they would set out for Srivalian and the Crystal Pyramid in good time. Dwarves too were making their way to the Cave of Marvels from their many mines and settlements around the world. In death, this sacred hall would serve as their collective tomb just as in life it had served as the ceremonial and social heart of the community.

Queen Scintilla had summoned her people to Senton Elftown; they honoured their ancestors and consoled themselves in a great out-pouring of recollection and grief. Famous bards recounted the ancient myths and legends in preparation for their forthcoming reunion with the gods and goddesses who had protected and guided the Elfin people from the very dawn of time — but who could protect them no more.

As for the Harbingers, that fun-loving fragile race had no notion of the tragedy about to overtake them and, to the last, would sing and dance in the rays of the ever-rising sun — though *ever* was destined soon to become *never again*. The Duke had tried to warn them of the coming disaster but his knowledge of their language had proved inadequate for describing a catastrophe of such awesome magnitude.

* * * * *

Only a couple of days now remained.

Calthea persuaded her consort to accept Dinkarspeak's invitation to visit the dwarves in their Cave of Marvels; she accompanied him into the dark tunnels and saw the astonishment on his face as he entered that glorious chamber. Chunka led him to the throne of firestone, then he and Dorka took their places on either side standing like two proud Imperial Guards. The Chief Dinkar welcomed their guest.

'Great Lord, you are our king. Ever since you rescued our people from the cruel tyrant, we have thought of you as our honorary king. At last we can tell you of our gratitude and devotion. Never before has an aristocrat treated dwarves with the respect you have shown us. Great Lord, will you permit your people to pay homage to you and to the Lady Seraphina?'

The Duke, thoroughly shocked, nevertheless had the presence of mind to agree to this strange request. Calthea was invited to sit on the adjacent throne; she felt like a queen as a seemingly endless file of dwarves came up and bowed so low that their heads almost touched the floor. Between them, Dorka and Chunka hurried the line through so that the process took less time than she feared it might from the vast numbers present.

The Duke made a moving speech in which he acknowledged his regard for all dwarves who had proved loyal and hard-working assistants. He also spoke of his pleasure and surprise at the great honour they had done him; he'd had no notion of the deep affection he had triggered in these faithful souls; in fact, he said all the right things. After many emotional farewells, Calthea and her consort were permitted to leave.

'I'm so glad you asked me to visit our friends, Calthea,' The Duke commented as they rested in his cliff-side cave. 'I had no idea that they regarded me as their king! I have always observed the loyalty of dwarves towards anyone who treated them fairly, but it's a sad indictment of our past treatment of this dependable people that they should feel such extraordinary gratitude in return for mere good manners.

'I also had no idea that that extraordinary chamber existed on our very door-step. When did you see it before?'

Calthea told him of the visit she and Chrysilla had made prior to the departure of the second expedition.

'Did you realise Versain, that you were sitting on a throne of firestone and that only the leaders of the dwarves are allowed to sit on that throne?'

'Was that where you first came across firestone?'

'It was; and because I'd seen it, I knew I'd be able to carry out my assignment in spite of the destruction of all my lovely gemstones. So many extraordinary things have happened in my life, Versain. I could write a book about them. But there's no time now to write it and soon there'll be no one left to read it either.'

'You should record your experiences Calthea, but rather than write them why not send them to Phillestra.'

'How? Phillestra is far, far away and I could hardly expect her to listen to my ramblings on her *mentori*.'

'You told me that fire-crystal and firestone can communicate with each other in some strange fashion. You know how to record into fire-crystal; why not record your experiences into one of your parapendia? You could dictate into a *peblo* and direct your thoughts to one of the parapendia. Would that work?'

'It's a very clever idea, Versain. You've given me an assignment at this very last moment. How cunning you are; I shan't have time to think about the meteor, I'll be far too busy compiling and dictating my life-story.'

'It's our memories we fear to lose by dying, don't you agree? We have no idea where we go after we die, only an inner conviction that we must go somewhere — that in some sense we are actually immortal. But what value does survival have if our memories don't survive with us? Would surviving have any value without our memories? It's questions like this that have been exercising my mind more and more in these last days. I'm not afraid of dying so long as some part of me will continue after death. What do you think?'

'I think you must have been talking to the prof! But I do agree about memory; my memories are so much a part of who I believe I am. It's why I shall always be grateful that you brought me here. I've acquired many very precious memories since coming to these mountains — and some very precious memories of the times before, not least, our marriage ceremony.'

'Some people believe we only live on after our death in the memories of those we leave behind. It would be insurance for your continued existence if you were able to record your memories into one of the parapendia; that should survive the coming disaster. The story of your life will become one of the precious gems we've saved for posterity.'

'Do you think we'll meet after death, Versain? Will we go to the Mentaillion and meet there as disembodied souls?'

'Who can possibly say? Oracle might have been able to

answer such a question, but I dare say her answer would have been framed to obscure rather than reveal the truth. I'm not sure we're meant to know these things. It's strange that we should have been given intelligence and curiosity but not allowed to use them to find out things that are of the greatest relevance to us.

'Anyway my dear Calthea, I think it's time I left. Kinver and the Master will be waiting; we need to take off before the sunlight weakens.'

'So this is *goodbye*. I hate goodbyes so please just leave, Versain. We have our peblos and can stay in touch till the end.' The Duke turned to leave but at the cave entrance he turned back.

'You know Calthea, I believe Girilayne would have been very proud of you, very proud of the way you have carried out your very difficult assignment.'

Not waiting for her response, he leapt into the air and flew across the canyon, heading for the plateau above its southern escarpment. He landed beside Professor Kritten, who was waiting at the open door of the shuttle.

'Where's Chorton?' The Duke asked.

'He's inside powering up the engine. We're ready to leave as soon as you are.'

The Duke bent down and scooped up a handful of sand.

'We'll not set foot on Stellaster again, Kinver — it's a small souvenir to remind me of our wonderful, unique and tragically doomed world.'

* * * * *

Just before sunset Calthea went out to the terrace of the Duke's cave to chant the *Mortissima*. This would be the penultimate time she would see Sol sink beneath the horizon.

She recalled the evening she'd taken Phillestra to watch the sun set; that was just over ten years ago yet it seemed like a lifetime.

Perhaps she should begin the account of her life-story with that sunset; it had certainly marked the beginning of the amazing adventure that had brought her to these mountains. She thought about the Duke's idea for sending her thoughts across interplanetary space to one of the parapendia now on distant Luna. Surely it should be possible to project her thoughts in a focused beam to one of her fire-crystal globes. She'd never know if she'd succeeded; in less than two days she would no longer be an embodied soul.

She continued to stand on the terrace long after the light had faded, watching the stars as they appeared like magic in the darkening sky. What a boon it had been to live on this wonderful world, even if that boon was soon to be snatched from her. She would pack as much living as she could into the few hours remaining.

Versain had told her that his twin planned to spend her final hours in his cave; Versilla would leave the southern sandlands and fly to Paradisia in the morning. Calthea decided she'd spend this penultimate night in her workroom; she'd spent so many happy hours there. Chrissy would join her in the morning and they'd spend their last day together, visiting anyone within reach, including the Empress.

They planned to spend their final night in Girilayne's cave, the terrace of which faced east; that would give them a chance to see the meteor before it slammed into the planet — that is, if Meon didn't slam in first. Astronomers around the world had noted Meon's increasingly erratic orbit; the gravitational forces of the approaching meteor were already creating disturbances in Stellaster's magnetosphere. It would be a close run thing; would the meteor or Meon hit the target first?

She realised that she'd have little time to carry out the Duke's assignment once Chrissy came; her time and attention would then be fully occupied. It was a waste to spend the coming night in sleep; she'd have the whole of Eternity for sleeping; better to spend the time recording her life-story with its many adventures and challenges.

She took her *peblo* in her hand and began: *It was twilight, that magical hour when the world morphs from colour-rich day into the monochrome of night....*

* * * * *

The tiny silver bullet that was shuttle no. 3 rose from the plateau and soared into the sky. Their plan was to speed towards the meteor so that Professor Kritten could learn all he could of its composition and momentum. They knew very well that there was nothing they could do to divert this massive object from its path but the Duke wanted to see for himself the culmination of its long journey through Space and final collision with their world.

This was no fool's errand: the information might be of little relevance to those on Stellaster whose lives now had hours rather than days to run; it would be of great interest to Devallian, in a similar shuttle some considerable distance away. The Duke had been far from happy when he'd learned — by means of his *peblo* — that Devallian was not safely on Luna but on a similar quest to his own to watch the cataclysmic destruction of a world that had existed for billions of years.

'Why didn't you stay on Luna, Devallian? Why risk serious damage to your craft from the collision? This is a foolhardy adventure. It would have been better to head away from a location that will soon be the scene of unimaginable devastation.'

'Because Phillestra wanted to witness the collision my Lord, and since this is an event unlikely to be repeated in our lifetime, I sought and gained permission from the joint commanders to take one of our shuttles so she could watch it for herself.'

'*What!* Are you saying that my daughter is with you? I find that irresponsible in the extreme. Why didn't you leave her on Luna? I'll give you a commentary from close by, so there's little to be gained by putting my daughter's life at risk. I'm surprised at your lack of judgement Devallian, after all my training.'

Devallian responded in a deliberately neutral tone, as if explaining a simple matter to a child.

'The reason Phillestra asked to be taken, and the reason I asked for permission to take her my Lord, is that Luna will be screened by Earth at the predicted time of impact. No one on Luna will see the collision. Most people don't want to see their old world blasted into thin air but Phillestra was adamant that she wanted to watch the drama with her own eyes. I have to admit I share her desire.'

'I appreciate how persuasive Phillestra can be, Devallian;' the Duke was more conciliatory, 'Anyway, I can hardly criticise since I've set out on a similar journey for precisely the same reason. Once we can get a closer look at this monster we'll have a better idea of the probable consequences. Please stay in touch.'

Two hours later, the Duke contacted Devallian. He shared a new concern.

'I'm afraid the Phobos garrison will bear the full brunt of the disaster. Kritten warned us years ago that the meteor's arrival might well coincide with a close approach by both Mars and Earth. Mars is now far too close to escape the blast.'

'That's not just bad news for the Phobos garrison, my

Lord;' Devallian replied, 'if Mars is in the firing line, what will happen to her biosphere? But I dare say that a shower of debris will cause less damage if it falls into water than onto solid rock.'

'That's a good point, Devallian. Let me ask Kritten what he has to say.'

The question was put to the astronomer who responded: 'We've spent so much time thinking about the impact the meteor will have on our own world Versain, that I dare say we've rather neglected its impact on Mars. I don't think the planet itself is in serious danger, but I believe there could be a very real risk to its biosphere.

'It's not debris that is the main threat,' he continued, 'it's the blast wave that will follow impact. I don't know if the Martian Ocean will protect its life-forms from the blast but it probably won't. It could well be that, of the three present biospheres only Earth's will survive this terrible catastrophe.'

As Stellaster continued to turn on her axis — orbited by Verastra and Meon — the Duke's shuttle continued to speed towards the oncoming meteor. Master Tang had rigged up a telescope and other instruments from the Verastra observatory in the nose-cone of the shuttle and the astronomer spent most of his time with his eye glued to the telescope or taking readings from his other instruments.

He was becoming increasingly worried as the meteor approached; from time to time he would call out readings from his instruments and Master Tang would make calculations, which they then discussed with growing incredulity.

'Versain,' the professor turned from his instruments, 'this thing is a even denser than I thought. It may be a fragment of a neutron star; at any rate it doesn't resemble anything I've ever come across before. If it's as dense as the readings suggest, there's going to be one hell of a bang when it collides with

Stellaster. I can't say how far the blast will carry, but I suggest that Devallian immediately takes his shuttle as far as he can and as fast as he can in the opposite direction.'

'Did you hear that, Devallian? Look, I'm giving Professor Kritten my *peblo*. He can tell you what you need to do.'

'Devallian? Imagine the Solar System as a flat disk with the sun at its centre and the planets orbiting at various distances within that disk. OK? Now I want you to turn your shuttle at right angles to the plane of that disk and head out of it — head in the opposite direction from the meteor's. Do understand what I'm saying?'

'I do, but I haven't the least idea *how* to do it. Master Tang had better talk to my pilot; then they can discuss the technicalities engineer to engineer.'

The *peblos* in both shuttles changed hands.

'Who am I speaking to?' the Master enquired.

'I am Pilot Trysen, Master. I was an assistant pilot on *Brave Endeavour* and when Commander Devallian needed a pilot for this shuttle, he chose me.'

'He chose well. I remember you Trysen; you were a good student. You're going to need your wits about you because you'll need to make some alterations to the control system. Have you any tools on board?'

'I have one of the emergency kits from *Brave Endeavour*. I know that's overkill but we could carry the extra weight; there's only the four of us on board.'

'I think you're going to be glad you did that. Now what I want you to do is.... '

A detailed technical briefing followed; the Master described the modifications required and Trysen repeated those instructions back.

'I don't suppose you thought to put any pods on board, did you?'

'Actually I did, Master. I thought we might need them in case we experienced turbulence from the blast.'

'That's fortunate. They're going to be needed. I believe you attended Professor Kritten's foundation course, am I right?'

'I did, Master — we covered basic navigation. I'd hoped to take other modules but the time arrived for the launch.'

'OK. Now I'm going to hand this *peblo* back to Professor Kritten. He will brief you on the course you must set to take you clear of the danger zone.'

Having completed this briefing, the professor announced that he'd seen all he wished to see and learnt all he was likely to learn from the meteor. The Duke asked the Master to take the shuttle out of the path of the advancing meteor; all that remained was to sit back, observe what happened and give a running commentary on the greatest firework display likely to have been witnessed in the Solar System in billions of years.

After that, who can say what would happen.

* * * * *

By morning, Calthea had finished recording, projecting her life-story into a parapendium on distant Luna; whether it arrived safely she had no way of knowing. Not feeling in the least tired, she began the day by performing the *Obeisance*. Sol would continue to reign in his kingdom but would rise no more over the horizons of the Great Mountain Range; one of his acolytes was about to quit his service.

An hour later, whilst waiting in the courtyard of Paradisia for Chrysilla, she spied the figure of the Empress flying overhead to the Duke's cave. Chrysilla arrived a few minutes later; Calthea hadn't seen her friend for two months. They flew to the roof of the west wing to bask.

'How's the prof, Chrissy? What does he plan to do today?'

'Oh Cal, he's gone! He went almost two months ago.'

Calthea put her arm around her friend's shoulders; she was clearly in distress.

'Tell me.'

'If you recall, I was on my way to Persinnia when we last met. The prof had invited me to attend his first *preparing-to-leave* lecture to students at the Institutes. It was brilliant. You know the plan: we'd present the preparation talk, then invite every-one present to discuss with a neighbour whether they wanted to leave immediately — if so they'd be invited to attend a farewell ceremony a couple of days later — or if they preferred to remain until the end.

'So much for plans! At the end of his talk, the prof invited anyone who wanted to leave to follow him into the caves. Just like that! No discussion, no *farewells*, no ceremonies, no changing one's mind at the last minute. He just walked to the nearest Cave and everyone — and I do mean everyone — followed. I followed too but he turned at the entrance and saw me.

'He said: *No Chrissy, you have work to do*. He called me *Chrissy*, Cal! He's never done that before.'

'My poor dear. Partings are *awful*; I said goodbye to Versain yesterday. We spent a wonderful day together but all too soon he had to leave, not for the Caves I admit, but I'll never see him again in this lifetime.'

'Yes, parting from friends and colleagues has been by far the toughest part of this whole business. But at least we'll be together till the end, Cal.'

'Talking like this reminds me of something Oracle said to the Seraphim on the evening she bid them *Farewell*. She said: *I urge you to remember always that your chief concern must be to arrive at the end of your life having attained what it was you came here to attain; each of you is aware of what that is, for the goal differs for each individual.*

'She also said: *The greatest challenge you will face in these coming years will be to keep hope alive even as annihilation approaches. Always remember who you are and who you are not; that knowledge will serve as your map and compass in the difficult terrain you will soon be traversing.*'

'Cal, that's amazing; *always remember who you are and who you are not*. Thank you for those words; I shall treasure them in my heart till whatever it is that's going to happen, happens.'

'The words that resonated with me were: *to arrive at the end of your life having attained what it was you came here to attain.* She said each of us would know what that was, but I wonder if I really know what my purpose has been. Girilayne said it was to make recordings of our culture for the expeditions. But who can say whether she was right or wrong? Do you have any idea what *your* purpose was, Chrissy?'

'I don't know about *purpose*; but I do feel I attained something very special in this lifetime through meeting the prof. I was extremely fortunate to study under such a wise and compassionate person. Perhaps being true to his teachings in these final hours might be thought a worthwhile purpose.'

They basked in silence for a while, then considered how they'd spend this last day. They would pay a visit to the Empress and discuss what they'd all been doing these past few months; on their way home, they'd visit the Crystal Chamber for a last word with Chunka then spend their final hours in Girilayne's cave.

'We must be sure to arrive well before sunset, Chrissy,' Calthea insisted. 'This will be my last chance to chant the *Solema Mortissima*. Who knows exactly when the meteor will strike but it's bound to be some time during the night. We'll honour Sol once more before Armageddon arrives.'

Neither Calthea nor Chrysilla slept that night; they stood

against the outer wall of the cave facing east. It was a clear night, though strange lights occasionally flashed across the sky, indications of increasing turbulence in the magnetosphere. The stars shone as brilliantly as ever. But Meon failed to rise at the scheduled time — that was no surprise, Meon had become increasingly unstable in recent days.

'I wonder how everyone is doing on Luna, Chrissy. Do you mind if I take a moment to contact Phillestra? I usually wait for her to call as I'm never sure when she'll be sleeping.'

It was then that Calthea discovered that Phillestra was with Devallian in a tiny shuttle, waiting and watching. She told her daughter of her recent attempt to add her story to a parapendium and asked her to check whether she had been successful on her return to Luna. She did not wish to prolong this further *goodbye*, so with one last assurance of her love, she ended the call.

After a while, Chrysilla claimed her attention.
'I wonder whether it will be the angel settlements or these weird hybrids who will be the torch-bearers of our culture, Cal. I very much hope it is angels but I can't help thinking of what the prof said about biospheres; Luna is an inhospitable world.'

'I think it will be the hybrids; intelligent beings ought to live in a biosphere. I have great confidence in Banderene; he's an extraordinary person on many levels. He understood Gylan's moral objections but he has a deeper vision of where Evolution might be heading. Let's send our blessings to our pioneers anyway, Chrissy; it's all we can do for them now.'

The end came at precisely 3.28 in the morning (Mountain Time) on the 10th day of the 10th month of the year 1864. Meon, streaking across the Great Sand Ocean at an ever-decreasing altitude, slammed into the massive wall of the Quartz Mountains... and that was that.

A third of the way around the globe in the city of Cander Imperia, a dozen watchers had chosen not to enter the Caves. The group included Emperor Constant; he stood on the roof of the ducal palace with his companions and faced the western horizon where Sol had just set for the last time. These brave souls then turned to the east and linked hands. Each night for the past month, they had come to watch the great meteor rise and speed its way across the sky, growing larger and brighter each night; they knew that tonight would be their final vigil.

Barely an hour after Meon had crashed into the mountains, *Armageddon* ended its immensely long odyssey through Space in the western reaches of Cander Valley. No one on the ground witnessed this final *coup de grace*; twenty minutes before, a blast of scorching air from the east had brought instant death to every living thing in its path; the wind was followed by a series of deep violent landquakes. The impact of the meteor completed the process of Stellaster's disintegration into rock and dust.

* * * * *

The explosion — the double explosion — that vaporised Stellaster and her moons was witnessed by seven souls, three very briefly and from very close and four from a tiny shuttle already speeding away as fast as it could.

The sight was beautiful beyond belief; indeed it was quite shockingly beautiful.

Devallian found the entire event totally mesmeric even though he knew the awful consequences for those who'd remained on the planet's surface and those in the shuttle that carried the Duke, Professor Kritten and Master Tang. He had stayed in touch with Lord Versain via their *peblos* until the last moment.

The meteor, villain of the drama, had been virtually invisible, too dark to spot from their distant viewpoint but its impact had been all too visible. The Duke had described the progress of the invader towards the doomed world; he'd also reported signs that Meon, the dark moon was becoming increasingly erratic, resulting in its final plunge into the surface of the planet.

The Duke had provided continuous commentary during those last moments; it would be a close run thing whether the meteor or Meon struck first; Meon won by a squeak, hence the double explosion and spectacular blossoming of that incandescent fireball that had expanded rapidly to engulf golden Stellaster and rosy Verastra in its greedy maw.

This binocular perspective — the Duke's commentary and his own panoramic view — seared into the very fabric of Devallian's mind an image vivid in scale and detail; undoubtedly that image would remain with him for the rest of his life. The explosion had taken the life of Lord Versain, his mentor and hero, which only added to the sharp poignancy of the image.

After the explosion, there'd been only an ominous and enduring silence.

THE STELLASTER ARCHIVE

Volume One:
The Wrath of Time

∼

Volume Two:
Seeding the Wind

∼

Volume Three:
Echoes in the Mists of Time

Part One:
HOMEWARD BOUND

Part Two:
GUARDIANS OF THE RUBY GLOBE

Part Three:
OF MEN AND ANGLES